THE CHOICES WE MAKE

ANNELL ST. CHARLES

THE CHOICES WE MAKE

For Permission requests, write to:
YBR Publishing, LLC
PO Box 4904
Beaufort SC 29903-4904
contact@ybrpub.com
843-597-0912

THE CHOICES WE MAKE

ANNELL ST. CHARLES

5

ISBN 13: 978-1-7339992-6-7
ISBN 10: 1-7339992-6-7

Cover design by Jack Gannon & Cyndi Williams-Barnier

Bill Barnier – Senior Editor, YBR Publishing
Cyndi Williams-Barnier – Production Editor, YBR Publishing
Jack Gannon- Production Manager, YBR Publishing

DEDICATION

As always, to my husband, Costas Tsinakis. I can always count on you for helpful comments and useful advice, whether I want it or not.

To my brother, Frank St. Charles, III. Your years of working in the banking/financial field inspired part of the story line of this book. I only wish you were here for me to talk to you about it. Your life was too short, my dear big brother. I miss you deeply.

And to my children – Sophia and Andreas Tsinakis. Watching you grow from sweet, interesting young children to still-sweet, still-interesting, wonderful adults has been inspiring. Being your mother is a gift I will always treasure.

ALSO BY ANNELL ST. CHARLES

9

The Things Left Unsaid: A Georgia Ayres Novel

The Chances We Take: A Georgia Ayres Novel

The Clam Shell: Poetry of a Relationship

Sunrise on Hilton Head Island: Coligny Beach (Photography)

Island Life: (Photography)

NOTE TO THE READER

This book is entirely a work of fiction. As in all good fiction, there are some facts.

For example, there is certainly a vibrant music industry in Nashville, of which the Country Music Association is an integral part. WSM is one of a group of radio and television stations that helped make Nashville "Music City," and spread the Nashville Sound across the world. Opryland USA was built on land that was formerly the site of a sausage factory, until it was demolished and replaced with a shopping mall. The Ryman auditorium was the original home of the Grand Ole Opry before it was relocated to a new venue next to Opryland. The Opryland Hotel and Convention Center was completed in 1977, and it continues to be one of the most impressive hospitality and entertainment complexes in the United States.

Fan Fair began in Nashville in 1972, and continues today as the CMA Music Festival. Music producers have found their way from the West Coast to Nashville from time to time, and have managed to lure music celebrities away from their current agents and producers. However, Glen Campbell, (and the fictitious Dottie and Kenny) never worked for a man named Tommy Owen.

The banking industry in Nashville has had its ups and downs, which can also be said about banks across the rest of the United States. During the seventies and eighties, a pair of brothers created a major scandal in Tennessee because of their financial dealings, which served as the inspiration for part of the story line of this novel. But the facts about their case have been changed to make them a better fit for the story.

Melodeon floridanus skeletal (pre-historical cat) remains really were discovered during the excavation of a building in downtown Nashville, and later became the mascot image for the Nashville Predators hockey team.

Local politicians have been known to hobnob with club owners of a criminal sort, and newspaper editors and publishers have not always played by the rules. But the tale that I have told here is completely fabricated.

Printers Alley and the Carousel Club are real, as are the Belle Meade Country Club, the City Club, and the Hermitage Hotel. I have borrowed them to give authenticity to the scenes I created. The Savage House was the previous incarnation of the Standard that is still in the same location.

J. Edgar Hoover died before the date of his fictitious visit in this story, but I bet he would have been right in the thick of things had he still been alive.

Centennial Park is a wonderful green space to the west of downtown Nashville and it does, indeed, boast the only existing replica of the Greek Parthenon, which stands in its center.

East Nashville previously suffered from an image of being on "the poor side of town". In recent years, however, it has become one of the most desirable areas of Davidson County.

The boutique, Gianna, does not exist. But if it did, I have no doubt it would be located in Belle Meade.

Former President Eisenhower was known to play golf in Nashville with some of his banking buddies, but his death preceded the time period described in this book.

As an author of fiction, I have taken liberties with the time and place of many of the scenes depicted in this novel in order to make them fit the story.

Having said all of that, I would like to thank my hometown for giving me so much fodder to fuel my imagination. You're quite a grand lady, Nashville!

I extend my deepest gratitude to Emily McCluskey and Lee Penuel for taking the time to be second draft readers. Your suggestions, impressions, and tips were extremely helpful. My thanks to Costas (my husband) for your male perspective of the story and for your valuable suggestions.

A very special thanks to Donna Clark: an incredible editor and dear friend who passed away after the release of this novel. Her "green pen" remarks on my first and second drafts were invaluable.

Finally, to the members of YBR Publishing: Bill Barnier, Cyndi Williams-Barnier, and Jack Gannon. I greatly appreciate your expert advice on the re-editing of the second edition of this book, and tireless efforts on bringing all three of my "Georgia Ayres" novels to print and digital life. Joining forces with you all has been invaluable.

THE CHOICES WE MAKE

CHAPTER ONE
JULIE'S STORY

My dad worked for the Cincinnati Financial Corporation for twenty years when he decided to jump ship and join the ranks of the First National Bank in Nashville. That was no small undertaking, considering it involved uprooting his wife, five kids, two dogs, a pet rabbit, and a house full of accumulated possessions, then hauling the lot nearly 300 miles away. The chaos it created was frightening, and my mind swam with thoughts of how I was going to keep it all orderly.

My oldest brother, Bill, led the way driving a station wagon loaded with the household pets and my twelve- year old twin sisters, Sherry and Carey, who could also be said to fit into that category. He was followed, very closely, by an Oldsmobile sedan driven by my dad, with my mother riding shotgun in front of a slew of suitcases. Bill had a tendency to drive with a heavy foot when his mind became fixed on a goal. He was hard driven to bulldoze a path toward whatever he set his sights upon. Dad just wanted to make sure he could slow him down with a few toots of the horn if he started to pull too far ahead of the rest of us.

The tail end of our convoy was a rented oversized moving van, driven by my other brother, 17-year old Mike. Being 15 and not yet legal to drive, I was assigned to ride with Mike to make sure he stayed on course. Mike was prone to daydreaming and distraction, which often resulted in his drifting off track. Getting lost, or ending up somewhere other than where he was supposed to be, was not out of the ordinary for Mike. But I was determined to keep him on track.

We finally pulled up in front of our new stark white, black roofed, two story home in Nashville, Tennessee, on a steamy, early summer day in 1965, I thought it was one of the prettiest, yet strangest, houses I'd ever seen. It was large and square, and sat back from the road on a small rise, an oak tree guarding the left flank. A garage attached to the right side was topped with a screened-in deck, and a wide staircase protruded off to the left of the house.

"Huh. Looks like a big box." Mike proclaimed.

"Yeah. It's big, alright. But I kinda like it. The neighborhood seems nice, too. A little bit like where we lived in Cincinnati. I wonder if that's why they picked this place."

"Nah. I heard them talking one night about how they wanted us to live someplace with good schools. Dad said he checked into it and found the perfect location." We both stared more closely at the house.

"I dread getting to know new kids all over again." I said.

Mike punched my arm and grinned reassuringly. "Aw, it'll be alright. You'll make new friends in no time."

I attempted to smile in return, but only managed a slight nod.

Since my parents staunchly believed in the value of education to give children a leg up on life, it was important the neighborhood where we were to live was zoned for top-notch schools. That meant private schools. They didn't believe public schools could provide the level of instruction they thought we should receive. They were concerned that the type of "life" education we might encounter in a public-school environment was not in our best interest.

In Nashville, as in Cincinnati, going to a private school in the 1960s meant we would be attending Catholic school. There were a few other choices for a private school education, but they were out of the price range that our family could afford, especially considering there would be five of us attending these schools at the same time. There was only one small problem; we weren't Catholic. I guess you could say we were nondenominational. Going to any sort of church was not a regular thing for us.

Our new house was located in Southwest Nashville, just a few blocks away from Holy Angels, the elementary school Sherry and Carey would be attending. An all-girls Catholic high school, St. Bernadette's was a similar distance in the other direction for me. The all-boys high school, St. Thomas Moore, was a few miles away for Bill and Mike. The neighborhood lay between two main streets; Hillsboro Road, and Belmont Boulevard. Hillsboro Road was home to the campuses of Vanderbilt University and Peabody College. Belmont Boulevard was named after Belmont College at its northern end, and was anchored on the south by David Lipscomb College.

My dad walked up beside our car and swept his arms out in a wide circle. "There are so many academic institutions close by that all you have to do to get an education is stand in the yard and absorb it like sunshine on a cloudless day." Mike and I rolled our eyes at each other, but the twins, who had walked up while he was making this announcement, began to jump up and down in celebration.

"Oh, don't put wishful thinking in their heads, Will Travers," our mother said as she walked up next to dad.

The First National Bank was located in downtown Nashville at the corner of Fourth Avenue and Union Street. It was considered one of the top three financial institutions in Nashville, along with Third American and Commerce & Trust banks. I later found out all three of these banking institutions had been in pursuit of my dad, but he never explained why he chose First National. When I asked him a year or so after we had moved to Nashville, he just said, "I had a good feeling about it."

My dad was well-known in our family for relying on what he called, his "gut instinct". In his typical fashion, he loved to expound on the scientific meaning behind the term. As he explained it, the gut has a mind of its own, which means that those little butterflies we feel in our stomach when we're on the verge of doing something, are actually chemicals trying to send us a message. The message could be we should stop what we're doing and run in the opposite direction. Or, the butterflies could mean we've stumbled across something very important that we should run toward. The point of it all, according to my dad, was that we should listen carefully to our gut because it rarely leads us in the wrong direction.

My brother Bill would always respond to my father's gut ramblings by patting his stomach and remarking the only thing his gut told him was he was hungry. That never failed to elicit giggles from the twins and an unsympathetic grunt from my mom. I found the idea that our gut could talk to us vaguely unsettling, but over time I began to learn the value of listening to it.

CHAPTER TWO

One of the upshots of being a member of a large family was the five of us kids had to learn to sort things out for ourselves at times, instead of depending upon our parents to fix every little wrinkle in our lives. We were as different from one another as we could possibly be when it came to figuring out how to do that. Bill's was into sports and tinkering with something mechanical he had taken apart in order to figure out how it worked. Mike gravitated toward the distraction of a good book.

For me, hanging out in my bedroom was the best antidote for whatever was bothering me. I could easily spend hours organizing my things or making lists of what I needed to do over the next week. I was also thrilled to find I had been assigned the bedroom overlooking the large oak tree that rose majestically from our front yard to the top of the roof. If I lifted the window, the room filled with the sweet smell of newly mown grass and a hint of honeysuckle. I was content to stare out the window for hours, watching the birds flittering about or studying the people who walked by in the street below. My room was my cocoon. I felt more comfortable within its confines than any other place in my life.

The twins usually turned to each other when they had a problem. They were the epitome of two peas in a pod. Sherry and Carey fit the description of identical in as many ways as two people could, yet still be separate individuals. The only time a problem arose they couldn't work out between them was when they found themselves on opposite sides of an issue. It didn't happen too often, but when it did, they were like two banty hens circling each other before a fight.

My parents were pretty even tempered. Not much bothered them, and they tended to take in stride any minor disagreements that erupted among the five of us, unless it seemed as though we weren't likely to reach a resolution on our own. I don't know why I couldn't follow their lead on this, but whenever there was dissonance in the house, I found it impossible to relax until it was "fixed". I would haul myself out of my self-imposed exile in my room and try to find a way to quickly restore order.

I used to wonder why I felt compelled to do this. No one else seemed to be bothered when these little tiffs occurred. I let them get under my skin, and inside my brain, to the point that I couldn't sit still or concentrate on anything else. I often wondered what this said about me until a magazine article gave me some insight.

The article described how middle children are often loners because they become accustomed to the first- and last-born children getting most of the attention. They tend to be diplomatic because they are usually in the middle of struggles between their siblings, requiring the use of diplomacy to resolve. They fall into the role of peacekeeper because, more than anything else, they want their lives to feel in control.

I had come to rely on the little routines I created in my life in order to help me feel secure and calm. It made me nervous unless I made my bed as soon as I got up. My pens needed to be lined in a row next to my notepaper before I could start my homework. If a piece of paper happened to fall on the floor while

I was working, I found it impossible to concentrate until I picked it up and put it where it belonged.

It took some time for me to be able to see the bigger picture of why I did these things. All I knew for certain was that mess caused me stress while order made me calm. I eventually began to understand my need for order was really a thinly-veiled attempt to hide that I didn't feel totally secure in my life, which was difficult for me to admit. It didn't mean something was wrong with me. It just meant I needed to figure out how to use my orderliness to my advantage, rather than let it bog me down. The realization that I could change my life gave me a feeling of hope, though I still had no idea how to go about making it happen.

It was mid-June when we finally finished moving into our new home in Nashville. My siblings made fast work of settling into their bedrooms by ripping open their boxes and dumping the contents on the floor, before tossing things haphazardly into closets and drawers.

My method was a little different. I lined up each of my boxes against one wall then opened them one by one, examining the contents carefully before deciding where they should be placed. I had packed my books alphabetically by the author's last name, which enabled me to place them in the same order on my bookshelves. I learned that trick from my mother who had been alphabetizing our spice rack for years. When it came time to pack my clothes, it was a simple matter of placing them in the correct box according to their color, type, and season. That was the way I hung them in my closet, which made it much easier to choose an outfit to wear. Nothing about this seemed odd to me. It was just the way I had always done things.

By the end of our third full week in Nashville, I drifted into the routine of spending most of my days in my bedroom, lounging on one of the twin beds with a book I checked out from the local bookmobile, or peering out the front window from a chair. When we lived in Cincinnati, I was always poking into one of my siblings' rooms to see what they were up to, or following them around the house to make sure they didn't get into any mischief. It never occurred to me they might not appreciate me inserting myself that way. It was just something I took upon myself to do.

When we first arrived in Nashville, I fell into this same pattern, until I realized my siblings were doing fine on their own. In fact, they all told me at one time or another they'd prefer I get my own life and stop trying to interfere in theirs. At first, I didn't believe they meant what they said. But after days of having doors slammed in my face or seeing the stony looks they gave me when I wandered into the middle of a private conversation, I finally gave in. I didn't know what to make of these changes. How had I gone from being the one they turned to whenever they needed help, to suddenly being the outcast? The universe had done an about face on me. So, I did the only thing I knew how to do; I retreated to the comfort of my room, where there was a place for everything, and everything had its place. Even me.

One day, as I sat in my favorite viewing spot staring out at the birds nesting in the oak tree, I began to sense someone standing behind me. I turned to find my mother looking at me inquisitively.

"Wouldn't you like to go outside for a while, Julie? It's a beautiful day."

I leaned against the window and attempted to smile. "Not really. I'm fine here."

She sat on the edge of the bed nearest to the door. "Your father and I are a little concerned about you. You've barely left the house since we moved in. You seem to be withdrawing from the rest of us more and more each day." She patted the bed next to her. "Tell me what's bothering you."

I reluctantly left my spot by the window and sat next to her. For a long minute neither of us spoke. The silence was broken when I felt a hand on my knee and turned to find my mother looking at me with a mixture of worry and understanding. "I know this move has been difficult for you. You've always had a tendency to carry the weight of the world on your shoulders, especially where your brothers and sisters are concerned. I just wish I knew how to help you understand you are not responsible for anyone but yourself."

I shrugged my shoulders. "They've always needed me to help them solve their problems. But since we've been here, they don't seem to need me anymore."

She nodded her understanding. "I know it may seem like that, but I'm sure you're just as important to them now as you've always been. Everyone is just trying to find where they fit into our new life. If you think about it, that's actually a good thing. It means you can be free to find your way, too, without feeling you have to worry about your brothers and sisters." She smiled and looked at me intently. "You know you're not their parent. There's no reason in the world you have to feel responsible for anything your brothers and sisters do."

She looked away as she seemed to think about what she was saying. "I guess your father and I are to blame for that. I'm afraid we have a tendency to get caught up in our own little world too often." She turned so she could take my hands in hers. "We're going to have to make some changes, starting with helping you lighten that load of worry you carry around. You're fifteen years old, Julie. This should be a carefree and happy time in your life."

I shook my head slowly. "I don't know how to be that way. Carefree, I mean. I feel if I don't keep things in order, my life will spin out of control."

She placed her hand under my chin and turned my head to look at her. "How long have you felt that way?"

I shrugged. "My whole life, I guess. When we were living in Cincinnati, everything was more certain. I had a schedule I could count on, and I pretty much knew what to expect. Moving here has thrown everything off. Nothing feels the same. It's as if someone pulled the floor out from under me, and I'm just floating in space." I looked around my bedroom. "Except in here. I feel safe when I'm in my room."

She leaned forward and wrapped her arms around me. A sob threatened to escape from my throat, and I could feel my eyes filling with tears.

"Oh, sweetheart, I'm so sorry. I had no idea you felt that way. I knew you seemed to feel things more deeply than your brothers and sisters, but I thought that just meant you were more sensitive." She pulled back from me slightly so she could look into my eyes. "I've always thought of you as the one of our children I didn't have to worry about. I can see now how unfair that's been." She put her hands on my shoulders and looked at me intently. "I promise you things are going to get better. Your dad and I are going to find a way to help you. I don't know how yet, but I promise you we will."

I swiped at the tears rolling down my cheeks. "It's okay, Mom. It's my fault. You and dad don't have to worry about me. I'll do a better job at being happy."

She sighed and stood up. "That's precisely the problem. We've allowed you to feel you have to fix everything wrong with the world, at least the world in this house. It's not your fault, Julie, and it's not something you need to take care of." She smiled at me reassuringly. "Now, how about coming downstairs with me? It's been a while since we've made homemade cookies together.

My eyes opened wide thinking about the savory wonder of fresh baked cookies. I could feel the tightness in my chest beginning to loosen, and I forced myself to take a deep breath. "Chocolate chip?"

She laughed and pulled me to her. I could feel her head nodding as she held me in her warm embrace. "Absolutely." She pulled back to look at me. "Go wash your face and meet me downstairs."

Her visit had been a surprise, and our conversation even more so. I felt a glimmer of the same hope I had begun to recognize after I read the magazine article. Maybe I didn't have to feel so confused anymore. Maybe there was a way to change. At least now I knew someone else was looking out for me.

CHAPTER THREE

Several days went by before I heard anything further about my conversation with my mother. During that time, I tried to appear as normal as possible, which meant I attempted to mimic the actions of my twin sisters instead of behaving like myself. That was no small feat, considering I had no idea what it meant to be a "normal" fifteen-year-old. At least I managed to get out of my room more often. Not that I ventured very far. I mostly sought refuge in the den on the main floor, tucking myself snugly into the window seat built into the bay window. Sitting there gave me the chance to watch what the rest of the household was up to without appearing to pry.

One day, I decided to wander out into our backyard. It was a bright, glorious day, and the den was washed in the colors of the midday sun. I could feel the warmth cover my face, and I leaned back against the cushions of the window seat and closed my eyes.

The house was unusually quiet, since all four of my brothers and sisters were out. Mike had come bounding down the stairs about an hour earlier, yelling something about a book give away in the parking lot of the local elementary school. My next-to-oldest brother was a far cry from what you might call a book worm, but he had a fascination with first edition copies of novels and was forever on the lookout for one that might show up in an unexpected place.

The twins followed close on his heels, begging him to "wait up" so they could tag along in hopes of running into some of their future classmates. Bill sauntered by about a half-hour later, his hands filled with an overstuffed ham sandwich that he crammed into his mouth as he mumbled a goodbye. I assumed he was heading down the block to meet up with a boy he had spotted taking apart a record player in his garage, just to see how it worked. That scenario was as enticing to my oldest brother as candy was to a toddler.

I wasn't sure where my parents were. I hadn't seen them since breakfast, but because it was Saturday. I suspected they were off somewhere devoting themselves to the pursuit of their favorite passions, which either meant each other, or their respective hobbies. I picked up the book I had been reading and headed to the back door of the house, stopping in the kitchen to fill a glass from the ever-present pitcher of iced tea my mother kept in the refrigerator.

The main floor of our house was laid out symmetrically. The front door opened into a small foyer that ended at the staircase. An opening to the right of the foyer led to a formal living room, although there was rarely anything formal that took place in there. The rear of the living room opened into a dining area with a large table that could easily seat ten people. Double doors opened off the right side of the dining room into the screened porch built on top of the garage.

The den was to the left of the front door, on the other side of the foyer. It housed our family's stereo cabinet and assortment of vinyl records, a comfortable sofa and two overstuffed chairs, and the window seat that had recently become my favorite place. There was a narrow hallway extending from the side of the foyer and running parallel to the staircase as it passed in front of the den. At the end of the hallway was a door that opened into a pantry where food and other household supplies were stored. A doorway to the left led into the kitchen, which was large enough to accommodate a small table used for snacks or meals when our entire family was not present, and served as a makeshift sewing table for my mother. On the other side of the pantry was the entrance to the dining room, and a small powder room was tucked into the area under the staircase across from the pantry.

A door at the rear of the kitchen allowed access to the backyard after passing through what was known as a mud room. I don't know why it was called that. I guess it was intended to be a spot to wipe off the yard's dust, dirt, and mud so they wouldn't be tracked into the rest of the house. Our mud room held a washer and dryer and our pet rabbit, Jackie. Jackie had been brought to our Cincinnati home by the twins after their teacher told their class that the rabbit would be set free in the woods the following afternoon. The twins were certain Jackie would never survive the "wilds" of urban Cincinnati, so they convinced the teacher to let them bring her home. Unfortunately, neither the teacher nor the twins checked with our parents first. Jackie became the source of many teary discussions until my parents finally relented and allowed her to stay. She was supposed to be the twins' responsibility, but her care and feeding usually fell to my mother.

Grabbing the book I had been reading and the glass of iced tea, I headed out the back door, stopping to scratch Jackie's nose between the wires of her cage. The backyard was at least a third of an acre in size and rose in terraced levels to an alley. A ramshackle garden shed sat in the far-right corner of the yard. When my father was home, he spent a lot of time in the backyard tackling the out-of-control condition of the gardens he inherited from the previous owners.

My mother's domain was the kitchen. She loved to cook and sew, and frequently had a pot of something delicious simmering on the stove while she was bent over a cut-out pattern of some item of clothing she had laid out on the kitchen table.

The entire backyard was fenced, which gave our two dogs, Barkster and Sunny, plenty of space to run about. However, after they had trampled a patch of vegetables my dad had painstakingly nurtured back to health, he erected a second fence to enclose the back portion of the yard next to the shed. The dogs didn't seem to mind too much when they were confined to that area. The enclosure provided a comfortable place for them to rest under the shade of one of the trees that grew next to the alley, and grass they could roll on when they wanted to enjoy the sun. There were even two dog houses located next to the garden shed where they could get out of the rain or bad weather, although they usually chose to snuggle into one of them together.

Barkster was a Chocolate Lab and Sunny a Golden Retriever. Needless to say, they took up a lot of space. Barkster was technically Bill's dog, and Sunny was Mike's. When the dogs first came to live with us in Cincinnati, my brothers spent countless hours playing with them and taking them on outings to nearby parks where they could run to their hearts' content. But as the boys grew older and other activities captured their interest, the dogs began to spend more time with my dad. I don't think he minded too much. He mentioned to me he always wanted a dog when he was a boy, but his parents had been against the idea. Now he had the pleasure of fulfilling his boyhood dream in duplicate.

I made my way out of the house and walked toward one of the shaded wooden benches located about halfway up the yard. My dad waved at me from where he was standing, peering down at a row of plants. He had on faded jeans, a well-worn, light blue chambray shirt that he wore un-tucked, and a floppy straw hat that I guessed had been left behind by the previous owners. It wasn't the type of hat a man would typically choose to wear, especially since it had a yellow and white plastic daisy woven into the headband. But my father seemed unconcerned about how he looked. During the week, he left for work wearing a perfectly pressed suit with a white dress shirt and tie. As soon as he arrived home he quickly changed into his "play clothes", as he called them, which consisted of some variation of what he was wearing this day.

From where I stood, I could hear him whistling a tune I recognized from one of the records kept in the den. The record collection included a diverse selection that reflected the taste of each member of the family. My parents' choices tended toward Big Band music, whereas my brothers were more inclined to select Elvis Presley or Chuck Berry. I recognized the song my dad was whistling as one by the Beatles. They were favorites of the twins and, I had to admit, mine, too. Since the twins frequently commandeered the choice of music being played in the house, a Beatles tune filled the air more often than not.

I sat my book and glass of iced tea on the wooden bench and made my way over to where my dad was working. As I got closer, I noticed his face appeared relaxed with contentment as he plucked away at the weeds that surrounded the plants.

"Hey, Dad."

He straightened up and greeted me with a big smile. "Hey yourself, Jubie."

"Jubie" was what I had called myself until I was around five years old. For some reason the l sound was difficult for my tongue to form, so I had inserted a "B" instead. Even after I was able to make the shift to pronouncing it correctly, my dad chose to keep calling me Jubie. I didn't really mind, at least when we were at home. But his use of this childhood nickname made me cringe when I heard him say it in public. I was always trying to break him of that habit. Parents can be so hard to train!

I stood next to him and peered down at the plants he was weeding. "What kind of plants are those?"

"Well, technically, they're tomato plants. But it's too soon to tell whether we'll get any fruit from them."

I looked at him curiously. "Don't you mean vegetables?"

He gave me a smile that said he was about to impart a little tidbit of knowledge. My dad was famous for his tidbits about anything and everything that came up in conversation, usually preceded by saying "Well, let me tell you about that," as his face spread into a broad grin. In this case, he launched into a description of how a tomato was really a member of the fruit family because it develops from the ovary of a flower and contains seed. The whole idea of a plant having ovaries made absolutely no sense, and I frowned at him in disbelief, causing him to burst into laughter.

"Hard to imagine, I know. The thing of it is, a tomato is considered the fruit of the plant, but it's classified as a vegetable when we eat it. The same can be said of eggplants, cucumbers, bell peppers, avocado, and olives, to name a few."

I looked at him closely to see if he was serious, but his face showed no sign that he was joking. I held up my hands in surrender and looked down at a patch of green-leaved plants next to the tomato. "What's that called?"

My dad crouched down so he could pinch off a leaf. "Basil. Smell this." He held the leaf under my nose. The aroma was a little peppery with a slight hint of something sweet.

"Umm. It smells good. Can you eat it?"

"You wouldn't want to eat it by itself, but pair it with a red, ripe tomato and a little oil and you'll think you've died and gone to heaven."

I couldn't help but grin at his enthusiasm. My father was definitely a peculiar man. Staunchly professional in his daily life, carefree gardener during his off hours. He reminded me of Clark Kent, Superman's alter ego, except this caped crusader wore jeans instead of tights. The image of my dad yanking off his work shirt to reveal his true identity made me smile.

"Oh Dad, you're such a character!"

A silly grin spread across his face. "I kind of like the idea of being a character. Especially if it makes me mysterious." He raised one eyebrow and squinted at me with the other eye. I suspected he was trying to mimic one of the detective characters on television, but he came across looking more like Popeye. I held my hand in front of my mouth in an effort to hold back the giggles threatening to spill out.

His expression shifted from playful to serious as he brushed his dirt-covered hands against his jeans. "I'm glad to see you smiling. Your mother told me you've been having a pretty rough time since we moved to Nashville."

I dropped my eyes away from his and pretended to study the basil. "I'm okay. I guess it's just taking me a little longer than the other kids to get used to being here." I glanced quickly at him, then stared down at my feet. "You and mom don't have to worry about me. I'll be fine."

He reached over and put his hand on my shoulder. "I'm sure you will. But maybe it would help to have someone to talk things over with. Someone besides your mom or me, I mean. Sometimes running things past someone with a more objective view can be helpful."

My eyes opened wide in alarm. "You mean a stranger? I wouldn't feel comfortable talking about my feelings with someone I don't know. That would be too embarrassing."

He nodded slowly. "I understand how you might feel that way. The only reason I'm bringing it up is one of my co-workers at the bank mentioned his son had a lot of difficulty adjusting to his new school when they moved here a year ago. They found someone for him to talk to who really helped him turn things around. I'm wondering if you would be willing to at least meet her. If you hit it off, we can arrange for you to see her regularly for as long as you want."

I looked at him in alarm. "So, she's a shrink? Everyone will think I'm crazy if I'm seeing a shrink!"

He smiled at me reassuringly. "I don't think she'd appreciate being called a shrink. She's a psychologist who specializes in working with young people. Just normal kids like yourself who need someone to help them sort things out. My co-worker said she did wonders for his son."

I was beginning to feel light-headed, and I realized I was holding my breath. I allowed myself to exhale slowly, and I could feel the tension in my chest ease. I knew my parents well enough to understand that suggesting one of their children might need to see a psychologist was not an easy thing for them. I also realized they never would have suggested it unless they felt it could help.

My parents had their share of shortcomings, but love for their children and the desire to do what was best for us were not among them. I decided I needed to muster up the courage to give their idea a try.

"I suppose it wouldn't hurt to meet her. Will I have to go by myself, or can you or Mom go with me?"

He smiled at me warmly and I could see a glimmer of tears in his eyes. "I promise you, one of us will be right by your side as long as you want us to be."

I nodded firmly. "Okay. When can I see her?"

He surprised me by pulling me close to him for a hug. "I'm so proud of you, Jubie. I'll get the psychologist's phone number from my colleague and ask your mom to give her a call tomorrow." He pulled back to look at me. "Now what do you say about going inside and bringing your old man a glass of iced tea? I've worked up quite a thirst out here."

"Sure, Dad. I totally forgot about mine." I trotted over to the bench where I left my glass. The ice had completely melted, and I decided to dump it out and get a fresh glass. As I got to the door, I turned and looked back at my dad. He was still standing where I had left him, with his shoulders slightly hunched and a faraway look in his eyes. It suddenly occurred to me that my parents had worries, too. Of course, I knew they did, but sometimes I forgot they were just as human as the rest of us. The idea that I had been the cause of some of their most recent worries didn't sit well with me. I decided I was going to have to do whatever it took to get things in control. Maybe if I started seeing this psychologist right away, everything could get back to normal. I could go back to being the strong, dependable daughter my parents were accustomed to.

I opened the door to the mudroom carefully, making sure it didn't slam behind me, and made my way to the refrigerator. I felt a newfound resolve forming in my mind. I was going to become the best adjusted child in the house. That way, my parents wouldn't have to worry about me anymore. Funny thing was, it took me several weeks to understand it was exactly this sort of thinking I needed to change.

CHAPTER FOUR

Five days later, I found myself in the waiting room outside of the office of Dr. Sally Blackburn. My mom agreed to come with me since my dad was working. In truth, she would have probably been the one to join me even if he was free. As great as my dad was, I still couldn't see him sitting comfortably in the waiting room of a psychologist who was about to scrutinize his oldest daughter. My mom, on the other hand, appeared to take it in stride, as if it were no different from waiting to see any other type of doctor.

We finished filling out some forms the receptionist had given us and were picking through the stack of old magazines on the coffee table, when the door to the doctor's office opened. A girl who appeared to be about my age emerged, followed by someone I assumed was Dr. Blackburn. The girl smiled at me shyly as she passed by and I returned her smile. Dr. Blackburn stopped where my mother and I sat and regarded us warmly.

"You must be the Travers family. I'm Dr. Blackburn." She extended her hand to my mother, who rose and took it in hers.

"It's nice to meet you, Dr. Blackburn. I'm Diane, and this is my daughter Julie." They both looked in my direction, causing me to bolt up from my seat.

"Pardon my manners." I held a hand out to Dr. Blackburn. "It's nice to meet you, Dr. Blackburn."

She looked down at my hand with a smile before taking it firmly in hers. "You have excellent manners, Julie. Would you like to come into my office?"

I looked from her to my mother, suddenly unsure of what to do. "Your mother is welcome to come in with you if it will make you more comfortable."

I glanced at my mother before answering. "No, I think I'd like to come in by myself. If that's okay, I mean."

My mother's face briefly registered her surprise, but she quickly moved to retake her seat on the couch. "That's perfectly fine with me, Julie. I'll be here if you need me for anything."

I followed Dr. Blackburn into her office. The room was pleasantly inviting, and I could feel myself begin to relax. Two windows on one side of the room were covered in lacy curtains, muting the harshness of the afternoon sun, while still allowing it to bathe the walls in light. The walls were painted a pale yellow that appeared to absorb the sunlight and reflect it onto everything it touched.

A large desk was at the back of the room. Two cushioned chairs faced the desk, and a small sofa sat off to the far right. All of the furniture was framed in dark brown wood, with pillows covered in yellow and white fabric that complemented the color of the walls. A faint scent of something flowery seemed to come from a small bowl on one end of the desk, and a tray holding a pitcher of ice water and two glasses sat on the opposite end.

Dr. Blackburn pointed to one of the chairs in front of the desk, indicating I should sit there, before taking a seat in the other chair. She produced a small notebook and jotted something on it.

"I'm just going to take a few notes while we talk."

I nodded in her direction, although I found it difficult to concentrate on anything except my sweaty hands. I tried to wipe them inconspicuously on my shorts, but that only made me aware of how they seemed to be riding up my legs. I tugged at the hems and shifted in my seat, wishing I had worn long pants instead. Dr. Blackburn didn't seem to notice my discomfort. Or if she did, she was doing a good job of hiding it. I guessed that was normal for a person in her profession. She probably had a lot of training at pretending not to notice when clients were acting nervous.

She stood and walked to the pitcher of water. "Would you like a glass of cold water before we begin? It's awfully hot outside, today."

She filled one glass halfway and held it out to me. I looked at it longingly, but I was afraid to take it for fear it would slip through my sweaty palms. "No, thank you."

"Okay then," she said, returning to her chair. "Tell me why you're here today. Your mother mentioned you've been having some difficulty adjusting to your new environment. I believe she said your family moved to Nashville about six weeks ago. Is that correct?"

I nodded. "From Cincinnati. My dad decided to change jobs, so we moved here."

"That's a big change. It's hard to leave your home and all of your friends to start over in a brand-new place. I imagine that was a very scary thing to do."

"Have you ever had to move away from your home?" I wasn't sure if I was allowed to ask her questions, but she didn't seem to mind.

"Several times. When I went to college and graduate school. Then again when I was first married. Since that time, I've been lucky enough to stay in the same place for several years. Nashville has become my home now. I couldn't imagine living anywhere else."

I looked at her curiously. "So, you like Nashville? Did you have a hard time getting used to living here?"

"At first it was a little difficult. After my children were born, it felt like I'd never lived anywhere further than where we lived now. When you live with people you love, it's easier to make a home wherever you happen to be." She looked at her notebook. "I believe your mother said you have four brothers and sisters?"

I nodded. "Bill and Mike are older than me, and the twins are a few years younger. I'm the one in the middle."

She wrote something on her notepad. "I imagine that can be difficult at times. Being the middle child can make you feel as if you have to referee arguments from either side."

I looked at her with surprise. "That's right! I always feel I'm being pulled in one direction or the other, and I'm supposed to be able to solve any problem that comes up. At least I used to feel that way. Lately it just seems like nobody needs me anymore." I glanced down at my hands and I realized I told her something I hadn't admitted to anyone but my mom.

"I see. What was life like for you in Cincinnati? Did you feel as responsible for your brothers and sisters there as you do here?"

I thought about that before answering. "Maybe more. Since we've moved to Nashville, everybody else in the family seems to be adjusting just fine. It like my brothers and sisters rarely need my help anymore. I'm not even sure they notice I'm around most of the time." I frowned as the truth began to sink in.

"Does that make you feel better or worse, knowing they are getting along well on their own?"

I couldn't answer her immediately. The thought that Bill and Mike, and Sherry and Carey didn't need me anymore, the way I thought they should, was confusing. It was a relief, but it made me feel as if I had just stepped off a cliff without a parachute. "I guess it feels weird. Like things changed when I wasn't looking."

She laid the notepad and pen on her desk and leaned forward so her elbows were resting on her knees, with her hands clasped in front of her. "Perhaps you've been defining yourself by your role in your family. With that role having changed, it leaves you uncertain who you are anymore."

Her comment puzzled me. "But why don't my brothers and sisters need me anymore?"

"I'm sure they still need you, but perhaps in a different way. Maybe they all just need you to be Julie, whoever she happens to be. Moving to a brand-new place was a big adjustment for all of you. I suspect your siblings are just trying to figure out where they fit in their new lives, the same as you. If you think about it, that gives you the freedom to find out who you are, without having to worry about anybody else."

I shook my head firmly. "But that doesn't feel right. It would be selfish for me to worry only about myself. Plus, if I don't keep an eye on what everybody is up to, things could get really crazy. You have no idea how much trouble five kids can get into."

She laughed. "It's true. I only have two children, but that still gives me a pretty good idea what you're talking about." She turned to a new page on her notepad. "Tell me more about your life in Cincinnati."

I spent the next several minutes describing what life had been like before we moved to Nashville; the school I attended, the people we knew, the house we lived in, and what our everyday life was like. The more I talked, the clearer it became. My life in Cincinnati hadn't been much different than it was in Nashville. My siblings hadn't really needed me to intervene in their arguments or check up on their whereabouts. They tolerated my intrusions into their lives, but they all had interests of their own that kept them happily occupied.

Dr. Blackburn listened patiently as I spoke, occasionally offering a comment or a reassuring nod of her head. As I finally reached the end of my story, she snapped her notepad shut, and leaned forward so her elbows were once again resting on her knees, her hands clasped below her chin.

"I'm very impressed by how well you were able to express your thoughts just now. It took a lot of courage to say those things out loud. Especially to someone you've just met." She sat up straight. "Here's what I want you to do. Between now and our next visit, I want you to think about what makes Julie special. You're not allowed to say anything about your siblings or your parents. I'm not saying they aren't an important part of your life, or you aren't special to them. Being a member of a family means we will always care how everyone is doing. But I want you to concentrate on what makes you, uniquely you. It might help to write your thoughts. Or, if you're artistic, you might feel like drawing a picture. But keep in mind this is not a test. There are no wrong answers."

At first her idea seemed ridiculous. But the longer I sat there, the more excited I became. Think about what made me, me. What an odd assignment. And that's exactly what it was…an assignment. I know she said I wasn't being tested. But when I thought of it as homework, I became very enthusiastic. I could do this! I was good at homework. Once I thought of it that way, I became extremely determined to excel at the assignment.

"Okay. I'm willing to give it a shot."

She clapped her hands together and stood. "Wonderful! Let's plan to see each other again next Wednesday. I'll let the receptionist know to block this time for you for the next several weeks."

My mouth opened in shock. "Several weeks? You mean it will take me that long to get fixed?"

She smiled and placed a reassuring hand on my shoulder. "There's nothing that needs to be 'fixed' about you. You just need a little time to get acquainted with yourself. Does that sound okay?"

I frowned and mumbled a solemn, "Okay." As we were about to leave her office, I stopped and turned to her once more. "What should I tell my parents?"

"Whatever you feel comfortable with. Just remember, this is your time. You don't have to feel obligated to explain anything about our sessions unless you want to. I'll let your mother know we'll be continuing to see each other, and you made good progress today."

I looked at her doubtfully, but her permission also made me feel relieved. It was going to be enough of a challenge to just concentrate on completing her assignment. If I had to explain it to my parents or to any one of my brothers and sisters, I wasn't sure

I could get through it. It would just be too embarrassing. That was a feeling I'd just as soon avoid.

CHAPTER FIVE

My sessions with Dr. Blackburn continued for a long time. At first, I was just trying to figure out who I was if I no longer had to be the peacemaker, mediator, or traffic controller of my siblings. That took a lot of work because I had never considered myself in any other way. Eventually, with Dr. Blackburn's enduring support, I began to realize that a whole lot was going on inside of Julie Travers that I needed to explore.

I became aware I didn't have many friends, which was to be expected since I'd just moved to a new city. But even in Cincinnati, I basically closeted myself off from everyone but my family, except for a few schoolmates I would study with on occasion. Eventually, I was able to understand this had a lot to do with my need to manage everything down to the last detail. Dr. Blackburn said that this needed to be in constant control, or compulsion as she called it; that it was a clear sign of insecurity. So, however much I told myself I didn't have time for friendship because my family needed me so much, the truth was; the idea of risking the level of vulnerability that making friends required scared me to death.

That's how I came to meet Georgia Ayres. When it was time for me to begin my freshman year in high school in Nashville, I entered the doors of St. Bernadette armed with a concrete plan. Dr. Blackburn had advised me to pick out one fellow student who looked even more ill at ease than I felt, and make friends with her. When I noticed Georgia sitting by herself in the school cafeteria day after day, I decided she would be my pick. I realized this was somewhat cowardly of me, since she was obviously at least as socially uncomfortable as I was. But it also helped me muster my courage to approach her. All I had to do was tell myself I would be doing her as much of a favor as she would be doing me, and it boosted my confidence.

It was around the third week of school when I set my plan into motion. On the appointed day, I loaded my tray with food from the cafeteria line and made a bee-line for the back table where Georgia sat alone, bent over one of our textbooks. I placed my tray on the table and sat across from her. Truthfully, I don't remember too much more about our interaction that day, except that she seemed surprised to see me, and more than a little grateful for the company. I also remember thinking, what an odd couple we made. She was clearly one of the tallest girls in the class in a sort of gangly, "just growing into herself" way, whereas I was short and skinny. Whenever we were together, we tended to resemble the cartoon duo Mutt and Jeff. That was also the time when I was wearing a pair of glasses way too large for my face that kept slipping down my nose whenever I would lean forward to take a bite. So, all-in-all, we were a rather comical pair.

From the first time I sat across from Georgia in the school cafeteria, I knew we were going to be best friends. She had a way of making me feel special, as if I was the only one she could turn to when she needed to figure out something. From my side of the relationship, her unconditional acceptance gave me the confidence to unlock some of the doors behind which I kept my true feelings. I felt stronger when I was around her, and less reluctant to show my insecurities.

Georgia used to say that our friendship helped save her from herself. For me, it helped lead me to myself. I didn't tell Georgia about my meetings with Dr. Blackburn, at least not for several years. Between the continuing encouragement of the doctor and the unabashed acceptance from Georgia, I steadily became more aware of what was special about me. I slowly began to loosen the swaddling blanket of control that I had depended upon for so long.

By the time graduation day was approaching four years later, I had not only made great progress on figuring out who I was, but also what I was really good at doing. It turned out I was a virtual whiz with numbers and could rival any of my classmates in contests involving mathematical calculations. I was also very detail oriented, which was no surprise to anyone who had ever spent any time around me. Instead of just using that talent to help me arrange my closet, I began to turn it toward developing a sharp precision for working out math problems. I wasn't satisfied to just produce the correct answer. I wanted to be able to outline in minute detail the steps taken to arrive at the end result. Luckily, that peculiarity was highly regarded in the academic world, garnering me the respect of my teachers and the attention of the guidance counselor, Sister Anaselma, who began to map out her idea of what my future should look like.

Part of the Sister's plan was to meet with my parents and describe how a college education could expand upon my mathematical talents and guide me into a productive career. That was one way in which I was fortunate to have attended an all-girls school. In the late 1960s, there was still a fairly pervasive societal attitude that it was more important for boys to have a career, than for girls. I guess the assumption was, a girl would just end up getting married, having babies, and taking care of her kids, husband, and home. Why waste time and money on preparing her for a job? Since all of the students and most of the teachers at St. Bernadette's were female, the attitude that placed girls in a secondary role to boys just wasn't tolerated. We were repeatedly told we had to plan for our future, rather than assume some eventual husband would fill those shoes.

I remember the day my parents came home from meeting with the guidance counselor. I was sitting in the den in what was still my favorite spot, engrossed in a book I picked up in the school library. I heard the front door open. They didn't see me at first, and I heard my mother say to my father, "I understand you're excited about the idea of having one of your children follow in your footsteps, but what if that's not the best thing for Julie?"

When they spotted me sitting in the window seat, they stopped abruptly in the doorway and looked in my direction.

"What are you two talking about?" I asked.

My mother glanced at my father, who was staring at me with an expression I couldn't read. "Your mother and I just came from a meeting with Sister Anaselma. She seems to think you should go to college so you can hone your mathematical skills. She also mentioned there's a Career Day next Friday at your school where you're allowed to visit a business where you might want to eventually work. I thought maybe you'd like to go to the bank with me."

I looked back and forth between my parents, waiting for them to tell me what they thought, but they remained silent. "I don't know if I want to go to college. I realize that's what Sister Anaselma thinks I should do, but I'm not sure if it's the right thing for me." I paused and looked at my dad, who was intently studying his fingernails. "I do like the idea of going to the bank with you on Career Day, Dad. I've always been curious to learn more about what you do, and maybe spending a day there can help me figure out if it's something that might be right for me, too."

When I finished speaking, he finally looked at me, and I could see a glimmer of excitement in his eyes. "I'd like that. But your mother and I also want you to give serious thought to the idea of going to college. I did, you know. If I hadn't gotten my bachelor's degree in business, I wouldn't have been able to move into a management position at the bank as quickly as I did. A college degree can give you a leg up on a career, and it's even more important today than when I was your age. Tossing that aside is not something you want to do lightly."

I let his advice sink in. "I understand, and I promise I'll give the idea of college a lot of thought. But, in the meantime, I'd still like to go to the bank with you next Friday. There's no harm in collecting as much information as I can about my options, right?" I looked directly at my mother, who had remained oddly silent throughout our conversation. She caught my eye and sighed audibly.

"No, there's no harm in that. But I want you to promise me you won't make a decision without talking with Sister Anaselma again. It might be a good idea for you talk to Dr. Blackburn about it, as well."

I could feel excitement beginning to bubble up in my chest. "You know me. I'll probably think this decision to death, like I do everything else. I agree it's a good idea for me to talk to Dr. Blackburn. I'll give her a call and set up an appointment for some time after Career Day."

My dad's face broke into a broad grin as he looked from my mother to me. "Okay, then! Now that that's settled, what do you say to some pizza? I have a craving for a sausage pie from The House of Pizza."

I jumped eagerly from the window seat. "Great! I'll tell the twins to get ready. Mike's not here. He left a while ago saying he was going to the library to study." Mike was in his sophomore year at Peabody College, but he was still living at home. Bill was the only one of us who had left Nashville. After high school, he entered Georgia Tech, where he was finishing his junior year.

The House of Pizza had become a family favorite from the time we moved to Nashville. Their claim to fame was an incredible thin crust pizza, loaded with the topping of your choice, which for us always meant sausage.

I ran upstairs to poke my head in the door of the twins' room to tell them to get ready, then stopped in mine. I peered into a small mirror that sat on top of my chest of drawers to check my reflection, grabbing a hairbrush to pull my straight, shoulder-length blonde hair back into a pony tail. I almost didn't recognize the girl who looked back at me. Her eyes were shining, and she had a happy grin on her face. I recognized an odd feeling in my chest and the pit of my stomach as excitement tinged with anxiety. There was a huge choice in front of me, with the potential of mapping out the road I would take for the rest of my life. That was incredibly exciting, but also terribly scary. I had been mulling over the idea of going to college since my guidance counselor first brought up the possibility. Now, I could see there might be a second option just as enticing as the first. I didn't know how in the world I was going to be able to choose between the two, but I couldn't wait to figure it out.

When the day came for me to visit my dad's bank, I felt surprisingly calm. The night before, I had carefully laid out the clothes I intended to wear, a black skirt and white blouse, (my idea of business attire), so I wouldn't have to worry about choosing them in the morning. We were planning to walk together to the corner to catch the eight-thirty bus, so I made sure to be downstairs by seven-fifteen. My dad was already at the kitchen table, sipping a cup of coffee while he scanned the morning newspaper. My mom had just taken a pan of muffins out of the oven and was attempting to keep my brother Mike from burning his hand as he tried to snatch one before she could even set it down.

When Mike was a junior in high school, he decided he wanted to be a writer, but the guidance counselor wisely directed him toward pursuing a degree in teaching instead. Bill had been able to get a full scholarship to Georgia Tech, mostly because of his prowess on the football field. Mike was not as lucky. His grades were pretty good, but his tendency to daydream through classes kept him from earning the marks that could have helped him get a scholarship. He set his sights on going to George Peabody College, which was located near our house and across the street from Vanderbilt University. Peabody's teacher education program was nationally recognized and highly competitive. Mike managed to get admitted to Peabody, but it was necessary for him to work part-time through the school's work-study program to help pay his tuition. Since Peabody was a private college with a fairly high price tag, he opted to continue living at home to cut costs.

Mike breezed past me on his way out of the kitchen, tossing off a "Hey, Sis! See you tonight. I'm late for class," as he grabbed his backpack off the counter and sprinted for the front door. My mom placed the muffin pan on the stove top and shook her head at his retreating back.

"That boy will be late for his own wedding. That is, if he ever gets his head out of the clouds long enough to seriously date anyone."

My dad looked up from his newspaper with a puzzled expression. He had apparently been so engrossed in what he was reading he totally missed the interaction between my mom and Mike. He looked around the room in confusion to see what the commotion was about. When his eyes rested on me, he smiled broadly.

"There's my girl! Are you ready to learn what the bank business is all about?"

I took a glass out of the cabinet, filled it from the carton of orange juice on the kitchen counter, and sat across from him. "I could hardly sleep last night. I know I've been in the bank a few times, but this is different. I almost feel like I'm starting work today."

A smile spread across his face, which he quickly squelched as my mother gave him a stern look. "Well, let's not get ahead of ourselves, Jubie. Today is just a fact-finding mission. Your mother and I want you to have every chance to consider all the possibilities for your future, so you're better equipped to make a decision."

My mother's back was turned to us, but I knew she was listening carefully to our conversation. It was no secret she wanted to see me follow in my brothers' footsteps by going to college. I wasn't totally opposed to the idea myself. I just felt reluctant to postpone starting a career, especially if having a degree wasn't absolutely necessary. I talked this over with Dr. Blackburn, even before the idea of my visiting the bank on Career Day had come up. She pointed out that my desire to bypass college for work could be another offshoot of my need to feel in control; even when there was no clear evidence that control was within my reach.

There was actually a clinical name for what I seemed to be struggling with. It was called the Illusion of Control, which, as she explained it, was the tendency to overestimate one's ability to influence the course of events that one actually had little or no control over. Surprisingly, according to Dr. Blackburn, this is considered one of the more positive illusions that a person can have, because it makes them persist at things that they might otherwise give up on.

Her explanation reminded me of a story I had always enjoyed as a child called The Little Engine That Could. It was a tale of a happy-faced, choo-choo train, that was always spouting "I think I can, I think I can," as it struggled up a seemingly insurmountable hill. I always admired that brave little engine, since I related more than a little to its optimistic outlook. So, I decided; if thinking I would have more control of my life if I started working sooner rather than later was merely an illusion, at least it was helping me have the courage to move forward toward an unknown future that might otherwise have stopped me in my tracks. I was enjoying replacing anxiety with courage, and I was beginning to really like the new Julie I was getting to know.

CHAPTER SIX

My dad's position at the First National Bank was financial manager. As he described it, that meant that on most days he spent the majority of his time developing and reviewing financial reports and budgets. He was also responsible for managing and auditing the profits and losses of several major organizations.

Once we were seated on the bus, he opened his briefcase and began flipping through a stack of papers, selecting one that appeared to be filled with columns of numbers. "I won't be able to spend much time with you this morning. There's a pretty important meeting that I have to attend, but after that I'll hopefully be able to break free for a while."

He went on to explain that the meeting was to take place with three men who were in executive positions with the Country Music Association and WSM radio, and a couple of others who had ties to the banking industry. "The Country Music Association, or CMA, as it's known locally, was started in the 1950s with the intent of encouraging radio stations across the United States to give more airtime to country music songs. WSM was one of Nashville's local radio stations whose claim to fame was being the first station in the entire U.S. permitted to broadcast on the 650 frequency, which was known as "clear-channel broadcasting". A clear channel station had the highest level of protection from interference by other stations, particularly at night, which meant the broadcast could flow unimpaired across the airwaves. One advantage to WSM using this type of broadcast was the music it featured would be able to reach thousands of fans living in rural areas who otherwise would not be able to pick up the station. WSM is owned by the National Life and Accident Insurance Company, which also owns the Grand Ole Opry."

I had heard of the Opry even before we moved to Nashville. My parents frequently tuned in to WSM on Saturday evenings to listen to what they called a "barn dance". At the time, WSM played a variety of music throughout the week, but switched to country music for that one night.

"Do you remember the station we used to listen to on Saturday nights?" I rolled my eyes as I recalled the countless nights that my siblings and I had sat through part of each broadcast until we could slip away without offending our parents. "That broadcast became so popular that National Life decided to move it into a building in downtown Nashville called the Ryman Auditorium. After that, the radio show became known as The Grand Ole Opry." He went on to explain how the broadcast quickly grew from just a Saturday night barn dance to a full-fledged concert, with a live studio audience and a line-up of comically designed commercial breaks featuring many of the country music stars. The advent of the televised Opry brought country music and the Nashville Sound, as it eventually became known, into homes across the United States.

"I can't tell you any more about the meeting but there's some exciting stuff brewing in Music City." He grinned at his use of the label that had been attached to Nashville since the 1950s.

We got off the bus at the main station downtown, and headed east to walk the few remaining blocks to the bank. It was housed in an impressive, five-story rectangular building at the corner of Fourth Avenue and Union Street. It was constructed entirely out of gray stone, with a series of tall columns that lined all four sides. The columns gave the building an ornate appearance, reminiscent of the replica of the ancient Greek Parthenon that stood in the middle of Centennial Park on West End Avenue.

The Parthenon had been part of the Centennial Exposition that took place in the park back in 1895 to commemorate the 100-year anniversary of the founding of Tennessee. When the Exposition ended, the city decided to keep the Parthenon, restoring it in a more permanent fashion in the 1920s and 30s. For most of the Nashville community, it represented civic pride in the "Athens of the South" nickname that had been bestowed on the city in the 1800s due to its emphasis on education. But for me, as well as countless other Nashville high school students, it represented a great place to gather with friends in the shade of its imposing walls.

I stepped into the lobby of the bank, stopping just inside the door to allow myself to take in the view of the entire space. The inside of the building was chilly, in spite of the heat of the day, and I imagined that was because the interior walls and floor were made of stone. It made me think of a cave I visited on one of our school field trips that felt chilly in spite of the warm temperature outside. Windows were positioned between each of the exterior columns allowing natural light to fill the room. Shades hung from the top of each window frame that could be raised or lowered, depending upon the angle of the sun. A desk sat to the left of the front door with an employee stationed behind it to greet customers as they entered the building.

A long, tall counter lined the right side of the room. There were six, open-framed windows across the front of the counter. Each window was manned by a teller, a man or woman who stood or sat behind each opening and handled customer transactions. There were two separate rooms at the rear of the main floor. The name, Tim Carson, Bank Manager was painted on one, and Will Travers, Financial Manager on the other. There was also a large enclosed area off to the left side of the main room. The door to that room was open, and I could see a sizeable wooden table at the center of the room, surrounded by leather cushioned chairs.

A hushed quiet pervaded the building, reminding me of being in a library. There was no laughing or loud talking. Everyone I saw, including the customers, was dressed in business attire, which meant suits and ties for the men, and skirts or dresses for the women.

It wasn't the first time I visited the bank. I had gone with my mother a few times when she needed to take something to my father, or arrange for a money withdrawal from their account. But this time felt different to me. Every image and sound seemed sharper than ever before, and I stood motionless in the midst of it, allowing myself to absorb the experience.

I had forgotten my dad was still standing beside me, and I turned to find him giving me an inquisitive look. "Would you like to look around? I have to get ready for my meeting soon, but I've arranged for the branch manager to give you a tour."

I nodded without speaking. My heart was beating rapidly, and my mouth felt dry.

I followed him to the long counter where a young man was talking with a woman standing behind one of the stations. "Harry Simpson, I'd like to introduce you to my daughter Julie. As I mentioned to you, her school is having a Career Day, and she thought she'd like to get a good look at what goes on inside a bank. I told her I've asked you to show her around."

Harry turned away from the counter and faced me. He appeared to be only in his mid-twenties, although I noticed his sandy-colored hair was beginning to recede from both sides of his forehead. He was of medium height, but he still appeared tall compared to my five feet two inches. He was compactly built, like some of the boys I knew who had been involved in wrestling at St. Thomas Moore. He was dressed similar to my dad with a navy-blue suit, a white shirt, and red and white striped tie. A genuine kindness in the way he looked at me put me instantly at ease, and I found myself surprisingly drawn to him.

Our eyes caught, and Harry held my gaze. "I would be happy to show your daughter around."

My dad nodded at Harry and gave me a gentle squeeze on the arm.

"I'll come find you if I get some free time. Thanks again, Harry." He began to walk briskly toward his office.

We stood for a few seconds just looking at each other before Harry broke the silence. "Is this your first time to visit our bank, Miss Travers?"

For a moment, my mind went blank as I found myself distracted by the sparkle of his green eyes. He stood watching me patiently with a slight smile on his face until I finally managed to collect my wits enough to mumble a response. "No. I've been here a few times before, but I feel like I've never really seen it until today. It's busy, but there's a peacefulness about it, too. It makes me feel at ease."

His eyes narrowed, as he seemed to consider what I said. "I remember feeling that way the first time I came to work here. I'd been in several banks before. Even worked in one of them. But this place is special. I don't know what there is about it, but when I'm here, I feel like it's where I belong." A sudden look of embarrassment crossed his face. "I'm sorry. I guess that sounded crazy."

I shook my head emphatically. "Not at all. I was thinking the same thing a few minutes ago. When I've been here before, I just thought of it as a place where my dad worked. Now I'm seeing it as a place where I might work, and that thought makes me feel really happy."

His eyebrows lifted in surprise. "Really? So, you're considering a job in banking. I assume that would be a few years from now?"

The implication that I might be too young to be ready to start working at the bank was slightly annoying, but I decided to shrug it off. My size tended to make people assume I was younger than my actual age, and I guessed he was just falling prey to the same conjecture. "No, I'm talking about soon. I'll be graduating from high school in a few months, and my dad thought I might want to consider a job in finance. I'm really good at math, and working with calculations interests me."

A smile lifted the corners of his mouth, which only added to his appeal. "Well, then. Why don't I show you around so you can get a better idea of what the day-to-day operations of a bank are all about?"

He gestured at the long counter on my right. "This is where the tellers work. Sometimes they're called cashiers, because they're the ones who handle the money transactions, but they're also our main link with the bank customers. They need to be well trained, not just in financial matters, but also in public relations, because most people's impression of the bank is based upon their experience with the tellers. If they're impatient, or irritated by something a customer says, we can lose business. But if they're friendly and welcoming, the customer leaves with a positive experience.

"The financial part of their job is pretty demanding, too. They have to be able to process transactions with a high degree of accuracy and pay attention to details, like the denominations of bills they're handling. You can't imagine how many times a teller has made the mistake of writing down the wrong deposit because they mistook a one-hundred-dollar bill for a ten, or even a one. Or, even worse for the bank, when they've handed out the wrong amount in a withdrawal. Customers won't often point it out when a mistake is made in their favor, but they're really quick to say so when the error goes against them. Either way, the bank reputation suffers.

"Tellers have to be security conscious, too. They need to learn to read people when they walk in the door, and when they come up to their window. They have to be able to recognize when someone tries to use a fake ID. Then, at the end of the day, they have to figure out the interest on each individual account and record it, and file it away. If they make a mistake, it can throw the entire operation into turmoil."

I watched the tellers at work while he spoke. A small, but steady line of customers stood in front of each station waiting their turn to be helped. When they reached the window, the teller greeted them with a smile and asked, "What can I do for you today?"

"I had no idea the job of a teller was so complicated. Do they have to go through a lot of training?"

Harry began to walk slowly past the counter, and I followed along beside him. "They have to complete six weeks of instruction and pass a fairly rigorous exam before they can even start working. Once they're hired, they're considered on probation for the first few months, during which time they are required to attend a series of classes held at each branch location on nights and weekends. There's a lot of on-the-job learning that happens, too. Occasionally, they have to go through some additional training when a new bank product becomes available."

As we arrived at the end of the counter, I noticed a desk that had not been visible before. Harry pointed to the man seated there. "This is Frank Reed. He's the bank's financial service representative. FSRs often start out as a teller, but they go through more extensive internal training in order to be capable of doing things like monitoring market trends and providing financial advice based on a customer's needs. They're also responsible for keeping track of the bank's assets and liabilities, although the person with the biggest responsibility for that is the financial manager. In this case, your dad."

Frank glanced up as Harry spoke and gave me a quick smile, before turning his attention back to the papers stacked in front of him.

Harry pointed to the office behind Frank's desk that was labeled Bank Manager. "That's Mr. Carson's office. He oversees the operation of the entire bank and supervises the senior employees, like your dad." He leaned closer to my ear and lowered his voice to a whisper. "Truth be told, he spends more time on the golf course than he does in his office. The bank's president, Mr. Browning, is an avid golfer. He and Mr. Carson meet at least three times a week to play out at the Belle Meade Country Club. Rumor has it, they've even played a few rounds with former President Eisenhower."

It took a few seconds for his words to register, because I was distracted by his nearness and the tantalizing scent of his aftershave. I recognized it as the same one a boy I had dated during my junior year had worn; a boy I had a huge crush on until he snubbed me just before the prom and took another girl instead. I inadvertently shook my head to clear it of these thoughts.

"What? You don't believe me?" I turned to see Harry regarding me with a sly smile.

"No. I mean, yes, I believe you. It's just hard to imagine President Eisenhower playing golf in Nashville. Does he come here often?"

"I believe he does. He's friends with Sam Flanders, the CEO of Third American Bank. They're old golfing buddies, and sometimes they invite Carson and Browning to join them. I imagine that has as much to do with business as with any sort of social contact." He looked at me out of the corner of his eye. "You know they say more financial deals are struck over a golf ball than a desk top."

I smiled at his attempt at humor. Even though Harry Simpson gave the impression of a serious, buttoned-down professional on the outside, there was clearly more beneath the surface of this man than was immediately obvious. Realizing that only tweaked my interest in him even more.

We continued walking past the bank manager's office to the door labeled Financial Manager. I pointed to it. "That's my dad's office. I remember going there a few times with my mom."

Harry looked where I was pointing and nodded. "That's right. Having his office next door to the bank manager helps them stay in close contact. That is, when Mr. Carson is on the premises."

I turned so I could look around the entire main floor from one end to the other. The only remaining office I could see was the one where the table and chairs were visible. "Where's your office?"

My question seemed to make him uncomfortable, because he shoved his hands in his pants pockets and looked down at the floor before answering. "I don't actually have one. My job is more hands-on with the tellers and FSR, so I mostly just wander around during the day. When I need to meet with someone, I either use the conference room or one of the file rooms upstairs."

I glanced overhead to the second floor, which was visibly open to the main level, separated only by an iron railing. A set of stairs, positioned between my dad's office and the bank manager's, led from the back of the main floor to the second level. There was also an elevator next to the conference room.

"I noticed from the outside that there are five floors to this building. Does the bank have offices on all of them?"

"Actually, there are six floors; a basement, the main floor, and four floors above the main one. The bank's vault is located in the basement. That's where money, records, documents, and other valuables can be securely stored. The floor just above this one is where you'll find restrooms, a break room, and the file rooms.

"The top three floors are rented to various attorneys who want space to work close to the Courthouse. Since they are able to access those floors from inside the building only during the hours the bank is open, there's a separate entrance outside leading to a staircase. All of the upstairs tenants are provided a key to that door, as well as to their individual offices. Having that separate entrance allows them to walk up to their floor when the bank is closed, at which time the doors leading into the main floor, as well as the elevator door, are kept locked for security."

As we were talking, I noticed my dad escorting five men into the conference room. They were an impressive looking group, all dressed in exquisitely tailored suits. I wasn't a very good judge of age, but I guessed them to be in their forties or fifties. I noticed that two of the men stood a little apart from the others. One of them was of medium build and had thick curly hair.

My dad gave a little wave in my direction as he stood aside to allow the five to enter the conference room, then closed the door behind him.

I heard a low whistle, and turned to see Harry staring in the direction of the conference room. "That's a pretty impressive group your dad is meeting with."

I looked at him to see if he was going to explain, and when he didn't, I asked him what he meant.

"The first three hold some of the most powerful positions in the music industry. The one with the mustache is Wes Plant. He's the chairman of the board of the CMA, and he's also on the board of directors for the First National Bank. Ronnie May, he's the one in the dark gray suit, is the founding president of the CMA. The third is Elliott Waldell. He's the president of WSM and has been a key player in both radio and TV in Nashville for quite a few years. The last two are the Taylor brothers, Hank and J.R. Junior. Their father, J.R. Senior, was a bank president in Union City, and the brothers worked for him for several years before branching out on their own. No one seems to know exactly what they're up to these days, but word has it they've been buying up stock in several banks across the state for the past few years." He folded his arms and frowned. "I wonder what that meeting is all about."

I wondered, too. My dad had mentioned that he would be meeting with representatives of WSM and the CMA, but he had only described the other two as having some involvement in banking. Just watching them at a distance gave me a creepy feeling, sort of like when you know you shouldn't walk down a certain street because there might be danger ahead. I wasn't sure if that feeling was an example of my gut instinct at work, but it made me want to find out more about why those two were in the bank.

I glanced at my watch and was surprised to see that it was almost ten-thirty. It had been a long time since the glass of juice that had been my only breakfast, and I was beginning to feel the need for something more substantial.

"Would it be okay if I stepped out to get a bite of something? I haven't had much to eat today." My stomach chose that moment to growl insistently.

Harry placed his hand over his mouth in an unsuccessful effort to cover the grin that spread across his face. "Sure. I have some work I need to take care of anyway." He reached in his back pocket and pulled out a wallet, extracting a twenty-dollar bill. "There's a sandwich shop on the corner that opens early. They make a really good turkey on rye. Why don't you let me treat you, and you can pick one up for me on your way back?"

I hesitated as I looked at the bill he thrust toward me, and realized I hadn't thought to bring any money. I took the bill from his outstretched hand and tucked it in the pocket of my skirt. "Thanks. Do you want mustard on your sandwich?"

He responded with a faint smile and shook his head. "Thousand island dressing, and a pickle on the side. They make the dressing themselves. Just bring it back to Frank's desk when you return. He has to leave soon to drop off some documents to one of our branch offices, so I'll be working there."

As I turned to leave, a question popped into my mind. "Say, Harry. Do you think it's a dumb idea to skip college in order to start working here?"

His mouth twisted in a frown. "Maybe. It depends on what you want for yourself, and how soon you want it."

His answer surprised me, because it was exactly what I had been struggling to figure out. Should I delay going after the career that really interested me because going to college first might prepare me for a better position down the road? Or should I jump at the opportunity to get started right away because who knew what the future would bring? How someone who had just met me could get right to the heart of my struggle was pretty amazing. Pretty disturbing, too!

CHAPTER SEVEN

That night, I could barely wait for dinner to be over so I could corner my dad to talk about my day at the bank. We hadn't spoken much about it on the bus ride home. He had been preoccupied with studying a file he brought with him from work, and I was grateful for the time to just stare out the window and allow my mind to wander back through everything I experienced that day. I hoped we could talk over dinner, but Sherry and Carey came home from school full of stories about how their freshman class president had been caught smoking a cigarette behind the school building; how the principal called her into her office, and how she eventually emerged in tears, with her scowling parents on her heels. Apparently, rumors were already circulating that she might be suspended from school for a few days, and would very likely be stripped of her role as class president.

I would have considered those things to be major, life altering issues, too. But given the bigger matter I was having to tackle, what I was going to do with my life, and how I should go about doing it, I found myself squirming with impatience waiting for their chatter to end. My mother kept casting studied looks in my direction, until she finally suggested that the twins help her clear the table, freeing my dad and me to vacate the room.

It was my dad's usual habit to go outside after dinner and check on his plants. He used to say that he wanted to see "how much they'd grown overnight," but I guessed he just wanted to enjoy a little quiet time after the hustle and bustle of his work day. Even with Bill away at college, and Mike gone most of the time, the twins had a way of filling up whatever space they occupied. I felt a little guilty for intruding on his quiet time, but my need to talk to him outweighed that concern.

He turned to me with an understanding look as we left the back door. "You were very patient with your sisters during dinner. It couldn't have been easy to wait for them to wind down so you could get a word in."

"I was hoping we could talk some about my visit to the bank today."

I walked beside him as he headed to the enclosed area at the back of the yard where Barkster and Sunny stood, wagging their tails expectantly and practically exploding with excitement as they watched us approach.

"Just let me let these two pups out first. I usually let them out when I'm working in the garden, but today they were trying to help me a little too much."

As soon as he opened the gate of the enclosure the dogs set off on a mad dash that had them circling the perimeter of the fence. They managed to make almost two complete turns before Barkster picked up a scent of something that caused him to pull up short and burrow his nose in the grass. Sunny trotted up to him nonchalantly to take a look at what he had found before heading off on her own hunt.

Dad turned two large ceramic pots upside down. "Have a seat. We need to keep an eye on what these two get up to." He carefully sat on one of the pots while I settled onto the other. "Harry Simpson said you seemed to enjoy your time at the bank today."

I nodded. "I did. I hadn't realized there was so much going on, and so many different jobs to be done. I had the impression that a bank was only a place to keep money until you needed it."

"That's how the banking business got started. People needed a safe place to store their money. So, for a long time, the business of banking mainly involved collecting money from individuals and businesses, then loaning that money to others who had credit needs. The person making the deposit had to be willing to accept a rate of interest; that means how much they would earn on the money over the time they left it in the bank which was lower than the rate paid by the one borrowing the funds. That way, there would always be a surplus of money to go around from deposits and interest rate differences. It's referred to in banking as assets and liabilities. Assets are what the bank owns, whereas liabilities are what a bank owes. It's extremely important that the balance between the two stays in the black. Otherwise, the bank would be at risk of insolvency."

I repeated the last word slowly. "In-sol-ven-cy. Harry mentioned that today. He said that's what it's called when a bank is at risk of failing because its debts outweigh its assets. He said that making sure that doesn't happen is one of the things you're responsible for."

"Generally speaking, that's true. Although the bank's president and the board of directors are officially in charge of monitoring the balance sheet in order to prevent that from happening."

I shook my head in amazement. "There's so much I don't understand."

He chuckled and patted me on the back. "And I've only given you the abbreviated version. But that's what school is for. Whether you pursue a college degree in Finance and Economics, or decide to dive right into the banking profession, you'll be required to attend a lot of classes and listen to a lot of lectures. And the need to learn will continue, even once you start working. I'm constantly having to read up on some new regulation or procedure that will cause a shift in the way things are done. For example, some pretty major changes began about ten years ago with the introduction of FAX transmission equipment, wire transfers, and money shipments. Then, more recently, when computers hit the market, the entire operating procedure began to change again. Most of the large cities, like Atlanta, New York, and Chicago, were able to move quickly to adjust to these innovations. Here in Nashville, we're still playing catch-up."

A little alarm went off in my head. "Does that mean that First National is at risk of closing?"

He paused before answering. "I don't think it will come to that. But we have to find a way to keep pace with our competition. I'm afraid some of what will have to take place won't be pleasant."

I studied his expression, but it was impossible to figure out what he was thinking. "What do you mean?"

"Well, for example, once we become more fully automated, we'll have machines that can process checks forty times faster than a person can do it. The more the bank changes to automation, the fewer people will need to be employed to do those same jobs."

"So, some of the people I saw today would be out of a job. Would all of those tellers be replaced by machines?"

He smiled at my question. "No, I think the tellers' jobs are safe for a while. It's harder to automate the handling of currency than checks. But that time will come. The key is for us to anticipate it before it does, and adjust accordingly. It's not just a matter of becoming more automated, the bank also needs to become more innovative."

I leaned forward on my makeshift seat and rested my face on my hands. It seemed to me that he was describing a revolution in the business of banking that had already begun, one that would eventually shake it to its core. That meant everything I had imagined I knew about working for a bank could be incorrect. It also meant, the limits I assumed existed in the profession were wrong, as well. If I chose to go to work for the bank, I could be completely helpless when it came to controlling my future, or I could end up in a situation that had more potential than I ever dreamed of. The back and forth possibilities of what could occur had my head spinning.

"Was that why you were meeting with those men today?"

His eyebrows lifted in surprise. "That's a pretty smart guess you just made there. I'm not really able to tell you much about it at this time, but I can say if what we were discussing today comes about, it could improve the bank's status in the community tremendously, and possibly even provide us with the means to shore up our liability structure."

I felt as if my head was crammed too full of new information, most of which I still couldn't fully grasp. "I don't understand what that means. Does it have something to do with helping the bank become more automated and innovative, like you were talking about?"

He paused before answering. "In simple terms, a bank's liability structure determines how much risk a bank can take without collapsing. It has to do with the input and outflow of funds, but also the type of funds that a bank is most dependent upon."

His explanation still confused me and gave me a glimpse into how little I really knew about the banking business. Luckily, I was given a break from having to figure it out any further, as I struggled to avoid being knocked off my seat by an overly enthusiastic Sunny. She came to a halt in front of me, rising on her hind legs so she could place her front legs over my shoulders. I threw my arms around her neck and pressed my face into her warm fur. "What a good girl! Did you find interesting things to chase today?" She answered with a joyful bark, then hopped down and began to sniff at one of the tomato plants that was beginning to hang heavy with red, ripe fruit. My dad stood and grabbed her by the collar, reaching with his other hand to snag Barkster.

"Oh, no you don't. I've spent too much time babying those things to have you chew them up. Let's get you two back where you belong, then I'll fill your bowls with some dinner." Both dogs began to dance around his legs as he attempted to move them toward the back of the yard. I jogged off toward the house so I could fill a bucket with the dried food that was kept in the mudroom. Once both bowls were filled with food and their water bowls had been refreshed, the dogs began to chomp away happily. We stood by and watched them for a few moments before my dad turned to me with a wistful look on his face. "One of the things I really appreciate about dogs is how straightforward they are. They either like something or they don't, and they never hesitate to let you know which one it is."

I wasn't sure what to make of his comment. Was he referring to the bank business again? Or was he talking about something completely different? Whatever he meant, I decided being straightforward was a good way to be; not just for dogs, but for people too. Which reminded me I had forgotten to ask my dad about the other two men who had been part of his meeting, and the strange feelings I had just from looking at them.

I started to bring it up, but decided to wait for a better time. Patience was something I had been forced to learn due to being part of a large family, but it was still something that didn't always come easy for me. In this particular case, my gut feeling told me this was not the time for that conversation.

CHAPTER EIGHT

The next few weeks were a flurry of activity. The school year was coming to an end, which meant the members of my senior class were frantically involved in deciding what their next steps would be. A few girls were engaged and planned to be married right after graduation. Others had received acceptance letters from colleges and were excitedly talking about buying things for their dorm room, or scouting out which sororities to consider pledging. Still others, like myself, were either caught in limbo between choosing college or career, or had already forsaken the path of continuing education for a secure job.

My best friend, Georgia, was in the latter category. Georgia was the editor of our school paper, and one of her articles had earned her a position working for one of Nashville's two local papers, the Nashville News. Her job would start almost as soon as school ended, which wouldn't give her much time to catch her breath before being immersed in a new challenge. That seemed to sit well with Georgia. Starting work right away would give her the chance to move into her own apartment. Life at home for her was a far cry from the loving environment of my own, so I couldn't blame her for wanting to get started on her new life as soon as possible.

Almost everyone in my class had been encouraged to send in college applications; everyone except those few girls whose grades did not suggest any chance of acceptance, or a few who had begun to show that motherhood was in their near future. I opted to apply only to schools in Tennessee in order to receive in-state tuition rates. I received acceptance letters from three colleges that offered degrees in Business or Economics: Vanderbilt University in Nashville, Middle Tennessee State University, located about an hour south of Nashville in Murfreesboro, and the University of Tennessee in Knoxville, a three-hour drive to the East.

The problem with Vanderbilt was it was just too expensive, and I was not offered any scholarship or financial assistance. MTSU was located in the middle of a corn field. At least, that's the way I viewed it. Murfreesboro was a quiet town in those days, with virtually nothing of interest to a teenager, unless you happened to prefer farm life, which I didn't. Commuting back and forth from Nashville was out of the question. It would take too long to make that trek every day, and my family was already down to just one car, since Bill had taken the second one to Georgia.

Knoxville posed a similar problem with respect to transportation, but it had the draw of the Great Smoky Mountains to its east. Among the three, Vanderbilt was my first choice, both in terms of location and the programs they offered, but after mulling over the financial picture with my parents, I realized I had to take it out of contention.

When I look back at those days, from that 20/20 hindsight that the future provides, I'm certain my choice of whether to go to college or plunge into a career was largely driven by practicality; although I can't deny there was more than a little of my ever-present desire to control things seeping in, as well. I wanted to learn more about the financial field. Specifically, I wanted to learn everything I could about banking. The small taste I sampled on the day I visited with my dad started a hunger in me that I was anxious to satisfy. Although pursuing a college education focusing on business was intriguing, I would have to wade through a long list of required non-business courses before I could even begin to delve into the topics that really interested me. When I matched the cost to my parents against the gain of my diving right into an entry level banking job, the balance began to clearly tip in the direction of the job. Still, it wasn't an easy decision to make.

What ultimately helped finalize the decision for me was a conversation with Dr. Blackburn. I had been describing how difficult I found it to make a choice between college and career, and how I was worried if I didn't make the correct decision it could ruin my life. In typical fashion, she allowed me to moan and groan over my dilemma for several minutes before she stopped me with a simple statement. I should allow myself to listen to the truth buried beneath my worries. It took me a little while to understand she was talking about that gut instinct thing my dad was so keen on. I still hadn't mastered the fine art of listening to it. On that particular day, I followed her advice to close my eyes, take a deep breath, and see if I could hear the message. To my great surprise, it come across loud and clear. I could choose to turn my anxiety into courage!

When the day came for me to tell my parents about my decision, I found myself practically vibrating with a mixture of nervousness and excitement. I chose a Saturday to talk to them, because I knew it was more likely they would both be at home, and Mike and the twins would not. I hung out in my room for most of the morning, telling myself that I was giving my parents time to themselves, though the real reason was I was trying to calm my nerves enough to talk to them. It was finally around lunch time when I could hear the faint sound of singing drifting up from the kitchen. I shook myself all over to try to release some of the tension I was feeling and headed down the stairs.

As I walked toward the back of the house the singing intensified, and I paused for a moment to allow myself to enjoy the sound of my mother's voice flowing uninhibited through the hall. It wasn't often I had the chance to just listen to her without the interference of other sounds. I realized it was something I would miss whenever I moved away on my own. I entered the kitchen to find her bent over the table, intently cutting cloth along a paper pattern.

"Hey, Mom."

She looked up and smiled before returning to her cutting. "Hey yourself. Do you want some lunch?"

"Umm. In a little bit. Is Dad around?"

"He's in his garden, I suspect. He passed through here a while ago, but I haven't seen him since."

I walked to the back door and peered out. Sure enough, I could see my dad's bent figure standing over a large, round container that looked like half of a wooden barrel. I headed to where he stood. As I got closer, I could see there were a few plants protruding from the soil, displaying large, green, heart-shaped leaves. My dad was using a trowel to mix something into the soil around the plants. He turned to look at me as I walked up. "Come see what we have!" He gestured emphatically with one hand, while the other kept digging around in the soil.

I leaned over the pot and looked closely, but all I could see were a lot of leaves. "What are they? More tomatoes?"

"Ha! No, no. This is zucchini. You've eaten it of course, but this is the first time I've been able to grow it." He pushed one of the leaves to the side. There was a tiny, finger-shaped green zucchini visible at the bottom of the plant.

"Oh! A baby zucchini!" It was so tiny I couldn't imagine eating it. I also noticed a bright yellow flower sticking up from one of the other leaves. "What's that?"

My dad looked where I was pointing. "Well, let me tell you about that. It's a zucchini flower. This one's a male. The bright yellow color attracts bees that carry pollen from the male to the female flowers." He carefully pulled the leaves of the flower apart so that I could see a long, fuzzy looking piece inside. "That's the stamen. The bees bump up against it causing pollen to stick to tiny hairs on their bodies, then they carry the pollen to the female flower. Once the pollen is transferred to a female flower it fertilizes the ovary, which grows into a small zucchini. Then the yellow blossom falls off."

I stood up straight and shook my head. "Why do I always feel like you're giving me a sex education lesson when we talk about vegetables? Can't you just tell me what they are, and leave it at that?"

His hearty laugh filled the quiet of the backyard. "What's the fun in that? Learning how these little beauties are formed is half of the pleasure. Eating them is the other."

I grumbled a quick if you say so, then remembered why I had come outside to start with. "Would you mind coming inside for a few minutes? I'd like to talk to you and mom while no one else is around."

He looked at me intently and blinked a few times. "Sure. Just let me finish spreading this fertilizer around and I'll be in. In the meantime, ask your mom if she'd mind making a sandwich for me. Might as well have a little lunch while we're talking."

I went inside to relay his request to my mom, turning down her offer to also make one for me. I'd always had a robust appetite, but eating anything while my heart was still stuck in my throat seemed impossible. After my dad sat at the table and taken a hearty bite of his sandwich, I cleared my throat and launched into the details of my plan. I told them about the acceptance letters and my reasons for deciding to decline all three. Then I carefully tried to describe my fascination with the banking industry and my desire to launch my career in that field as soon as possible.

My parents listened quietly until I finally wound down and leaned back against my chair, exhausted with the effort I put forth. My dad placed the remainder of his sandwich aside and looked directly at my mother, pausing as if to gauge her reaction before speaking.

"I'm very impressed by the amount of thought you've put into this, Jubie. While I would have been pleased to hear that you've decided to go to college, I have to admit, I'm tickled to death that you've chosen to go into banking. I always hoped one of you kids would follow in my footsteps. I can't say I'm surprised you're the one to do so, given your proclivity for details." He looked at my mother again, his eyebrows raised in question.

My mother folded her arms across her chest and let out a deep sigh. "I've been holding my breath ever since you came downstairs this morning. I saw the letters from the colleges, and I've been wondering what you were going to do." She glanced from me to my father. "I have to admit I'm a little disappointed in your choice, although I understand your rationale. Like your father, I'm pleased you seem to have taken a very logical approach to making this decision. I just hope it's the right choice for you. You're such a bright girl. I have no doubt you could excel in college. I also have every confidence you'll do well in whatever you choose to pursue."

I could feel tears beginning to well up in my eyes as she spoke, and I swiped at them as they threatened to roll down my cheeks. Their response was even more than I had hoped for. Their support, though it was couched in caution, was a welcome relief, and helped to bolster my confidence in my decision. I could feel my tension ease as a wave of happiness began to wash over me.

"I'm so glad you're both supportive of my decision. I know it's not exactly what you may have hoped for, but I appreciate your willingness to give me a chance to follow my dream. Dad, can you help me figure out what I need to do to apply for a job at the bank?"

"Certainly. I'll arrange for Harry Simpson to look into it for you. I know there's a six-week training program you'll have to complete before you can be considered for a full-time job. You'll have to sail through that program with flying colors if you want to have a chance at employment. The starting position for someone with only a high school diploma is as a teller, and those jobs are in pretty high demand right now."

I frowned at his remarks. "Does that mean that even if I spend the six weeks completing the course I might not be hired?"

"There's always that possibility. But you have to pass an entrance exam even to be admitted into the course. So, the chances are good, if you get in, you will be employed once you finish the training program. I'm only mentioning the risk that you might not, because I'm aware of a few instances when that has happened. Usually, it involved someone who was approaching it with only half-hearted interest anyway, or who changed their mind about what they wanted to do partway through the training. I'm sure that won't happen with you. I've seen how focused you become once you set your mind on something. I have no doubt you'll not only pass the entrance exam, but also do extremely well in the course."

He stood up from the table and stretched. "My back's telling me I've done enough gardening for one day. I think I'll clean up and take a little nap. Care to join me, Hon?" He wiggled his eyebrows at my mother, who attempted to give him a stern look in reply.

"That's enough of that, Will Travers. I'm going to put these lunch things away and see if I can finish cutting out the pattern I was working on before Mike and the twins come charging in. There'll be no chance of getting any work done once they're home."

My father smiled and kissed her on the cheek. "You know where to find me." He turned to look at me. "I'll talk to Harry first thing Monday morning. I should be able to let you know something by the time you get home from school."

I watched my dad walk down the hall and heard him whistling as he headed up the stairs. Something struck me as odd about the whole thing, but I couldn't quite put my finger on it. My mother was also looking in his direction.

"I don't believe I've heard your father whistling in the house in quite some time. He usually does that only when he's in his garden." She gave me a warm smile. "Must mean he's very happy about something."

I realized she had hit the nail on the head. My dad never whistled unless he was outside, doing something he loved to do. The thought that my announcement had given him an equal amount of pleasure as his gardening, filled me with joy.

CHAPTER NINE
SUMMER, 1969

The fact that both Georgia and I would be foregoing college to immediately embark on a career path drew us even closer together during our final weeks as high school students. I also realized the differences in our future plans were threatening to create some distance between us, if not in spirit, then at least in the geographical sense. Georgia's new job at the Nashville News would be starting right after graduation, so she had arranged to move out of her parents' house into her own apartment a few days after our graduation ceremony. That meant her future was about to kick into high gear, whereas mine was delayed by the need to first pass the entrance exam for the training program, then attend six weeks of classes.

At my father's request, Harry Simpson arranged for me to take the entrance exam the week before I officially graduated from St. Bernardette's, which I passed with a surprisingly high score. As a result, I was admitted into the training program with no problem. Since the program would not begin until the first of July, my parents decided to reward my achievement, and mark my high school graduation, with a short trip to visit my grandparents in

Cincinnati. That meant I would be away when Georgia was moving into her new apartment.

Since we had become friends our freshman year, Georgia had gotten into the habit of staying over at our house almost every weekend. My parents didn't mind having her around. They liked Georgia, and to them, having six kids in the house, instead of the usual five, didn't make much difference. Besides, Bill left for college at the beginning of my junior year, and Mike and the twins were so involved in their own activities they were away from home more often than not.

Georgia told me more than once how much she loved being at my house. She seemed to thrive on the noise, which surprised me in the beginning, since it was so different from what she was used to. I spent the night at her house a couple of times after we first became friends. It wasn't an experience I particularly enjoyed. Being in her house made me feel like I should speak in a whisper, even when her parents weren't home. There were no sounds of laughter or argued shouts from siblings to fill the void. Her parents never sang or whistled while they went about their chores. In fact, there were no sounds at all, other than the nervous clearing of her father's throat, or the background hum of the television when her parents allowed it to be on.

It didn't occur to me until many years later how odd the change from her house to ours must have been for her. She always seemed completely at ease whenever she came over, from the moment she set foot in the front door, until the time for her to leave. Even though I knew what life was like in her house, I guess I just pushed it out of my mind. Out of sight, out of mind, as the saying goes. It was easier to just pretend she was a regular member of our family. Once we both moved out on our own, I began to realize what a toll her past had taken on her. The stern disapproval of her parents had a tendency to hang around her neck like a talisman. Instead of attracting good luck and warding off evil, it served to engulf her in a cloud of self-doubt and insecurity. It took many years, some serious counseling, which gave us another thing in common, and the loving presence of Jon Barnett, before she was able to break free of those burdens.

Since I would be away during the time Georgia would be moving into her apartment, we decided I would go to her parents' house with her before we left for Ohio, so I could help her pack her things. My parents agreed to let me use their car so Georgia and I could pick up some empty cardboard boxes from the local grocery store. When we showed up at her house and began to unload the boxes onto her front porch, we were greeted by her mother, who crossed her arms and gestured with her nose at the pile.

"What do you girls plan to do with all of that?"

Georgia seemed to grow visibly tense at her mother's words. "Julie's going to help me pack my things."

Her mother nodded. "You'll have to keep them out of sight in your room. Your father won't be happy if you make a mess."

Georgia's cheeks reddened as she looked at the boxes. "Yes, ma'am. I promise they won't be in the way."

Her mother looked as if she wanted to say something else, but turned on her heels and went back into the house. I had witnessed the stiffness of her parents before, but it never failed to surprise me and caused me to look with respect at the girl who stood beside me. It was certainly true I had struggled to overcome my own share of worrisome insecurities, especially after we first moved to Nashville. I couldn't imagine what it would be like to live every day in the environment in which Georgia had grown up. It made me admire even more that she had found the courage to follow her dream of going into journalism. I was sure she had taken that step as completely on her own as she appeared to be forced to do everything else.

I decided the best thing I could do for my friend at that moment was to pretend as if nothing was wrong, so I lifted one of the boxes and forced a cheeriness into my voice. "Let's get these boxes inside. The sooner we get started, the sooner we'll finish."

She let out a deep breath and nodded her agreement. "Can't be too soon for me."

Packing her things turned out to be fast work. Her room was fairly small, and the only things she would be taking away from it were a couple of boxes of books, a clock radio, some trinkets she'd collected over the years, a small suitcase, and a few boxes of clothes. When we'd finished packing the last box, we plopped on the bed next to each other and gazed at the collection in front of us. Georgia glanced at me awkwardly.

"Not much for eighteen years of living, huh?"

I tried to shrug nonchalantly. "At least you won't have too much to unpack. And it'll give you a chance to decorate your new apartment in your own style."

She gave me a look which said she knew what I was up to. "Right. Well, it's a furnished apartment anyway. So, there's not a lot of room for extra things." She shifted suddenly so she could look at me directly. "Guess what? I'm going to get a cat!"

"A cat? Since when? Are you sure your parents will let you?"

She frowned and shook her head. "It doesn't matter what they think. I'm not going to do it until after I move. It will be MY cat, in MY apartment. Nobody else has anything to say about it."

I was pleasantly surprised at the determination in her declaration. I leaned forward to hug her tightly. "I think that's great. Do you have one picked out yet?"

She nodded eagerly. "I went to the animal shelter last weekend. There's a precious little black kitten there named Ebony. I'm going to call her Ebie. They said she can stay there until I move next week. I've already paid the fee and everything."

I smiled at her with true delight. "That's wonderful. I can't wait to meet her." I glanced at my watch. "Gosh. I didn't realize it's so late. I promised my parents I'd have the car back by five." As I stood to go, I felt a wave of emotion wash over me. This would be one of the last times I would see Georgia before our new lives began. I felt sure we would remain friends no matter what, but I knew nothing would ever be the same again. I struggled to hold back tears as I turned to look at her. "Promise me we'll stay close. I mean, I know our lives are going to change, and we're both going to be really busy. Promise me we won't lose our friendship in the process."

Georgia's face mirrored my feelings as she pulled me into a quick embrace. "I promise. I couldn't have gotten through these last four years without you, and I don't intend to start now. Call me when you get back from Ohio. I'll be in my new apartment by then, and you can come over and meet Ebie."

Her promise filled me with relief, and I smiled at her happily. "It's a deal."

I walked hurriedly from her room and out to where my car was parked. When I started the engine and began to back out of her driveway, I abruptly felt gripped by anxiety. It was a feeling less familiar to me through my years of therapy. In the aftermath of my goodbye to Georgia, it returned with the urgency of an old acquaintance. When one runs into them again, they insist all the unpleasant things you remember about them should be forgotten, and they really just want to be friends. You find yourself wanting to believe them, but your past experiences make you regard them with caution.

I put the car in park, and leaned my head back against the seat, practicing the slow, deep-breathing exercise Dr. Blackburn taught me to use at those times. The thoughts whirling through my head had no clear substance, but I knew the causes of my tension were the upcoming changes ahead of me. Change was still difficult, even when it was my choice. It made me feel out of control. I closed my eyes and tried to focus on the rise and fall of my chest as my lungs filled and emptied. After a couple of minutes, I felt noticeably calmer. I put the car into gear and drove slowly out of the driveway.

Georgia's house was on the other side of the Cumberland River from ours, in what was called East Nashville. It wasn't actually on the "other side of the tracks", since there was no railroad line that ran parallel to the river. The idea of crossing the river from the West to the East held pretty much the same connotation to most Nashvillians. East Nashville was viewed as the less respected stepchild to the West. I wasn't sure why it came to be thought of that way. I figured it must have something to do with the fact that the downtown, with all of its impressive buildings and financial centers, was located on the West side; whereas the East area closest to the river was marred with factories spewing smoke, and large public housing developments with a reputation for crime. Georgia's family didn't live close to the river, and their house was a simple ranch style that was a far cry from the apartments making up the housing blocks near the Cumberland. In those days, everyone on that side of the river was subject to the same level of disrespect from the media and many of the residents to their West.

My family didn't live in what you'd call a rich neighborhood. I had always been keenly aware of the difference in attitude our address received, compared to Georgia's. I heard some girls at school making snide remarks about it a few times, which I quickly tried to squelch before Georgia could hear them. Their comments were hurtful and I often wondered if living with that kind of prejudice had been a contributor to her parents' stern reserve. Being the target of prejudice of any type could harden a person over time, and "hard" was definitely a label that fit her parents.

When I finally reached my home about twenty minutes later, I sat in the car for a while, just gazing up in appreciation at the large white house. It seemed like an eternity since we first pulled up in front of it after our move from Cincinnati. It was odd to realize it was only a little less than four years. I had grown to love our new home and the city where it stood, and I was grateful the next chapter of my life would not require me to leave too soon. Though I managed to loosen my need to control everything in my life, thanks to the weekly, then monthly ministrations of Dr.

Blackburn, I was still more comfortable when change took place slowly.

My thoughts were interrupted by the slamming of a door, and I looked up to see Carey and Sherry bolting down the front steps in my direction.

"Julie! Mom says you have to drive us to Sears so we can pick up some gifts for Gran and Gramps!"

They both struggled with the front door handle in an effort to win the coveted "shotgun" seat, before Sherry finally let go with a sigh and settled into the back. I turned to look at them curiously.

"And what exactly are we supposed to buy? Did Mom give you any money?"

Carey held up two ten-dollar bills. "She said to buy some type of lacy handkerchiefs for Gran, and a couple of boxes of Goo Goo Clusters for Gramps! AND another box for us to share!"

I had noticed that everything the twins said these days sounded as if it was punctuated with an exclamation mark, which I chalked up to youthful exuberance. Funny, I thought, I didn't remember ever being as young and carefree as they seemed to be. Now, I was about to begin an adult job.

As I held that thought for a minute, feelings of anxiety started to fill my chest again. I made a vow to phone Dr. Blackburn the next day and arrange a time to see her. One of the things I learned during my years of working with her, was to get a jump on my apprehension as quickly as I could. The only way I knew to do that was to talk it over with my therapist until the reasons behind it became clear. Then, and only then, would I be able to begin the task of getting it under control. Yep, there was that word again.

CHAPTER TEN

I hadn't realized just how uncomfortable the idea of diving into the unknown made me feel, until I was faced with Georgia moving, starting the training program, and the uncertainty of whether it would lead me into a job, or out of luck. It was bad enough when the changes involved moving hundreds of miles away from the only home I had ever known, starting a new school, and trying to navigate the murky waters of adolescence while attempting to fit into a totally new environment. Now, I was facing the challenge of an uncertain future. Something that Dr. Blackburn said came to my mind: "You can't go forward without leaving something behind." I was just having trouble keeping myself from looking over my shoulder instead of focusing on the road ahead.

I eventually figured out what I was really afraid of was the prospect of finding out I wasn't perfect, my choices could be wrong, and the tomorrow that looked so promising now might end up being a flop. When I expressed these things to my Gran during our visit to Cincinnati, she wrapped me in a hug and said, "Trust me, Honey, that's not what you're going to regret if you reach my age. We each get about as many chances in life as we're willing to take. It's the opportunities you pass up when you're young that may come back to haunt you later."

Her council made a lot of sense to me. If I hadn't found the courage to approach Georgia in our school cafeteria four years ago, I would never have known how wonderful it is to have her for my friend. If I had decided to forego the opportunity to take the training course that could allow me to embark on an exciting career, I would likely wonder for the rest of my life what I'd missed. The truth is, there are no guarantees that whatever choice we make is going to be the best one. Sometimes we just have to trust that voice in our head, and in our gut, that says, "Go for it," but also accept that we're not going to be right every time.

So, that's what I did. I took a leap of faith and jumped right into the training program, which turned out to be even more challenging and fascinating than I had anticipated. Each of the six weeks was devoted to a specific topic about which I was expected to develop, at the minimum, a rudimentary understanding. Week one focused on the Principles of Banking, followed by Cash Handling, Financial Operations, Electronic Calculations, Customer Service, and Business Communication.

The course was offered through the American Institute of Banking, which was the educational arm of the American Banking Association. The main instructor for the course was a retired bank manager who, as he explained it, was just looking for a way to pass his time during retirement and impart a little of his hard-earned knowledge. His name was Ted Nielson, but he indicated on the first day of the course that we should call him Professor, even though, according to the course booklet, he was lacking a college degree (or any other sort of training that should have earned him that title). His claim to fame was that he had taught the training course for five years, and I must say, by the end of the six-week program, I felt he deserved to be called whatever he chose.

During our first week of the program, Professor Nielson informed us we would continue to receive instruction through both on-the-job training and weekend classes when the training program ended. All-in-all, it would take the equivalent of three semesters of study to complete the training before I would be awarded a Bank Teller Certificate. This meant, though I would begin work as a teller at the conclusion of the six-week course, I would still be considered on probation until I received my certificate. It also meant my salary would be about half of what I would eventually receive as a Certified Teller.

When the six weeks ended, I was thrilled to learn I had passed the course with flying colors, and I allowed the tide of enthusiasm to carry me into a job as a teller-in-training at the branch of the First National Bank where my dad worked. Getting a job there was what I hoped for, but it hadn't looked like there was much chance of it happening until two of the tellers announced they were getting married to each other, and leaving the bank.

A month after I started working at the bank, I moved into my own apartment. It was located off West End Avenue, not far from the campus of Vanderbilt University and within walking distance of a bus route that would take me directly downtown.

The apartment was in the attic of a house owned by the parents of Debbie, one of the other tellers at the bank. The attic wasn't very big, with just one main room, a small bath and closet on one side, and a kitchenette on the other. It was furnished with a double bed, a chest of drawers, and an overstuffed chair with a hassock in front of it and a floor lamp behind. The bed was situated under the pointed part of the ceiling, which was the tallest area of the apartment. The roof sloped down on either side of the center, but it still left plenty of room for someone even several inches taller than me to stand up straight.

The biggest plus about the apartment was its private entrance, reachable from one side of the main house by way of a set of stairs. Unfortunately, the stairs were uncovered, which meant they didn't provide any protection from rain or snow or, God forbid, ice. There was also a pull-down staircase that could be accessed from the main floor of the house, in case of an emergency.

A decent sized landing at the top of the outside staircase provided just enough room to accommodate a couple of folding chairs. The landing overlooked a small, grassy lawn with a concrete, pedestal birdbath that attracted an assortment of thirsty visitors. The landing provided a sunny spot to enjoy the view during the morning hours, and a couple of trees which cast shade over the landing when the afternoon sun grew too harsh.

When Debbie mentioned the availability of the apartment, I surprised myself by quickly expressing my desire to rent it. That little voice in my gut shouted "Just do it, Julie!" I responded without hesitation. Perhaps it was the parting words of my Gran that propelled me forward: "Never let fear guide your present, or decide your future." Or maybe it was just my years of therapy finally beginning to take hold. Whatever the reason, I acted quickly and moved forward without regret. It was a good feeling.

Since I was still in the probationary period as a bank teller and not yet certified, my income was just barely enough to cover the rent on my apartment, with a little left over for essentials. I suppose it would have made more sense for me to live at home until my salary improved, but it was hard to shake the feeling of still being in high school until I moved into my own place. Dr. Blackburn encouraged me to take that step toward independence, not because I was fearful of doing so, but because she believed it would help give me a chance to continue discovering who I was when I wasn't defining myself by my role in the family.

My parents seemed to understand my need to move out sooner rather than later. They helped ease things for me financially by having me over for dinner on a regular basis, and sending me home with a hefty sack of leftovers and an assortment of extra items from the pantry. The odd thing was, even though money was sparse, I felt a sense of contentment as I settled into my new life. I knew what was expected of me, both at work and in the ongoing training classes, and I was enjoying living on my own. I had to admit, it was a little like playing grownup, but in the process of playing like I was grown up, I began to feel I actually was.

On those rare occasions when I found myself with a little money left over at the end of the month, I would call Georgia and arrange to meet her at one of the long-standing Nashville haunts where we knew we could count on getting tasty food at a low cost. The rest of the time, our get-togethers included walks in one of our neighborhoods or end-of-work visits at either her apartment or mine, armed with whatever snacks and drinks we could scrounge up.

Georgia's job at the paper hadn't turned out to be all she was hoping it would. A month into it, she still hadn't been assigned any reporting duties and, by all indications, it looked as if it would be some time before that was likely to happen. Georgia hadn't counted on how engrained the gender and age biases were in the newspaper business, but she was determined to tough it out until things took a turn for the better.

My job, on the other hand, took off like a rabbit chased by a hound. Each day, I was expected to be at my station just before the doors opened at nine in the morning, ready to greet the line of customers with a friendly smile and gracious attitude. Business was steady at the bank, which made the hours disappear quickly. I was given a thirty-minute lunch break at noon, then remained at my position at the teller's window until the bank closed at three. Most afternoons, I was required to stay at the bank until five o'clock to attend one of the continuing education classes, while those tellers who were already certified completed the laborious task of calculating and recalculating the day's tallies. Since many businesses were in the practice of paying their employees at the end of each week, the bank stayed open until six o'clock on Fridays to allow customers to cash their paychecks or make a deposit before the weekend.

I was also required to attend an occasional training class on Saturday. Those classes were held at the bank in the conference room, under the instruction of Harry Simpson. The content of those sessions was more focused on specific responsibilities of bank tellers, but they also provided a general idea of the day-to-day activities of the other employees of the bank, along with a good overview of the business at large. I found the Saturday classes the most interesting because they gave me a chance to better understand the big picture of the banking business. Harry was also a welcome contrast to most of the other instructors we had during the week, who made no effort to hide how unenthused they were with their assignment.

My dad explained to me that the class instructors were paid a small stipend, but most of them didn't feel it properly compensated them for their time. Harry always appeared nonplussed at having to show up on a Saturday to instruct a bunch of greenhorns. His demeanor was cheery, and he managed to instill enthusiasm in those of us attending the class, most of whom gave the impression they'd rather be back at home asleep in their beds. I have to admit, I wouldn't have minded sleeping another couple of hours myself. But my ever-present internal alarm clock that warned me when I was going to be late for something, never failed to propel me out of bed. I was usually the first one to show up at class, often even beating Harry, which was a little embarrassing given that I had to wait for him to unlock the door.

Strict punctuality was another unfortunate characteristic of my Illusion of Control. It made me extremely uncomfortable to be late for anything, so I often arrived early for appointments. I suppose some people would consider that a good problem to have, but those people would never have to see the laughter on their classmates' faces when they would spot me standing on the sidewalk anxiously awaiting the school doors to be unlocked. Like several other traits I had developed, it wasn't something I chose to do. It was just something I couldn't help doing.

On one of the Saturdays of the continuing education classes, I left the bank to find that the skies had opened up and were dumping a deluge on the streets outside. I took the bus to the bank that day, as I did most mornings of the week. I stood on the front steps of the bank staring out at the downpour, hoping it would taper off soon. I found the prospect of having to slog through several inches of rain to reach the bus stop unappealing. Since the morning paper hadn't mentioned the possibility of rain,

I left home without an umbrella. I was still standing on the steps digging through my purse in hopes of at least finding one of the plastic rain caps my mother always urged me to carry, when I heard the door open behind me.

"This is unexpected! Good thing I found this."

I turned to see Harry standing behind me, attempting to open a large umbrella. It was blue with wide, white stripes, and looked like it belonged on a beach somewhere.

He gestured to the right of where we were standing. "My car is parked just down the street. Can I give you a lift home?"

I looked at him uncertainly. He was technically my boss and my instructor, and it didn't seem appropriate to share his umbrella, much less his car.

"No, thank you. I'll just wait here a little while until the rain stops."

He looked up at the sky with a frown. "I think you'll have a long wait. This doesn't look like it's going to blow over any time soon." He flashed a reassuring smile. "Come on. Let me give you a ride home. Your father would never let me hear the end of it if I let you head out in this."

His mention of my dad made me feel more at ease with his suggestion. I had forgotten that my father was his boss. He was surely right in thinking my dad would expect him to look out for me. I nodded in appreciation. "Okay. Thanks. That would be great."

He unfurled the umbrella and held it overhead.

"I've never seen such a large umbrella!" I looked at it in amazement as I moved a little closer to him. When it was fully opened, it appeared to be at least five feet wide

"It's actually a golf umbrella. Mr. Carson keeps it here in case he gets an invitation to play a round unexpectedly. Lucky for us, he didn't use it yesterday." He held it high overhead. "Hop in. There's obviously room enough for a small party under here."

We set off down the street in the direction of his car, stepping carefully around puddles along the way. I was surprised when he stopped next to a red pick-up truck. It wasn't the type of vehicle I imagined he would drive, not that I had spent any time considering him driving anything at all. A pick-up truck made me think of boys in baseball caps heading out to a farm, with a cooler full of beer and a goofy dog hanging out the passenger window. Nothing about that picture seemed to fit the impression I had of Harry Simpson. The fire engine red color screamed "Look at me!" which also didn't jive with my image of the man walking next to me. There was nothing flashy about Harry Simpson at all. Not that he was boring. He just wasn't the kind of person who tried to draw attention to himself.

He unlocked the passenger door and opened it, stepping aside so I could get in, before hurrying around to the driver's side. He tucked the umbrella neatly into the space behind the seat, before jumping into the cab. I glanced at him as he started the truck. Water was dripping down his face, causing splotches to appear on his light blue polo shirt. He didn't wear a suit to the Saturday classes since it was technically his day off, usually appearing instead in jeans and some version of the shirt he wore on this day. He must have noticed me looking at him, because he turned the rear-view mirror sideways so he could study his appearance.

"I guess that umbrella wasn't as big as I thought it was. If you'll open that glove compartment, you'll find a wad of napkins in there."

I reached into the compartment and located the napkins, which I offered to him. He rubbed his hair with them vigorously, causing it to stick out from the sides where the hair was considerably longer than the top. The look was quite a change from his usual, tidy appearance, and I guess I was staring at him a little too long, because he suddenly stopped and regarded me with a grin.

"What? You're not fond of the wet dog look?" he swiped at his hair again with the napkins, and then used his fingers as a makeshift comb. "Better?"

I couldn't bring myself to tell him that his grooming attempt had only made things worse. "Um hum. Much better."

He wadded up the handful of wet napkins, cramming them into the space next to the gear shift, before turning the key in the ignition and reaching to turn a nob on the dashboard. "Brrr! This rain makes it feel like winter is already here. It's too early in October to be turning the heat on, but I don't want either of us catching a cold because of our wet feet."

"And wet hair, in your case."

He took another look in the mirror and ran his hands over the sides of his head.

"Well, at least it'll dry fast. That's one of the advantages of not having a lot of hair." He turned sideways in his seat. "Where to?"

I gave him directions to my apartment. We didn't speak much on the drive there. The rain continued to fall steadily. The combination of the warmth of the car and the melodic swish of the windshield wipers made me feel drowsy, and I struggled to keep my eyes open. I must have drifted into a half-sleep because the next thing I knew I was being gently shaken awake by a hand on my shoulder. My eyes popped open in alarm, as I turned to look at Harry.

"I'm so sorry! I guess I must have dozed off."

"No problem. It was so cozy in here I almost felt like joining you, except I was driving."

I looked to see if he was joking and was relieved to see a smile on his face. "Thanks for the ride." I gathered my things, and started to reach for the door handle.

"Wait a minute." He hopped out of the truck and grabbed the umbrella, hurrying around to open my door. "It's still coming down pretty hard. Why don't I see you to your door? I would just give you the umbrella to use, but I need to get it back to the bank first thing Monday morning before Mr. Carson notices it's missing." We huddled together under the umbrella as we made our way up the stairs to my apartment door. I fished my keys out of my purse and unlocked the door, pushing it open so I could duck inside.

"Thanks, Harry. I really appreciate the ride."

"You're welcome, Julie. Enjoy the rest of your weekend."

I closed the door and peered out the small window next to it. Harry made his way carefully down the stairs and then tossed the umbrella back in the cab, jumping in after it. I watched until his red truck disappeared down the street, then shivered as I became aware of the dampness of my clothes. I moved towards the bathroom, undressing along the way, and wrapped myself in the robe I kept on a hook on the door.

I looked in the bathroom mirror and was surprised to find a smile lighting up my face. What was I so happy about? The training session had been interesting, though I couldn't say it had been fun. Certainly, it hadn't been anything that would make me grin like an idiot. A knot suddenly appeared in the pit of my stomach. Was I smiling about Harry? That wasn't possible. He was my boss, and he was at least four years older. And even if the age difference wasn't enough to worry about, our boss-employee status made him strictly off-limits.

I shook my head and turned away from the mirror. He was just being friendly. That's all there was to it. I was smiling because I found his kindness touching. Yet, while these thoughts registered with my brain, my gut kept insisting there was more to the story.

CHAPTER ELEVEN
SPRING, 1970

Despite the nagging insistence of my gut, a trait I most likely inherited from my dad, Harry and I stuck strictly to our roles of boss/employee for some time. Life just became too busy to allow me the luxury of mulling around in that particular quandary. The demands of learning to be a bank teller, as well as mastering the ins-and-outs of the banking business in general, took a lot of time and energy. So, there was little left over for much of anything else. That was fine with me. I enjoyed the consistency of my daily work at the bank. Many of my nights and weekends were filled with continuing education classes, which meant my life felt full and rewarding.

When the probationary period ended, I was awarded the status of Certified Bank Teller and allowed more freedom to do that particular job without constant supervision. Harry was a comforting presence in the bank during this period; overseeing the row of tellers, stepping in when someone had a question or needed advice, and checking the end-of-day figures for accuracy. He also made time to meet with each of us separately at least once a week to gauge how things were going. I looked forward to those meetings. Seeing Harry made me happy. I could tell there was more simmering just beneath the surface of our superficial interactions by the way a smile seemed to linger on my face after our weekly meetings. He always appeared disappointed when our allotted time was up. Luckily, we were both doing a great job of ignoring what was really happening between us. At least that's what I told myself.

I didn't see much of my dad at the bank during that first year. Of course, I saw him at a distance, usually engrossed in conversation with someone or heading into the conference room for one of his frequent meetings. But we kept our interactions strictly professional while we were at work.

From time to time, I noticed the same five men, or some combination of the five with whom I had seen him on Career Day, showing up to meet with him. Sometimes all five would join him in the conference room. Just as often the meetings would include the three who Harry said worked with WSM and the CMA, without the other two. Truthfully, I didn't think too much about it. I was still trying to find my way in the banking business and I was just as happy to not add my odd response to those two to my list of "things I still need to figure out". That list kept growing longer and longer.

I visited my parents on most Sundays for the treat of a home-cooked meal and the chance to catch up with what was going on in the family. The twins were usually home on those occasions. They were in their junior year at St. Bernadette's where they were involved in writing a weekly column for the school newspaper. It was appropriately called Double Vision, and it described their joint impressions of what had been happening around campus during the previous week. They were also on the double's tennis team, and on the weekends they frequently went on double dates with two boys from St. Thomas Moore.

It seemed they always did things together, which I guessed was pretty standard for twins. In fact, they stopped participating in the school choir after their freshman year, choosing instead to practice singing and playing guitar as a duet;

either at parties given by their classmates' parents, or at the Sunday folk masses held at their former elementary school. Whether they just found it more comfortable to do things together, or were affected by the invisible thread of chromosomes that linked them before birth, it was clear they had an undeniable connection that transcended the simple fact that they were sisters.

Bill graduated the previous year from Georgia Tech with an engineering degree and immediately went to work for a company in Atlanta that manufactured equipment used by heating, ventilation, and air conditioning systems. He was also seriously involved with a young woman whom he had been dating since his sophomore year at Georgia Tech, and whose father was the owner of the same company that employed Bill.

Mike had just graduated from Peabody College and was teaching high school English at Montgomery Bell Academy, a private boy's school located in West Nashville. He moved out of our parents' house the previous summer and was living in a small apartment shared with a roommate, Josh, whom he met at Peabody and who taught first grade at Eakin Elementary School, a few blocks from Vanderbilt.

Their apartment was in the Hillsboro Village area of Nashville, within walking distance of Eakin, and close to Dr. Blackburn's office. In fact, I developed the habit of meeting Mike for coffee or a soda at his apartment after some of my sessions with her. I didn't see Dr. Blackburn as often anymore, but I still scheduled an appointment every month or two. I found that keeping some level of contact with her helped me stay balanced in my perspective of life. It was like getting regular maintenance on my brain, and I still looked forward to those recurring check-ups.

During one of my weekly Sunday visits with my parents, I was surprised to find my dad seated at the dining room table, engrossed in several pieces of paper spread out in front of him. It was uncharacteristic for him to be inside on the weekend instead of tending to his backyard gardens. I was curious what sort of work took him away from his usual Sunday routine. I stood at the door of the dining room, hoping he would notice my presence and invite me in. When it became evident that he was too wrapped up in what he was doing to be aware of me standing there, I began to walk toward the table.

"Hey, Dad."

He looked up with a frown, which was quickly replaced by a smile when he saw me. "Hay's for horses, Jubie."

I rolled my eyes at his attempt at humor and moved closer to where he was sitting. "What are you working on?"

He leaned back in his chair and surveyed the papers in front of him. "Do you remember our discussion about how the banking business is changing, and how our bank will need to change with it or be left behind? Well, I'm working on something that will, hopefully, help us keep pace with that change. A group of investors approached the bank a while back to seek our help in backing some pretty impressive projects. I've been meeting with them for over a year, and it looks as if things are finally falling into place." He pulled one sheet of paper out of the pile in front of him and pushed it across the table. "Have a seat and take a look at this. It's called a prospectus, and it outlines the key points of their plan."

I pulled out the chair across from him and sat. For the next several minutes, neither of us spoke as I studied the paper. It contained a list of bullet points that outlined a joint venture between the CMA and the owners of WSM. The CMA was interested in starting a music festival that would be a spin-off of the CMA awards show currently held downtown in the Municipal Auditorium. The festival, which was to be called Fan Fair, would be a four-day event, with the first fair scheduled to take place in April 1972, a little more than two years away.

The paper described how WSM would provide radio and television coverage of the festival, with backing from the National Life and Accident Insurance Company, abbreviated in the report as the NL&AIC. I knew of the National Life Company, but I couldn't understand what interest they could possibly have in promoting country music. When I paused in my reading long enough to pose this question to my dad, he explained that NL&AIC also owned WSM and had been instrumental in starting the Grand Ole Opry. That certainly gave the company a prime interest in the future of the Country Music industry.

Under the bullet point that listed the involvement of National Life, there was an explanatory paragraph describing how the festival would target fans, not just from the United States, but from the entire world. The big draw was they would have the unprecedented opportunity to attend numerous live music events over the four-day festival, as well as visit booths where they could personally meet, be photographed with, and secure an autograph from their favorite stars. All-in-all, the festival promised a tremendously exciting and unfathomable experience for fans of Country Music. What that meant for the NL&AIC and the First National Bank was the return on their initial investment should be quite impressive.

The final points of the prospectus outlined how the joint financial support of First National and NL&AIC would also allow the Grand Ole Opry to be relocated from the Ryman Auditorium to Donelson, Tennessee, a small suburb about six miles east of downtown. The property targeted included several acres on the southeast bank of the Cumberland River on what was the former home of Rudy's Farm – a locally owned, homemade sausage factory.

The first step of the plan for relocating the Opry involved the development of a theme park, to be called Opryland USA, followed by the construction of a music venue to be positioned next to the park. The final step called for the creation of a grand hotel and convention center, slated to be located adjacent to the park. It would carry the name, The Opryland Hotel. I silently shook my head in amazement at what would clearly be a remarkably complex, but a well-laid out plan even I could see promised tremendous potential.

I laid the paper back on the table and looked up at my dad. "Is this why you've been meeting with those men I saw you with when I visited the bank on Career Day? Harry mentioned something about what a high-powered group that was, and I've noticed that you've met with them several times since then."

He had been walking around the dining room while I read the prospectus, but sat back down as I finished. "Harry was right. Three of them represent some of the most influential people in the music and entertainment industry in Nashville. They pretty much control WSM and the CMA. One of them, Wes Plant, is the chairman of the board of both CMA and First National, and he was able to influence the others to come to our door with these plans. He was also instrumental in bringing the other two, Hank and J.R. Taylor, to the table.

"The Taylor brothers have a family history in the banking industry that started with their daddy, J.R. Senior. The brothers began buying up stock in several Tennessee banks back in 1968. They've been sniffing around Nashville for another opportunity and, for some reason, they set their sights on First National. I suspect they must have caught wind of some of these plans in front of you. When they approached Wes, he filled them in on what the CMA and WSM had in mind. Wes thought they might be able to help us arrange the finances. It turns out, in addition to their other investments, they also hold controlling interest in NL&AIC.

"When they first met with Wes, they suggested an arrangement whereby they would facilitate a brokered deposit from NL&AIC to First National to fund our prearranged loans for the construction of the Opryland properties. When Wes first brought their offer to the rest of us it sounded pretty good. Until we became aware of a federal regulation restricting how much money of that type can be deposited in any one bank. Now, the Taylors are suggesting that the remaining money we need could be divvied up among several other banks, which they also hold controlling interest in. That money could then be freed up for our use as needed."

A lot of what he was saying was going over my head, but I knew a little about brokered deposits from my classes at the bank. "But aren't brokered deposits considered fairly risky? I remember reading they're more affected by interest rate fluctuations than other types of deposits." I could see the pleasure on his face as he realized I had at least some grasp of the concept. "That's right. Core deposits, which include things like checking and savings accounts, are safer, but also yield lower return and contain smaller amounts. Totally relying on them to fund a venture of this scope would be impossible."

More facts began to fall into place as I listened to his explanation. "I remember the Federal Deposit Insurance Corporation placed a $100,000 limit on single brokered deposits. Since I'm sure the projects you've described will require a lot more than that, doesn't it mean you and the others will be depending upon the solvency of several different banks in order to have the funds at hand?"

He nodded solemnly. "I'm afraid you've hit the nail on the head. It's not unheard of for investors to make a run on a bank's funds if they believe the bank is on shaky grounds, or the entire marketplace has become uncertain—similar to what happened during the Great Depression. If that were to happen, we would not only lose the potential of tapping into the rest of the funds we need to finish our projects, but we'd also be liable to repay the money we used, plus a hefty add-on for the interest it accrued. All-in-all, it's a very risky plan and not one that I'm totally on-board with."

A thought suddenly occurred to me. "What do the Taylor brothers get out of all of this?" He leaned back in his chair with his hands laced behind his head and stared at the ceiling before replying to my question. "I guess you could say that's the catch-22 in this story. The Taylors want to buy a significant amount of stock in First National, which would give them controlling interest of the bank. Their willingness to broker the funds from National Life would be contingent upon that happening. And to tell you the truth, I'm just not so sure that's a good idea, although my misgivings about it are not totally shared by Wes or the other members of the board. They see the whole thing as a gold mine. I see it as a potential sinkhole."

"You know that gut instinct you're always telling me to listen to? Well, it spoke to me pretty loudly on Career Day when I saw you meeting with those five men."

His eyes opened wide as he leaned his elbows on the table and gave me his full attention. "What do you mean?"

I was suddenly hesitant to finish what I started. What did I really know about any of these business dealings? What if something I said caused him to make a move he might regret?

"Tell me what you're thinking, Julie."

I took a deep breath before speaking. "I didn't have any reaction to the first three you mentioned. But when I saw the last two, the Taylor brothers, my gut clenched and I could feel my heart beating too fast. It was almost as if some kind of evil presence was surrounding them." Even as I spoke, I could hear how crazy my words sounded.

My dad stood and walked to the door of the screened-in deck, stopping to gaze out with his back to me. I wondered if he was angry about what I said. I was getting ready to offer him my apology, when he turned back around to face me.

"I appreciate your telling me what you felt that day. Truth is, I've been having similar feelings about them myself. I just haven't been able to come up with anything concrete that I can present to Wes and the others to justify my feelings." He returned to the table where he began to collect the scattered papers into a pile. "If this project goes well, it could help secure the future for the FNB. But if there are problems, it could push us over the edge with a catastrophic conclusion." He stopped shuffling the papers and folded his arms across his chest. "I don't know if you've had a chance to spend much time downtown recently, other than at the bank, of course. There's a big hole in the ground on Deaderick Street that's going to become our new location. For a while, it looked as if it was going to remain a hole for the foreseeable future because the funds, pinpointed to support construction of the new building, dried up. This venture will give new life to the plan. One thing we stand to gain from this project is a 28-story skyscraper that will be called The First National Center."

I looked at him in disbelief. The story he shared with me, along with the plans outlined in the business prospectus, suggested my dad had been carrying around a lot of secrets for some time. I knew from experience that even trying to keep one secret without spilling it to anyone else was exhausting. I could only imagine the toll that keeping one of this magnitude had taken on him. I looked at him with new appreciation and with a greater awareness of the responsibilities his job required.

"What are you going to do?"

His mouth formed a tight line as he shrugged his shoulders. "The only thing I can do, which is to put more thought into the whole thing. I may have to do a little investigative research into the Taylors' background. See if anything turns up that could sway my opinion one way or another. In the meantime, I'll ask you not to discuss this with anyone. As you can see, it's a very delicate situation that needs to be handled carefully."

I nodded emphatically. "Of course. What about the new building you mentioned? Does that mean we'll be moving to a different location soon?"

"That's not going to happen for a while yet. As I said, the construction has just been approved. It will likely take at least a couple of years before it's completed. In the meantime, we'll have plenty of time to organize ourselves for the eventual relocation, assuming everything moves ahead as planned." He stood and lifted the stack of papers, placing them carefully into an old leather briefcase. "I think I'd better clear this stuff out of the way. It's nearly time for dinner. I'm surprised your mom hasn't been in here fussing at me for making a mess of her dining room. Why don't you go tell her I've cleared out of her way and offer to help her? I'm just going to put these things upstairs and make a quick call. Tell her I'll be down shortly." He started to walk from the room, but paused at the door and turned to look at me once more. "And Julie? Thank you for sharing your feelings with me. I want you to know that I won't take what you said lightly."

He walked out at that point, leaving me sitting at the table by myself. I still wasn't sure I had done the right thing by telling him about my gut reactions. What if I was completely wrong about the Taylors, and sharing what I felt about them caused my dad to call a halt to something that could have been the best thing ever for the bank? But what if I was right? The only thing I knew with certainty was that trusting in something as undefined as a feeling in the vicinity of my stomach was hardly reassuring. Dr. Blackburn explained it once. These feelings don't actually start in the gut. They begin when we have a perception about something outside of ourselves; an expression on someone's face, a tone of voice, an awareness something is just not right, or a golden opportunity just crossed our path. According to Dr. Blackburn, those perceptions cause signals to be sent to our brain, which performs a rapid scan of our memory files in order to assign an interpretation to what we have sensed.

She said some people call this intuition, which is really just a knee-jerk reaction to something based upon our past experiences. The more experience you have in a particular arena, the more reliable your intuition. I had little to no experience when it came to making life-altering decisions. My dad, on the other hand, had a couple of decades of accumulated experience in pretty much every issue we discussed. So, the idea of trusting his gut instinct, his intuition, was a no-brainer. Or a full brainer, to be more accurate.

I suddenly realized all I could do was to turn the weight of the decision over to him. Once I reached that conclusion, I became aware of how good it felt to relinquish control of something I really had no control over, anyway. I was surprised.

CHAPTER TWELVE
1972

I've heard some people say that time passes slowly when we're waiting for something, but it speeds past when we are happy with where we are. If that's true, then I guess the last two years of my life have been pretty satisfying. It seemed as if one day I had just started my job at First National, and the next I was fully entrenched in the life of a bank teller. A lot of changes took place over those two years, and knowing how uncomfortable unplanned change makes me, it's a wonder I survived it as well as I did. The truth is, I finally began to realize that without change, life becomes stagnant. As my Gran once said, that's a certain recipe for killing time.

When the New Year rang in the start of 1972, it also heralded the arrival of a few other significant events. Construction was well underway on the First National Center. There had been a slight delay in the beginning when some workers discovered a cave beneath the bedrock with the skeletal remains of a saber-toothed cat. At first glance, the bones were thought to belong to an animal of more modern origin. Radiocarbon analysis, performed by some members of the archaeology department at the University of Tennessee, determined the skeleton had once been part of an animal called Melodeon Floridanus that lived more than 11,000 years ago.

This discovery stirred up quite a lot of excitement among Nashvillians who clamored to the excavation site in hopes of catching a glimpse of the remains. However, the scientists from U.T. convinced the authorities the bones should be removed and preserved in the Museum of Natural Science in Washington D.C. Removing something that native Nashvillians considered their own caused quite a stir in the local media. The hubbub that followed did not manage to dissuade the removal of the bones, but it did convince the architects of the First National Center to alter the original building design so the cave where the skeletal remains were found could be protected. Eventually, an acrylic window was installed in the floor above the cave to allow visitors to look down into the remnants of the excavation.

The early part of 1972 also marked the first time that Georgia had an article printed in the Nashville News. The story covered a Victorian Ball held at the Belle Meade Mansion. When we spoke about it, it was clear her reporting of the event, and that she earned her first byline in the newspaper, took a backseat to the fact this was also the night she met Jon Barnett.

Her relationship with Jon got off to a pretty rocky start, in part because of his mysterious connections to the eventual closing of the Daily Courier, the only competitor to the News in Nashville. A large part of their initial struggles had to do with Georgia's reluctance to trust Jon, or pretty much anybody else; an unfortunate remnant of her childhood. She eventually sought the help of my therapist, Dr. Blackburn. It was her influence, combined with the loving support of an elderly woman, Ida Hood, who became a dear friend to Georgia, which eventually enabled her to move forward in her relationship with Jon.

In April '72, the first Fan Fair was held in the Municipal Auditorium. Unfortunately, the timing of the event coincided with a stagnant weather front that dumped a deluge of rain on Nashville for three out of the four days of the festival. Luckily, it seemed Country Music fans were not discouraged by mud and ankle-deep water. The final report indicated that more than 5,000 of them attended the event. Nonetheless, the weather fiasco was enough to cause the organizers to decide to avoid the risk of April Showers and hold Fan Fair in June in the years to come.

I spoke to my dad a few more times about the issues we discussed that Sunday in the dining room. It was pretty clear things were proceeding as planned with respect to the projects outlined on the prospectus. It was also evident my dad hadn't become any more comfortable with the idea of the Taylors being involved. The last thing he said to me about it was he'd reached the point where he couldn't discuss it with me anymore, and I needed to trust him when he said things would turn out for the best. I wasn't sure what he meant by that, and I had to battle with myself not to press him on it any further. I made a promise to myself, and to Dr. Blackburn, to try really hard to let go of the things I couldn't possibly control, and I was determined to keep that commitment.

By the time summer rolled around, the First National Center was nearing completion, and everyone in our branch was scurrying about frantically trying to organize things for the big move. The actual date was yet to be set. There were so many things to take care of, while we remained open for business, that life became more than a little hectic.

Most weekends, I didn't even manage to make it to my parents' house for dinner. The tellers had been delegated responsibility for packing up the files. That turned out to be a huge undertaking, considering they took up two entire rooms on the second floor. The files had to be boxed up, and each box meticulously organized and labeled so an individual file could be quickly located if needed. Once the other tellers saw how happily I dove into this task, they left the majority of the job to me. I was okay with that. Putting things in order made me feel calm. It also meant I had to devote countless extra hours of work in order to finish the project on time.

One afternoon, I was about to finish up my work before leaving for the day when I heard the door to the file room swing open. I turned in the direction of the sound, expecting it to be one of the other tellers returning to give me a hand. To my surprise, I saw Harry walking in my direction.

"I thought I might find you in here. You know, this was supposed to be a job for six people, not one." He stopped next to where I was crouched over, preparing to lift a box to add to the others stacked against the wall. "Here, let me get that for you." He reached past me, and lifted the box easily before placing it on the stack. "You've made a lot of progress on this. It must have taken you a long time."

I pressed the palms of my hands against the sides of my hair in an attempt to smooth back the tendrils that had fallen out of the pony tail I made when I began working on the boxes. The room was kept quite cool in an attempt to protect the contents of the files. I managed to work up a sweat during my hours of packing, which only made my already straight hair stick against my face. I glanced at Harry who was staring at me with an odd expression.

"Is something wrong? I must look like something the cat dragged in."

His face broke into a silly grin. "I haven't heard that expression in a long time. My grandmother used to say it whenever my brother, sister, and I would come in from playing outside and plop on the sofa before dinner. She'd swat us with a dishtowel she always seemed to have over her shoulder and tell us there would be no way on earth she'd sit at the dinner table with us looking like something the cat dragged in. Of course, we would jump up immediately and hurry to get cleaned up. I guess it was a little game we played because we knew sitting our dirty selves on the sofa would get a rise out of her, and she knew we would jump right up once she scolded us." He grew silent, as a wistful expression passed over his face.

"Do you still see your grandmother often?"

He shook his head. "She passed away several years ago. She lived near us when I was a kid, and she was over at our house a lot because both my parents worked. I guess it was unusual in those days for the mother to work outside the home, but it seemed normal to us because our grandmother was always there to fill in." He frowned slightly and turned his face away from me. "I guess I took her presence for granted, and before I realized how important she was to me, she was gone."

The sweetness with which he described his grandmother filled my heart with emotion and made me struggle to catch my breath. Finally, I choked out a question. "What about your grandfather? Did you spend a lot of time with him, too?"

His eyes caught mine, and he seemed to look deep into me, as if he was aware of the intensity of the emotion I was feeling. "He died of a heart attack when I was really young, so I never got to know him. After that, my parents made sure my grandmother was close by so she wouldn't be too lonely." He shoved his hands into his pockets and studied the floor for a moment before he returned his eyes to mine. "How about you? Are you close to your grandparents?"

"My father's parents live in Columbus, Ohio. We used to see them at least a couple of times a year when we lived in Cincinnati, but I haven't seen them at all since we moved to Nashville. I'm closer to my mother's parents because they live in Cincinnati near our old house. We still get together whenever we can, usually for holidays. My grandfather is still driving, so most of the time they come down here." I looked around at the stacks of boxes and realized I had been working for a few hours. The growling in my stomach also reminded me I hadn't eaten since lunch.

"Well, I guess I'm going to head home now. Did you need me to do something?"

That same imperceptible look I had seen when he first entered the room came over his face. "Not exactly. Although I did want to ask you something. I've been invited to a dinner party at the Belle Meade Country Club. Its main purpose is to celebrate the opening of the First National Center, although it looks as if that's still several months away. Anyway, it sounds like it's going to be a pretty swanky affair, and I was wondering if you'd like to go with me? I mean, I thought you might enjoy it."

My eyes grew wide in surprise. An invitation to dinner wasn't at all what I was expecting, and the idea that it would be held at one of the most exclusive spots in Nashville was a little scary. "I don't know. I work for you. Wouldn't that be considered inappropriate?"

A slight smile crossed his face. "Not at all. You have no idea how many office romances have taken place behind the scenes in this building. Not that I'm saying this would fit into that category! But there's no reason why we couldn't attend the dinner together. That is, if you'd like to go."

His comment about office romances gave me an odd feeling in the pit of my stomach. I hadn't thought about Harry in that way. Well, I had thought of him like that, but not since the day he rescued me from the rain by giving me a ride home. I guess I hadn't allowed myself to think of him like that again. Yet, I had let those feelings cross my mind and even enter my heart, but I was determined to keep them from expanding any further. Now, his unexpected invitation threatened to shake my resolve.

"I don't know. It sounds like it will be pretty fancy. I'm not sure I have anything to wear."

His smile showed his relief. "Don't worry about that. We have a bank customer who owns a women's clothing store near Belle Meade. I'm sure she can find something appropriate for you to wear. So, is it a deal? You'll go to the dinner with me?"

His enthusiasm was contagious, and I found myself excited at the thought of getting dressed up to go to a fancy dinner, at a fancy place, with a man I found more than a little interesting. "Yes. It sounds like fun. What day is it?"

"A week from Saturday." He pulled a pen and a piece of paper out of his jacket pocket and scribbled something on it. "Here's the name and number of the person who owns the clothing store I mentioned. Just tell her I told you to call, and she'll know what to do."

The name on the card read *Rosa Decavanta. Owner & Proprietor, Gianna: A Boutique.* "I've heard of this place. It's supposed to be very nice, but also very expensive. I'm not sure I can afford to buy a dress from there." I held the card out, but he dismissed it with a wave of his hand.

"Don't worry. As I said, she's a customer of the bank. I'm sure she'll be able to take care of you."

I reluctantly put the card in my pocket. I wasn't convinced I could afford even the lowest priced dress in her shop, but I didn't want to admit it to Harry. "Okay. I'll give her a call."

"Great." He glanced at his watch. "I didn't realize how late it is. Can I give you a ride home?"

His offer was tempting, but I felt I needed to put a little distance between myself and Harry Simpson in order to process what just happened. "No, thanks. I'm meeting a friend for dinner, and she's going to pick me up." It was a little white lie that I hoped to turn into a truth if I could convince Georgia to come to my rescue.

"Okay. Then I guess I'll see you at work on Monday."

I nodded numbly. "Yes, Monday." I'd suddenly found it impossible to form a complete sentence. The fact I'd just been invited to dinner shouldn't make me feel so discombobulated. After all, it was business related. Harry probably just didn't want to go stag to such an important event. I couldn't fathom why he picked me out of all of the other single girls at the bank.

By the time I left the building to meet Georgia, who had luckily been available and eager to get together, I convinced myself that the invitation from Harry was strictly business. For some strange reason, that didn't make me feel better.

CHAPTER THIRTEEN

At Georgia's urging, I made a call to Rosa Decavanta the next morning. Ironically, Georgia had written an article for the Nashville News on Miss Decavanta. The story had earned praise from the editors of the paper and gratitude from Rosa, who had been trying to clear her name from being connected to the less-than-stellar dealings of her family members back in New Jersey. When I explained I was a friend of Georgia's and had been encouraged by Harry to phone her, she practically jumped through the phone in her eagerness to help and invited me to come in that same day. Since it was Saturday, that worked out perfectly for me.

I hadn't given much thought to what I would wear that morning. I dressed in a clean pair of jeans and a neatly-pressed, light blue button-down shirt. It was what I would have put on if Georgia and I were doing something together on Saturday morning. Since I was going to shop for a dress, I didn't think it made much difference what I wore. As soon as I walked in the front door of the shop, I realized my mistake.

When I arrived at Gianna, I was surprised to find the front door locked. A small sign directed me to ring the doorbell. The door was opened promptly by a smartly dressed woman, who showed me to a lounge area where she said I could wait for Rosa. As I followed her through the front room, I couldn't keep my head from turning side-to-side at the numerous displays of clothing and accessories attractively arranged on shelves, tables, and hanging racks. The items themselves were striking, but the manner in which they were presented resembled a work of art. I had to stop myself from lingering behind to gaze at them.

The lounge was located through an open doorway to one side of the main room. It was luxuriously decorated, but it managed to be inviting at the same time. At the end of the room, directly opposite the doorway, sat two arm chairs covered in white, plush fabric. An antique brass table with two glass shelves was positioned between them. It held a stack of magazines on one shelf, and a ceramic bowl of flowers on the other. A large, round hassock sat in front of the chairs. It was covered in the same fabric as the chairs, and the top was sewn in a pattern of tucked indentations that gave it the appearance of a pin cushion. A glass tray sat on top of the hassock, holding a plate of assorted cookies and a small pitcher of water with slices of strawberries, and some type of green leaves, floating on top.

Filmy, pale green curtains covered three floor-to-ceiling windows behind the chairs, and an elegant chandelier, consisting of rows of teardrop-shaped crystals in an inverted pyramid design, hung over the hassock. The crystals caught the sunlight streaming through the curtains, casting prisms of light across the pale green walls.

My casual attire made me stand out in stark contrast to the lavish surroundings of the shop, and not in a good way. I picked up a magazine, and sat carefully on one of the chairs. I found myself flipping through it without seeing anything as I struggled to calm my nerves. Everything I viewed since I'd walked in the door screamed of extravagance, which meant the clothes I was about to see would likely be tagged with a price consistent with that impression. Though Harry assured me I would be able to find something to buy within my budget, I couldn't fathom how that would be even remotely possible.

While I was tormenting myself with these thoughts and wondering if I could make a discrete exit before things went any further, I heard the sound of high heels clicking on the hardwood floor and looked up to see a woman enter the room. She appeared to be in her thirties, of slender build and medium height, with the perfect posture of a model. Her hair was so dark it was almost black, and it made a striking contrast against her flawless olive complexion. Her dark eyes sparkled with warmth as she looked directly at me.

"You must be Miss Travers. I'm Rosa Decavanta."

I stood to accept her offered hand and was instantly aware of how my jeans and buttoned-up shirt looked next to the elegance of her black slacks and pale pink, silk blouse.

"Thank you for seeing me today, Miss Decavanta." My mouth had gone dry, and the words came out sounding hoarse.

She smiled at my obvious discomfort, but made no mention of it. "Please call me Rosa. Harry tells me you work at the bank with him."

I tilted my head in a slight nod. "I'm a teller at the bank. My dad also works there as the financial manager." I suddenly realized how my words must have come across. Telling her I held such a lowly position, but that my dad was one of the executives, must have given her the impression that Harry had an ulterior motive in inviting me to the dinner. That is, if she even knew why I was in her store. Maybe she just thought Harry had referred me because I needed a dress for some occasion.

Rosa was looking at me expectantly as these thoughts were speeding through my head. Was she waiting for me to explain why I was in her shop? Should I tell her Harry must have made a mistake sending me there because I couldn't possibly afford to buy anything she sold? I knew I needed to say something because her gaze was unwavering. "I'm sorry. I guess I got distracted for a moment."

She smiled and waved her hand. "It's quite all right. This place tends to have that effect on me, too, and I'm in here almost every day. Why don't we sit and you can tell me about yourself? I find it helps to know a little about my customers before suggesting an outfit."

We each took a seat. Rosa gestured at the pitcher of water. "Would you like a glass of our strawberry-mint water? It's very refreshing on a warm day like this. Or I can offer you coffee, or some champagne?"

"Some water would be nice." I leaned forward to accept the glass she offered me, taking a long drink before placing it carefully on the floor at my feet. I didn't trust myself to set it on the tray for fear I would cause the whole thing to topple over in my nervousness. "This is a really nice place. Have you had it a long time?" I regretted my question as soon as it came out of my mouth. I remembered that Georgia had written an in-depth article about the background and history of both Rosa and Gianna, and I was afraid she would take my question as disingenuous, since I mentioned that Georgia and I were good friends. Luckily, she didn't seem to find it odd I would ask her about something that I should already know.

"We've only been open a little over a year. I moved here from New Jersey, and I was surprised I couldn't find anywhere to shop of the same quality as some of the stores I used to frequent in Manhattan. There was an old building on this spot that the owners said used to be a café of some sort. It was in such a state of disrepair they were asking an excellent price for it. I couldn't possibly do anything with the existing structure, so I brought in a construction crew that leveled it and started over from scratch. I suppose I might have been able to find something in better shape that could have been renovated, but I fell in love with the location. We've had such an overwhelming response since we opened, so I've asked an architect to draw up some plans to add space for a hair salon in the back. I thought that would be an ideal match for a dress boutique. One-stop shopping, so to speak, where a woman could come in and choose everything she would need for an evening out, then have her hair and makeup done while she was waiting for our seamstress to make any necessary adjustments to her outfit."

I suddenly remembered something from Georgia's article. "Your shop is named for your mother, isn't it? Was she also interested in fashion?"

A look of pure love, tinged with a little sadness, crossed her face. "My mother loved nice clothes, but she couldn't afford them. When I was young, she used to make everything our family wore, even the suits and ties my father and brothers needed. I always dreamed of the day when I could take her to an elegant store and buy anything she wanted. Unfortunately, she passed away when I was just a teenager. I promised myself, one day I would have my own shop and name it in her memory." She paused to look around the room. "Everything we sell here is something I think she would have loved. It gives me pleasure to think she is smiling down at me in approval."

Understanding the reason behind the shop and its name made me look at it in a new light. It wasn't just a high-end clothing store with designer labels, it was a loving tribute to someone's mother. I glanced around once more, but this time I didn't see the cost of the items on display, I saw only the love with which they were chosen.

"It's a beautiful shop. I'm sure your mother would have been very happy that you've named it after her."

A tinge of red colored her cheeks as she dabbed at the corners of her eyes. "Thank you for saying that." She straightened her shoulders and directed her gaze at me once more. "Now. Let's talk about what we can do for you. Harry told me you need something formal for a dinner at the Belle Meade Country Club. Did you have any particular style in mind?"

I took another sip of water in hopes of buying a little time. Style? I didn't know a thing about formal dresses, and even less about what would be considered appropriate for dinner at the Country Club. "I was hoping you'd have some suggestions for me."

She nodded her understanding. "I have a few things in mind." She looked at me carefully. "I would guess you to be a size six. Is that correct?" I nodded without speaking, dumbfounded that she was able to guess my size just by looking at me. She turned toward the doorway to the lounge, where the same woman who had first shown me into the shop waited patiently. "Jenny? Would you please bring in the Halston, the Alice and Olivia, and the Valvo in a size six?"

Jenny made a quick exit, and returned carrying three dresses folded over her arm. She hung each one carefully on a rack standing against one wall, and stepped aside to wait. Rosa walked toward the rack. "I thought any one of these would be a good choice for a summer formal. Each is quite different from the others, but I believe they would look equally stunning on you with your blond hair and blue eyes." She lifted the first dress from the rack and held it up for me to see. "This is made by Carmen Marc Valvo. It's a color-block gown with a black crisscross-halter on top and a full ivory skirt on the bottom." She replaced it on the rack and lifted the second dress. "This is by Alice and Olivia. It's a floral embroidered, sleeveless maxi dress, in a lovely shade of turquoise blue with multicolored flowers across the bodice and skirt." She replaced the gown, and removed the third dress. "Finally, we have a sleeveless, V-neck belted gown by Halston in a striking mandarin orange." She returned the last dress to the rack, and stood aside to wait for my response.

What a tough choice she had given me! She was certainly right in saying that each of the dresses was unique from the others, but they were all strikingly beautiful. I walked to the rack so I could see them closely. The black and ivory gown was simply elegant, so much so I couldn't quite see myself wearing it. The turquoise with the embroidered flowers made me think of a spring garden. It looked fresh and simple, but still gorgeous. The mandarin orange was beautiful, and I loved the unique color, but the V-neck plunged a little further in the front than I felt comfortable with.

"I'd like to try the turquoise Alice and Olivia, please."

Rosa smiled happily. "An excellent choice. That's the one I would pick for you, too. Jenny? Would you please show Julie to a dressing room?" The salesperson nodded and picked up the gown, indicating I should follow her. We walked out of the lounge and into the back of the shop where there were three identical white, paneled doors in a row. She opened one of the doors and carefully hung the gown from a brass bar attached to one wall of the dressing room before stepping aside so I could enter. "Let me know if you need anything. I'll be just outside."

I stepped into the dressing room and closed the door behind me. It wasn't like the dressing rooms I had been in before in places like Harvey's and Cain-Sloan. The room was larger and more comfortable, with a padded bench and thick carpet, and it was infused with calming strains of classical music that drifted in from the rest of the shop. Even the lighting was subtle and, instead of making me feel like I wanted to avert my eyes from the harshness of the image reflected back at me from the three-sided mirror, it seemed to coat my appearance with a flattering glow.

I removed my sneakers, jeans, and shirt, and pulled the gown over my head. It slid effortlessly down my entire body and, to my great surprise, was a perfect fit. The mirror allowed me to see my appearance from the sides and from the back by turning slightly. As I stared at my reflection, all I could think was, I'm beautiful! As Rosa had predicted, the turquoise brought out the blue in my eyes and complemented my hair color. The flowers embroidered across the skirt and bodice were a playful touch that made me smile.

Thirty minutes later, I was leaving the store with the gown in a garment bag over my arm and carrying a box containing a pair of cream-colored sandals with two-inch heels and a matching handbag. The dress had been a little too long for me, but the onsite seamstress quickly altered the length while Rosa was advising me on the shoes and bag. When the final price for the items was rung up, I almost choked. It came to just under three hundred dollars. At my expression, Rosa had quickly taken the bill from me and marked out the total, replacing it with a more affordable sum. She handed it back to me with a warm smile. "These items are on sale, so I made an adjustment to the amount."

I glanced down again at the figure she had written on the receipt. It was still more than I should be paying for an outfit I'd probably only wear one time, but if I was careful with my spending the rest of the month, I could afford it. I looked up at her gratefully. "Thank you, Rosa. The dress is beautiful and I'm excited to wear it." I followed Jenny to the check-out counter and handed her the money to cover the bill.

I had taken the city bus up West End Avenue to the shop, and I felt a little funny standing at the bus stop knowing I was holding the equivalent of two week's salary in my arms. But it was an exciting feeling, and I found myself smiling in anticipation of wearing my new purchases at the dinner with Harry. I wondered what he would be wearing. A tuxedo I guessed, because that was what men usually wore to formal occasions. I allowed my mind to drift into a fantasy where we were standing next to each other, and he was leaning toward me whispering something. I shook my head to clear it of these silly thoughts. I told myself it was just because I had been visiting a fantasy world at Gianna, which some women might find comfortably familiar. But it felt like a fairy tale to me.

I moved closer to the curb as I spotted the bus approaching and silently reproached myself for giving in to such pointless fantasies. I wasn't Cinderella about to go to her first ball. Harry, regardless of how nice he might be, was certainly no Prince Charming. Well, he might be charming, but he wasn't a prince. We were just a couple of ordinary folks who were going to play dress-up for an evening. I climbed the steps into the bus and sat on an open seat, carefully folding the garment bag in my lap. Still, I continued to argue silently with myself. There was no harm in allowing myself to feel excited about the upcoming dinner. I turned to gaze out the window, smiling at the reflection of my happy face in the glass.

CHAPTER FOURTEEN

On the night of the dinner, I convinced Georgia to come over to my apartment so she could help me get ready, but mostly to provide me with some much-needed moral support. The dinner was at 7 p.m. with cocktails starting at 6. Harry said he would stop by to pick me up a little before 6, since the Country Club was just a short drive from my apartment.

Georgia arrived about an hour before Harry was due, armed with a large paper bag that she placed on my bed before plopping next to it. I had already taken a bath and washed and dried my hair, and I was wearing a robe over my underclothes. My dress was hanging over the bathroom door, still enclosed in the garment bag. I hadn't tried it on since bringing it home, telling myself that I might jinx the evening if I did. Truthfully, I was afraid if I saw myself wearing it outside of the unreal world of Gianna, I might be disappointed. I sat on the bed next to Georgia and glanced at the bag she brought.

"What do you have in there? Something to eat, I hope."

She looked at me with wide-eyed disbelief and shook her head. "I can't believe you're thinking of food at a time like this!

No, I didn't bring you something to eat. I did bring reinforcement of another kind." She lifted out a small bottle of champagne and a plastic bag that appeared to be full of every type of makeup I could imagine. "The bubbly is to help calm your nerves, and the rest will help your face match the glamour of your dress, which, by the way, you haven't shown me yet."

I frowned at the bottle she was holding. "I'm not sure champagne is a good idea. I'm afraid it might make me too relaxed, in which case I might say or do something stupid."

She shrugged and put it back in the bag. "No problem. We'll just save it for an after-first-date celebration."

I grimaced at her use of the word date. "Do you really think that's what this is? A date? I thought he just asked me to go with him because he was trying to earn points with my dad."

"That may be part of it, though I'll bet he has more than just a business reason for asking you. I've never met the man, but from what you've told me, he doesn't seem like the sort to play games. If he asked you to go to the dinner with him, it means that he wants you to go with him."

I could feel a knot of apprehension growing in my stomach. If what she said was true, then this evening carried even more significance than I thought.

Georgia must have sensed my growing anxiety because she placed a reassuring hand on my arm. "Look, my friend. Do you remember in high school when you had a crush on that boy who asked you to the prom, then he broke your heart by canceling his date with you so he could take someone else? Well, you survived that, didn't you? Do you remember what you told me after he called to cancel?"

I couldn't help but smile at the memory. "I told you I was devastated, but if he didn't want to go with me it must be because he was an idiot. I can't believe you remember!"

"It stuck with me because I had never heard you say anything quite so positive about yourself in the entire time I'd known you. You've grown ten times stronger since high school. You're a fabulous girl, an incredible friend, and anyone would be lucky to go out with you. You need to remember that tonight. Whatever happens; whether Harry is just using you to get in your father's good grace, or he has a genuine interest in getting to know you on a personal level, you're a catch! If he can't see that, then he's not worth worrying about."

I laughed at the ferocity of her speech. "Thanks for the pep talk. I needed to hear that." I stood abruptly and went to the garment bag. "Let me slip this on, then you can work your magic with that bag of tricks you brought."

"Deal! I may not use much makeup myself, but I'm quite handy at suggesting what would work on someone else. I guess those charm school lessons my mother insisted I take must have rubbed off on me after all."

"I thought those lessons just showed you how to walk with a book balanced on your head."

She laughed out loud. "That was certainly a big part of it. But there were also classes in makeup, how to dress, hair style, and manners. Makeup was the only one I had any luck with. I guess you could say I flunked the rest. At least that's how my mother put it. She must have had visions of me turning into some sort of debutante, but there aren't enough classes in the world to make that happen." She jumped up from the bed and headed for the dresser. "Let's get this show on the road. You get dressed while I lay everything out. This is going to be fun!"

I looked at her doubtfully as I lifted the garment bag from the bathroom door, unzipping it to remove the gown from inside. I had forgotten how pretty it was, and I stood for a moment just gazing at it before I took off my robe and slipped the dress over my head. It slid easily down my body, and felt as comfortable as my well-worn cotton nightgown. One look in the mirror told me it looked nothing like anything I had ever worn.

Georgia's reflection appeared beside mine in the mirror. "Wow! That's gorgeous! The color really makes the blue in your eyes stand out, and it fits perfectly. Take a seat at the kitchen table and let me work on getting the rest of you to look worthy of that dress."

For the next fifteen minutes or so, I sat as still as I could while Georgia took various items out of her makeup bag, applying them to my face in strokes and swirls. I couldn't see what she was doing, and my nervousness began to build as the minutes passed. Harry would be arriving soon, and I wanted to be completely ready before he showed up. Finally, she stepped back so she could scrutinize her work, before turning to me with a smug look of satisfaction.

"Perfect, if I do say so myself. Take a look." She moved aside and gestured at the bathroom mirror. I walked over to it hesitantly, stopping abruptly as I caught sight of my reflection. It was definitely me, but a more sophisticated, glamorous version of my usual self. I walked closer so I could study my face. Whatever she used around my eyes made them appear larger, and my cheeks had a rosy glow as if someone had pinched them. My lips were covered in a subtle, pale pink color that accented their shape. Overall, the result was flattering without appearing the least bit overdone.

"You're a wizard! I love how I look."

Her face showed her pleasure. "There's just one thing missing." She reached into her paper bag and lifted out a pair of earrings. They were silver, open teardrops, in a sinuously curved design. "They were my Nanna's. She gave them to me not long before she died."

She placed the earrings carefully in my hand, and I gazed down at them in awe. "I can't wear these. What if I lost them or something?" I held out my hand to return them to her, but she stepped back and raised both her hands.

"I want you to wear them. They'll look great with your dress, and my Nanna would be proud. Please, wear them for me, for her."

I started to protest, but I could see her mouth was set in an expression that said her mind was made up. "If you're sure." I leaned close to the mirror, and placed them carefully on my ears. They swung slightly from side to side, causing the silver to reflect the turquoise color from my dress. "They're beautiful." I turned to embrace her in a hug. "Thank you. I promise to take care of them." I pulled back to look at my friend and noticed the faint glimmer of tears in her eyes, which I felt certain matched my own. "I wish you were going to the party with me."

She rolled her eyes at me. "Right… Just you, me, and Harry makes three. I'm sure he'd be thrilled with that."

I shook my head at her. "You know what I mean. It would be more fun if you were there." Just then I heard a knock on the door. "Oh no! That must be Harry. You get the door while I finish getting ready." I hurried into the bathroom, grabbing my shoes on the way.

I heard her mutter under her breath as I bolted out of the room. "Sure. I'd like nothing better than to entertain your date while you're hiding in the bathroom."

"Please, Georgia!" I yelled through the closed door.

I could hear the muted sounds of conversation while I hurried to brush my hair and pull it back on the sides with silver barrettes. I carefully slipped on the sandals I bought to match my dress and took a deep breath before opening the bathroom door. Georgia and Harry were standing just inside the door in what could be called my kitchen/dining area. They turned in unison to look at me as I walked toward them.

"There you are. I was just telling Harry how we first met, and how cute you were with those hubcaps you used to wear for glasses."

I looked at her askance. "Thanks for painting such a pretty picture of me." I glanced at Harry, who was staring at me with such a stunned expression I began to grow uncomfortable. Georgia must have noticed it, too, because she quickly added, "But doesn't she look good now?"

As she spoke, Harry seemed to pull himself out of his frozen state. "Yes. She looks fantastic. You look fantastic, Julie. That dress is gorgeous. You're gorgeous!"

Georgia caught my eye to give me a smug wink, which I chose to ignore.

"Thank you. Rosa Decavanta suggested it."

"Well, she made a good suggestion. It really makes your eyes look blue. I mean they ARE blue. But the dress really makes them stand out." He fiddled with the collar of his shirt as if it had suddenly grown too tight.

I had never seen Harry quite so flustered. I selfishly found it made me feel a little more at ease. "Thanks. You look really nice, too."

He looked down at his suit as if he was trying to remember what he was wearing. He had on a pair of crisply pressed black pants with a matching cummerbund, a pleated white shirt with black buttons, a black bowtie that was hanging a little crooked from where he had tugged at his collar, an off-white tuxedo jacket with a shawl collar, and a pair of black patent-leather shoes that were polished to a high gloss. The only touch of color in his ensemble came from a pale turquoise pocket square that was tucked into the chest pocket of his jacket.

I had always that a tuxedo made any man look dashing, but there was something about the way Harry filled it out that made my mouth go dry. I found myself searching for something half-way intelligent to say, finally blurting out, "Your handkerchief matches my dress."

He smiled somewhat sheepishly. "I have to admit I had a little help with that. I called Rosa to find out what color dress you'd be wearing."

The fact he would go to that trouble surprised me. I had the sudden thought that maybe he did deserve the comparison to Prince Charming, after all.

"Well, I guess we should be going," he said.

We stood staring at each other awkwardly for a moment, before Georgia broke the ice by blurting out, "You kids have fun," causing the three of us to laugh in relief. Harry held the door open for me, and offered his bent arm to help me down the stairs. I accepted gratefully, glad for the steadying support of his arm to help me maneuver the steps in my heels. When we arrived at the bottom, I looked around expecting to see his red truck, but there was only a silver convertible parked in the driveway. He led me to the passenger side and waited while I slid onto the seat before closing the door carefully behind me. Once he was inside, I turned to him curiously. "Did you get a new car?"

He smiled as he backed out of the driveway. "No. I borrowed this one from my brother. I didn't think it would be suitable to show up at the Belle Meade Country Club in my truck."

"I forgot you said you have a brother. A sister, too, as I recall."

He smiled. "My sister, Angie, is a year younger. She lives in Knoxville with her husband and baby girl. My brother Brian is two years older than I am. He's a lawyer with a private firm downtown. He's still single, but he's been seeing the same girl for more than two years, so I don't imagine it will too long before that changes."

I considered what he said. "So, you're the middle child. Me, too! You know what that means about us, don't you?"

He glanced at me out of the corner of his eye. "That we're a little shy, diplomatic, like to be in control, and usually find ourselves in the role of peacekeeper with our siblings."

I looked at him with surprise.

"What? You don't agree?

"I absolutely agree. I'm just amazed to meet someone else who understands what it's like to be a middle child."

"I used to have a really hard time with it. When I was a teenager, I started acting out a lot. You know, that can be another trait of middle kids. I got myself into some pretty big trouble a time or two. Luckily, I had a guidance counselor at school, Mr. Dudley, who helped me understand I was just trying to get attention. He helped me channel my attention-seeking impulses into something more positive. I joined the wrestling team and managed to do really well. The discipline wrestling required helped me focus on my schoolwork, which enabled me to get into college. That's when things really began to come together for me."

His mention of college made me think back to my own decision to forego that particular pathway, and I could feel doubt start to creep its way into my thoughts. "Why did you decide to go into banking?"

He shrugged and frowned. "That's something I didn't exactly plan. I majored in Economics in college, and intended to become a Certified Public Accountant after graduation. I thought I could go to work for some firm that deals with financial planning, mergers, acquisitions, and investments. Those things really fascinated me. I hoped to eventually go into business for myself, once I got enough experience under my belt. Unfortunately, the girl I was dating at the time convinced me I should go into banking. Her father is the VP over at Third American. So, I followed her lead, became an assistant branch manager for Third American, broke up with the girl, transferred to First National, and was promoted to branch manager. Not the first time some lug let himself be led down a rosy path, out of a sense of obligation to the object of his affection, only to find out she wasn't who he thought she was, after all."

I was surprised to find the idea of Harry having a romantic past made me slightly uncomfortable. He was an intelligent, attractive man. Of course, he would have gone out on dates with a lot of girls before me. That is, if I allowed myself to admit that what we were on was a date.

"What happened? With the girl, I mean. Unless you don't feel like talking about it."

He turned and gave me a half smile. "No, I don't mind. It's been more than four years now. It turned out she wanted to mold me into an imitation of her dad. When she discovered that wasn't going to work, she dropped me for a guy she met at the Country Club. They got married not long after that. I guess it all worked out for the best."

I could sense a note of regret in his voice. "That must have been hard."

He shrugged. "At first. But then I began to realize what I was mostly feeling was relief. It was as if a weight was lifted off my shoulders, a weight I hadn't realized I was carrying around. I just regret I took so long to figure it out."

"But it's not too late, is it? I mean, couldn't you still become a CPA, and run your own business, if that's still something you want?"

"I've thought about it. But things at First National have been going really well. I want to wait to see what opportunities might be for me there before I make any other plans."

I nodded. "The bank's involvement in bringing about Fan Fair and Opryland USA has been pretty exciting, and of course we're all waiting to see what the new building will be like. I don't know if everything that's going on will be for the best." As soon as I spoke, I realized I'd made a mistake in mentioning something my dad told me not to discuss.

Harry looked at me blankly. "What are you talking about? Is there something going on I should know about?"

I could feel my happy mood slip away as I realized the extent of my mistake. "I'm not sure. My dad told me some things a while back, but he also told me not to talk about it with anyone. I guess I just screwed that up royally. Can we just forget I said anything?"

I could see the muscles in his jaw flex. "I don't guess I have a choice. But you have to know how hard it is to hear something's going on, then be told you can't, or won't tell me what it is." He pulled into a circular driveway that led to a long, white building, and stopped the car.

"I'm really sorry. I promise, if I find out anything I'm able to talk about, I'll come to you right away."

He smiled at me reluctantly. "Well, since I don't really have a choice, I'll just have to be satisfied with that for the time being." He opened his door before turning to me again. "The thing is, I trust you. So, I'm willing to put this aside for now so we can enjoy the evening."

His concession filled me with relief, and surprised me more than a little. He said he trusted me, after I had just shown him I couldn't be counted on to keep my mouth shut about something I had no right to mention. Something my Gran once said to me flashed through my mind: For someone to place their trust in you is an even greater compliment than for them to love you. If that was true, then Harry had just given me an invaluable gift. One I was not sure I deserved.

CHAPTER FIFTEEN

The Belle Meade Country Club wasn't very old, by most standards. It had been built the same year I graduated from high school, in 1969. The golf course surrounding it, from which it took its name, opened in 1901. When the clubhouse first opened, it quickly gained the reputation of being THE gathering spot for wealthy Nashvillians, and being allowed into its hallowed halls was not easy. You had to be a member in order to access most areas of the facility, and the membership fee was around $3,000 a year for a couple. Even if someone was able to fork over that kind of money, an invitation to join had to be extended from two existing members. New members had to be approved by the Board of Directors. In other words, just because you wanted in, didn't mean you would be allowed in.

Although technically Belle Meade was not part of Nashville, the Belle Meade County Club sat smack in the middle of some of the most desirable acreage in all of Nashville. It was considered an independent city which had its own police force, famously known for handing out speeding tickets to drivers who ventured even a few miles over the 25 to 30 mph limit enforced on its streets.

The clubhouse was bordered on the front by Belle Meade Boulevard, which ran from West End Avenue to Percy Warner Park. The building was designed in a traditional Southern plantation style, which meant it was huge and sprawling, with a front porch replete with white, wooden rocking chairs, perfect for wiling away a summer evening with a cold beverage close at hand.

As soon as we stepped into the lobby, Harry and I were greeted by a waiter holding a tray of assorted drinks. His white coat made a sharp contrast to the darkness of his face, and I suddenly remembered that the country club also had a long-standing policy that prohibited black people from being members. That thought made me stop abruptly in my tracks, causing Harry to come to a jerking stop beside me since I was still holding onto his arm. He looked at me in alarm.

"What's wrong?"

I wasn't sure how to answer him with just a few sentences. How did I tell him that the blatant evidence of prejudice made me ashamed of my color? The fact was, I had been fairly naïve about matters of racial segregation before moving to Nashville. Cincinnati was somewhat less affected by the racial disparities so rampant in the South. So, it was a pretty strong eye-opening experience when I encountered evidence of it in Nashville. There was one particular memory that stood out and haunted me from time to time, which I decided to share with Harry.

"Shortly after we moved to Nashville, I went to the Sears store with my mother and a woman she knew from church. The woman's daughter was going to be in my class, so my mother suggested we go shopping for school uniforms together. It was a really hot day, and after we finished making our purchases, I suggested we stop for something cold to drink in the cafeteria located on the main floor. My mother gave me a warning look and said we'd have to wait until we got home because it was getting late. Since it was still early afternoon, I didn't understand what she meant, but I could tell she wanted me to drop the subject.

"My mother barely said a word until after we dropped my classmate and her mother at their home and pulled up in front of ours. Then she turned to me with a sad look and explained the woman and her daughter would not have been allowed to enter the Sears cafeteria because of the color of their skin. I thought she was joking at first, until I saw the seriousness of her expression. After that, she sat me down and explained that even though a law had been passed in the mid-1950s that mandated racial desegregation of public schools in Tennessee and elsewhere, more widespread social integration of the races was still incomplete. There were many businesses that insisted on holding on to their right to prohibit blacks from using public facilities, like toilets, water fountains, and restaurants.

"My first reaction was to become angry with my mother for going to a place with such a rule, but she helped me understand that by taking our friends to shop there, we were helping to chip away at the fear that formed the foundation of segregation. As she put it, the more whites and blacks were able to interact in everyday activities, the more comfortable everyone would become. At least, she chose to believe that would happen."

Harry raised his head in order to scan the room. "I hadn't noticed it before, but the only black people in here, other than the workers, are one of our tellers and his girlfriend. Actually, he was the first black person hired at the bank. Maybe we should go over there and help them feel welcome."

The teller's name was Jerome Bennett. He was assigned the window two spots down from mine, and we had exchanged polite greetings most mornings as we went to our respective posts. He had been working at the bank only a few weeks, after transferring to our branch from one in Memphis. Jerome was soft spoken and polite, and he had a smile that could light up a room.

"That's a good idea. I wouldn't want them to feel uncomfortable."

Harry looked pointedly at the two standing alone with awkward smiles on their faces. "I think it's too late for that." He took my hand and led me in their direction.

Jerome introduced his date as Gloria Rayford and explained they had been going out since high school, and were planning to marry as soon as they saved up enough money. They were obviously crazy about each other, which was evident in the tender looks they shared. I felt an instant affinity with the slender young woman whose dark eyes sparkled with mirth as she listened to Harry and Jerome banter back and forth about their favorite sports teams.

Harry flagged down one of the waiters, lifted two drinks from the tray, which he offered to Jerome and Gloria, then chose two more, presenting them to me.

"I didn't know which you'd prefer, so I got one of each."

I looked at the drinks he held. One was clear and slightly fizzy with a wedge of lime pressed onto the rim. The other was an amber color with slices of orange and lime, and a maraschino cherry floating on the top.

"I'm afraid I don't have much experience with fancy alcoholic drinks. You'll have to tell me what they are."

He lifted the glass on his right. "I'm pretty sure this is a gin and tonic, and the other is probably some type of rum punch."

I regarded them with uncertainty, until Gloria sidled over next to me and pointed to the amber colored drink. "Jerome has a cousin who's a bartender. He's always trying out new concoctions on us. Try that one. It's one of my favorites."

I lifted the drink and took a careful sip. It was sweet, but also slightly sour. I caught Gloria's eye over the rim of my glass as I took another sip. "Um. It's good." I looked at the other glass Harry was holding and gave him an impish grin. "Can I taste that one, too?"

He smiled and held it out to me. It was also a combination of sweet and sour, but not as fruity as the first one. I held up the amber drink. "I think I'll stick with this one." I took another sip and looked around at the other guests. "There are a lot of people here I've never seen before."

Harry scanned the room. "Some of them are members of the bank's board of directors. Others are top stockholders, investors, and people who have some type of association with the bank. As you can tell, this dinner is about more than just the move to a new building. I can bet you there's a lot of high-powered hobnobbing going on, too."

I continued searching the crowd in hopes of seeing my parents, who I knew were planning to be at the dinner. I eventually spotted them standing on the opposite side of the lobby, engaged in conversation with a man I didn't recognize. I nudged Harry and pointed in their direction. "Let's go over and say hello."

We turned to Gloria and Jerome to invite them to join us, then made our way across the lobby. Reaching them was no small feat, considering there was barely enough room to maneuver through the crowd without turning sideways to avoid spilling drinks and stepping on toes. When we finally made it to where they stood, my dad turned to us with a grin. "There you are. I was wondering when you two would get here. Tommy Owen, I'd like to introduce you to my daughter, Julie. This is Harry Simpson, our Branch Manager at the bank."

Harry quickly stepped forward. "It's a pleasure to meet you, Mr. Owen. I've heard a lot about you." Tommy replied with a nod and an offered handshake.

I'm sure my face showed my puzzlement as I looked from Harry to my dad. Since neither of them offered to explain who Tommy Owen was, I stepped forward as well. "It's nice to meet you, although I have to say that I haven't heard anything about you."

Mr. Owen's face broke out in a wide grin and he laughed loudly.

"I appreciate your honesty, Miss Travers. Actually, I'm new in town, and your father has been kind enough to help introduce me around."

I looked at my dad, whose face was a mask of secrecy. He held out his hand to Jerome. "Hello, Jerome. It's nice to see you again. Who is this lovely young lady you're with?" He turned his attention to Gloria.

"I'd like to introduce you to my girlfriend, Gloria Rayford."

Gloria nodded at my father with a demure smile. "Mr. Travers. Mrs. Travers. I'm so pleased to meet both of you."

My mother smiled warmly at her. "And we're both glad to meet you." She linked her arm with Gloria's and steered her in the direction of the ladies' room. "Why don't you join me while I powder my nose? You can tell me how Jerome managed to catch your eye." She turned and gave my father a knowing look.

The five of us stood watching them walk away. I turned my attention back to the man my dad had introduced as Tommy Owen.

"What brings you to town, Mr. Owen?"

He rattled the ice cubes in his glass before taking a long sip and placing the glass on the empty tray of a passing waiter. "Music, Miss Travers. I'm in the music business."

My dad made a sound like a grunt. "That's putting it mildly. Tommy was a bit of a teen idol in Los Angeles. You may have heard the song "I'm Sticking With You'?" We all looked at each other and shook our heads. "Well, maybe that's because it was on the B-side of the number one hit, "Party Doll." His song did make it into the top 20, but he decided to forego a career as a singer and switch to the production side of things. Before he left L.A., he produced hits for folks like Frank Sinatra, Dean Martin, and Sammy Davis Jr. Now, he's ready to take on Music City."

Mr. Owen smiled broadly and raised his shoulders in a shrug. "Well, at least I'm going to take a stab at it. I've never been terribly interested in Country Music, but I believe there's a tremendous amount of talent in Nashville that hasn't been featured to its best advantage, and a range of music that goes way beyond country." He turned his attention to Jerome. "I've heard there are some pretty hopping joints on Jefferson Street where you can catch some great jazz and blues."

Jefferson Street was in a predominantly black part of Nashville. His comment was obviously directed at one of the only black members of our little group, which caused an awkward silence to descend over us. Jerome glanced at Gloria, who had just returned from the ladies' room with my mother, then looked directly at Mr. Owen.

"Yes, Sir. That's true. Although I haven't had a chance to go to many of them myself."

"Really? Well, we'll have to remedy that. Maybe I could give you a call next week, and we could arrange a night to take in that scene. Your lovely lady could go with us."

Gloria's eyes opened wide in surprise as she looked back and forth between Jerome and Mr. Owen.

"We'll have to think about that, Mr. Owen. I thank you for the invitation."

Tommy squinted at Jerome as if he was trying to decide what to make of his comment, then shrugged as he turned his attention back to my dad. "Will, I need a refresher. What say you and I head over to the bar before this shindig gets underway?"

My dad smiled politely. "Sure. Would anyone else like a refill?" The rest of us shook our heads, then stood watching while my dad and Mr. Owen made their way through the crowd toward the bar. My mother turned and looked directly at Jerome and Gloria. "I don't think he meant anything by his question. He's from L.A., you know. They view things differently out there."

"I suspect you're right, ma'am. It just took me by surprise, is all." Jerome clutched Gloria's hand in his and looked at her apologetically. At that moment we heard the tinkling of a bell, indicating it was time to head to the ballroom for dinner. Harry stepped between my mom and me, extending a bent arm toward each of us. "Ladies?" We each accepted his offered arm and stepped into line behind the rest of the crowd, with Jerome and Gloria following just behind.

CHAPTER SIXTEEN

One of the biggest draws of the Belle Meade Country Club, other than bragging rights to being a member, was a spacious, rectangular-shaped grand ballroom with the capacity to seat 200 people. It was most commonly used to host private parties and special club functions, but it was also the site of a weekly buffet dinner open to non-members on Friday evenings; a gesture I was sure was intended to show how welcoming the club could be. To some people, that is. The only time I had ever been inside the clubhouse was to attend a wedding reception in the same ballroom for the daughter of one of my mother's church friends. I was barely sixteen at the time, and I can still remember feeling dumbstruck, and more than a little bit intimidated, by the grandeur that surrounded me.

As we made our way into the ballroom for dinner, I was again struck by the lavish décor. The wooden floors were polished to a high gloss, reflecting the glow from four crystal chandeliers hanging down the center of the room. Fireplaces were located at each end, with two more on the sides. On this evening, because it was too warm for actual fires, they were lit by hundreds of twinkling candles.

Ornately carved crown molding capped the walls all the way around the room where they met the ceiling. The walls were painted pale gold, which seemed to catch the gleam of candlelight and reflect it back. There were six windows on the outermost wall, with six doors facing them on the opposite side. Three windows were carved into the walls at the far end of the ballroom, whereas the side where we entered was a solid wall broken only by a set of double doors propped open to allow the guests to flow freely into the ballroom.

Cream-colored drapes were hung across the tops of the windows and doors, falling in loose folds along the sides where they were pulled back by braids of gold-toned rope. Tablecloths of the same color as the drapes covered numerous round tables, set with an assortment of silver flatware and crystal glasses. A crystal fishbowl, filled with white tulip buds floating in water, sat in the center of each table on top of a piece of round, mirrored glass. The glass was surrounded by four votive candles in glass holders, and the overall effect made the room seem to sparkle with wavering light.

As we came through the doors of the ballroom, Harry pointed in the direction of a vacant table, midway up the right side of the room, and suggested we head that way to claim it as our own. Luckily, there were no assigned seats for the guests, except at one long table that stretched the length of the far end of the room. Each of the round tables was set for eight people, which would easily accommodate our party of seven. As we took our seats, I glanced curiously at the reserved table. All of the chairs along one side had been removed allowing the featured attendees to face the rest of the room. The bank manager, Tim Carson, and his wife, Evelyn, were already seated at one end of the table. The bank president, P. Brock Browning, and a woman I assumed was his wife were seated at the center of the row of chairs. On either side of them were Mayor Brill and Governor Lunt, with their wives. The rest of the table was quickly filling with the five men who had been meeting with my dad, accompanied by women who were either their dates or spouses, with the exception of the Taylor brothers who came alone. Two other men I didn't recognize, filled up the remaining seats. All in all, it was a pretty impressive bunch. I had to wonder why my dad wasn't seated among them.

Numerous waiters were roaming among the tables, offering to fill glasses from pitchers of a chilled, rose-colored beverage with slices of fruit floating in it. The drink was ice cold, as evidenced by the sheen of moisture covering the outside of the pitcher. I took a sip from my glass and discovered the taste was fruity and refreshing. I looked up at the waiter who was continuing to fill glasses at our table and asked him what it was, and he responded it was called Sangria.

The noise in the room had risen considerably with sounds of conversation mixed with the scraping of chair legs, clinking of glasses, and swishing of long skirts as the guests made their way to their seats. The combination of noises made it nearly impossible to carry on a conversation with anyone who wasn't seated close by. I sat next to Harry and Gloria, so most of my conversation was directed to them. My mother sat on the other side of Harry, and Jerome was to Gloria's right. My dad and Mr. Owen had returned to fill two of the vacant spots on the other side of my mother, leaving one empty chair next to Mr. Owen. He looked at it pointedly as he sat down. "Well. It looks like I'm going to have to rustle up my own date for the night. Anybody know any single gals here?"

His attempts at humor were beginning to grate on me. He was definitely what you would call "rough around the edges". I decided to give him the benefit of the doubt, since he was obviously someone who impressed both my dad and Harry. Gloria must have read my mind because she leaned in close to me and whispered "If I knew any, I'd tell them to get as far away from that man as they could." She gave me a wide-eyed look and we both stifled our giggles.

Harry turned his attention away from my mother, who had been keeping him enthralled with stories about the misadventures of the twins, and gave me an inquisitive look. "What are you two talking about?"

I returned his look with what I hoped was an innocent expression. "Oh, nothing. We're just talking about all the different people here." Well, it wasn't a complete lie. But it wasn't exactly the truth either. Harry gave me a look that said he wasn't buying what I said for one second.

A line of waiters paraded through the open double doors carrying trays loaded with small bowls, stopping to place one in front of each guest. Soon the sounds of spoons scraping against china joined the other noises in the room. I looked down at the bowl that sat in front of me, bending over it in an attempt to sniff the aroma. The soup appeared to be tomato based, with a slightly rough texture. There was a small amount of chopped vegetables in the center, topped by a spoonful of what appeared to be sour cream. I tried a small taste. I was surprised to find it was cold! I had never had cold soup, but it was delicious, with a slightly tangy flavor that mellowed once I stirred in the sour cream.

I looked sideways at Harry, who was devouring his soup with gusto. He glanced up sheepishly when he noticed me watching him. "Sorry. I didn't realize how hungry I was. This is one of my favorite dishes."

"Really? What's it called?"

"Gazpacho. It's a Spanish word. I had a friend in college whose family came from Mexico. His mother used to serve it to us whenever we would go over to their house, which was as often as possible, since neither of us had much money to spend on food. I watched her make it once. She tossed a lot of tomatoes into a bowl with onions, garlic, bell pepper, and various herbs, then blended them until they turned into a thick liquid. Then she added some oil and a little vinegar. Sometimes she'd top it with chopped tomatoes, cucumber, and avocado, then serve it with thick, sliced bread. It was amazing! This is almost as good. She never added sour cream to the top, but I like the creaminess it adds to the taste."

I looked at him with admiration. "That description makes my mouth water."

He smiled before digging into the remainder of his soup. "Actually, I've made it a few times myself. It never turns out as good as I remember, but I keep trying to improve my recipe."

This man just continued to amaze me. There was obviously a lot about him I still didn't know, but so far, I wasn't disappointed in anything I was learning. "So, you cook? I'm embarrassed. The most creative thing I've ever made was a salad."

"Maybe someday you can come over, and we can put together a soup and salad meal."

I looked at my bowl and smiled. "I'd like that."

He lifted one of the pitchers of Sangria the waiter left on our table and raised his eyebrows in question.

"Yes, please. That's something else I've never had before. Is the name also Spanish?"

"It is. It's usually served in the summer to accompany other Spanish or Mexican style dishes, like this gazpacho. I guess the chef is going for a Mexican theme tonight."

His guess was correct because the rest of the dinner consisted of an assortment of dishes I had never tasted, but Harry described as meals he had encountered in the home of his friend. Luckily, he was there to identify each one as they were placed before us. The soup was followed by a chopped salad made of red onions, fresh roasted corn, zucchini, red bell peppers, fresh cilantro, and something called Jicama, that gave the entire dish a sweet crunchiness. It was tossed in a dressing of lime juice and vegetable oil.

The main dish was baked chicken in salsa, with black beans and yellow rice. Fresh, hot tortillas accompanied the entrée, along with small bowls of guacamole, salsa, and sour cream, which could be spooned on top of the chicken or rolled inside of the tortillas along with the rest of the ingredients. I noticed several of the women in the room were forgoing the use of the tortillas for the safer option of a knife and fork, while most of the men layered the tortillas with as much as they could hold before taking hearty bites of the rolled tubes. I personally found the entire meal to be absolutely delicious, despite its potential messiness. But I had to wonder at the choice of menu considering the elegance of the surroundings.

As the dinner plates were being removed, a saucer containing a creamy custard dessert with a caramel topping was served. Harry called it Flan. The room began to grow quiet in anticipation of comments from the main table. The bank president, Mr. Browning, stood and clinked his knife against his water glass to get everyone's attention. He stood quietly for a moment, waiting for the table conversations to die down, before speaking.

"I'd like to welcome all of you to the Belle Meade Country Club. Please join me in a round of applause to thank them for providing us with such a wonderful meal." He stood waiting for the sound of loud applause to subside before continuing. "We have several things to celebrate tonight. Any one of them alone would have warranted a special celebration, but when you put them all together, they're cause for a grand gala such as this. The first thing I'd like to mention is the success of Fan Fair this past April. The reports indicate that more than 5,000 people attended the inaugural event, even though the weather gods weren't looking out for us. We plan to take heed of this year's experience and move Fan Fair to June beginning in 1973." The sound of applause rose again.

"A month later, we saw the grand opening of the Opryland USA theme park, which was designed to celebrate not just Country Music, but American music of all types. Those two events marked the first phase of an ambitious plan, developed by the illustrious group sitting at this table tonight. The next phase will include the relocation of the Grand Ole Opry from the Ryman Auditorium to a new venue on the edge of the theme park, followed by the construction of a hotel and convention center slated to be the biggest in the entire United States. In addition, in 1971 we saw construction resume on the new location for the First National Bank, and we're anticipating completion of that building, to be known as the First National Center, a few months from now." Loud clapping and cheers rose from the group until Mr.

Browning raised his hands palms down and patted the air in an indication that the applause should come to a halt.

"None of this would have been possible without the support of Mayor Bradford Brill and Governor William Lunt. But of course, the real heroes in this story are the men who put their heads together to come up with this grand plan then managed to pull together the finances to make it all possible. That group includes our bank manager, Tim Carson; Bill Winters, the president of The National Life Company; Charlie Davis, the chairman of the boards for National Life and WSM; Wes Plant, the chairman of the CMA; Ronnie May, the founding president of the CMA; Elliott Waldell, the president of WSM; and the two men who are responsible for making sure there was enough money on hand to allow these projects to come to fruition, Hank and J.R. Taylor."

As each of the men was introduced, they acknowledged the recognition with a slight nod, or wave of a hand. All, that is, except for the Taylor brothers, who sat smugly through the introductions with their arms folded across their chests. I looked at my dad to see how he was reacting to it all, and to see if he would give any hint as to why he had been not only left out of the introductions, but seemingly ignored for the critical role he played in all of the events Mr. Browning mentioned. He was sitting quietly in his chair, his face unreadable except for a slight twitch in his jaw. Mr. Owen leaned over and whispered something in his ear, to which my dad only nodded solemnly.

When the applause died down, Mr. Browning began to speak again. "Now, some of you are probably wondering why I haven't mentioned another key player in this whole project. He's someone who was instrumental from the start at pulling together the individuals I've already introduced, and making sure everybody's ducks were kept in a row; which, believe me, was no small undertaking. The reason I don't have him up here at this table tonight is because he's going to announce a special surprise guest who has some very exciting news to share with all of you. Will Travers is our financial manager at First National and the point man on the projects mentioned here. Will, why don't you come on up here to the microphone?"

The room filled with mumbled comments and enthusiastic applause as my dad stood and began to make his way toward the main table, gesturing with a wave of his hand that Tommy Owen should join him. I looked at my mother then Harry to see if either of them was as surprised as I was at what was happening. They both studiously avoided making eye contact with me.

My dad stopped next to Mr. Browning, accepting his offered handshake with a smile before turning to address the room. "I'd like to thank Mr. Browning, and all of the other gentlemen gathered at this table, for helping to make what started out as a bunch of wild dreams into an exciting reality for Nashville. The creation of an event that managed to draw Country Music lovers from around the world to our doorstep was unprecedented. The conceptualization, then realization of Opryland USA extended our reach to fans of Country music, as well as American music as a whole. Both of these venues have brought attention to the Nashville Sound and to our self-proclaimed 'Music City' within the United States and throughout the entire world." A loud burst of applause punctuated his last statement.

"Inviting the world to recognize Nashville as one of the top sites for musical entertainment and production also carries a lot of responsibility. It means we need to make sure we can match, if not exceed, the quality of music found in places like L.A., Detroit, and New York City. It means Nashville must go out of its way to find creative and innovative ways to bring music to the world.

"To that end, I have been in contact with someone who is able to bring to the table both his personal experience of the performance side of the music business, as well as his proven skill at producing that music. Tommy Owen first became involved in the music industry as a singer-songwriter when he was a teenager. In the 1950s, he had a hit record that sold over a million copies and won him a gold record before shifting his efforts to the production side of the industry. In the 1960s, he launched his own record company in L.A. where he has spent the last few years working on ways to revolutionize how music is recorded.

"He originally hails from New Mexico, which I understand is the reason for the unique and delicious menu we were offered tonight. Please join me in welcoming Tommy Owen."

My dad stepped aside to make room for Mr. Owen to move up to the microphone, which he did with the same flourish and bravado I had witnessed from him when we first met. He raised his right arm above his head, swept it down toward his waist in an exaggerated bow, then lifted both arms above his head as if inviting adulation from the crowd. The assembled guests responded to his antics with wild clapping and whistling. When the din finally died down, he leaned provocatively over the microphone and in a deep voice said, "Hello Music City. Where have you been all of my life?" which solicited the predictable response of more whistling and loud applause.

"When Will Travers first phoned me out in L.A., I had no plans to leave that thriving metropolis for what I considered at the time to be a sleepy little town. But the more he told me about the exciting plans underway, that were almost guaranteed to put Nashville at the forefront of music entertainment in the world, I started to see the city in a different light.

"As Mr. Travers mentioned, I started my life in Santa Rita, New Mexico and, truthfully, I don't think I've had Mexican food as good as they served here tonight since I left there." This prompted another outburst of applause until he held his hand up to signal quiet. "My family moved to Texas when I was just a little boy, and I left there to attend college in Pennsylvania. Yes, I said this good ol' boy went to college, and even managed to graduate with a degree in Business before I finally landed in Tinsel Town. Let me tell you, everything they say about living in L.A. is the truth: it's brash; it's busy; and you have to be able to take a lot of hard knocks before maybe landing on your feet. And that's a big maybe."

"In my case, I was one of the lucky ones. When I was still a teenager, I paired up with the very talented Bobby Nash who, as you may recall, had a number one hit with his recording of "Party Doll." My recording on the flip side of his didn't do too badly but I quickly realized I didn't have the pipes to perform like Bobby. What I did have was a pretty good feel for what would make a record sound good.

"During the 1960s, I was able to produce hits for a few names you might recognize, like Dean Martin, Sammy Davis Jr, and Frank Sinatra." A loud shriek punctured the air, followed by laughter. "Thank you, ma'am. My success at producing records for those three gave me the impetus to start my own record label.

"Well as I said, I had no plans to leave L.A. until this gentleman standing behind me made a convincing argument in favor of moving to Nashville. As he put it, "The music scene in Nashville is ready to explode and leave L.A. in its dust."

"Isn't that what you said, Will?" He turned to glance over his shoulder at my dad who shrugged with a smile. "I plan to contribute to that explosion by revolutionizing the way music is recorded. I believe both the technology it will entail and the modernization it will bring to the final product will help propel Nashville to the forefront of the music industry. So, in closing, let me just say, I think Nashville and Tommy Owen are going to make some beautiful music together." He stepped away from the microphone, turning to shake my dad's hand before waving to the gathered attendees who had risen to their feet to applaud his final statement, then sauntered slowly back to his seat.

My dad moved closer to the microphone again, waiting for the applause to die down before speaking. "Thank you, Tommy. Now, if you can just manage to overcome your bashfulness..." The crowd laughed enthusiastically. "All kidding aside, I've had a chance to get a preview of some of the things he has in mind for Nashville, and I think we're in for an exciting ride. With that said, I'll turn things back over to Mr. Browning."

My dad made his way back to our table, stopping frequently along the way to accept an offered hand to shake. I found it difficult to concentrate on what else Mr. Browning was saying. I suspect it was of little importance, since no one else seemed to paying much attention either. Shortly afterward, people began getting up from their tables and heading towards the lobby where bar stations had been set up for those wanting to enjoy an after-dinner drink before heading home. My dad said something to Harry, who nodded and steered us in the direction of a lounge located on the Southside of the club, near the tennis courts.

The room was dimly lit and smelled like a combination of cigars and cologne. A large television screen hung on the wall behind the bar. It was broadcasting some national tennis tournament that had the attention of a group of patrons occupying the stools lining the front of the bar. Harry pointed to an empty, round table at the far corner of the room and ushered us in that direction.

Once we were settled, Tommy Owen raised his hand and signaled for a waitress. "Two bottles of your best champagne, darlin'." The waitress looked at him with a smirk and replied, "Right away, hon," which drew a brash guffaw out of Tommy. "I do like a woman with spunk!" He glanced around the table, letting his eyes settle on me. "How about you, Sweetheart. Do you have spunk?"

I could feel my face flush from a combination of embarrassment and irritation. I opened my mouth to reply, but my dad, who was sitting next to me, placed his hand firmly on my arm. "Tommy, tell us a little bit about what you have lined up for the coming weeks?"

Tommy grinned at him knowingly and winked at me before responding. "I've set up a meeting next Thursday with Glen Campbell's manager. He said Glen hasn't been real satisfied with the sound quality on his recordings, and he wants to discuss my ideas for how it might be improved. I'm also going to be visiting a couple of recording studios that are supposed to have the most modern equipment in the area so I can see what I'm dealing with. I don't know yet if I'll have to start building the technology I need from scratch, or if there might be some things available that can be altered. In other words, I should know more about where we are after this week." The waitress brought the champagne, placing the bottles and glasses in front of Tommy, who popped open the corks and poured a healthy amount in each before passing them around. Once everyone had a glass, Tommy raised his. "Here's to new beginnings." When we had clinked glasses and taken a sip to seal the toast, I turned to Harry.

"Do you think it would be all right if we go soon? I'm feeling tired."

"Of course." He pushed his chair back and stood, stepping behind me so he could pull my chair out. I hadn't expected him to react so quickly to my request, and I felt awkward as I attempted to stand, gathering my skirt in one hand, and pushing up from the chair with the other. I was searching for an explanation for our abrupt departure when Harry came to my rescue.

"We're going to take off now. Mrs. Travers, it has been a pleasure to see you again. Jerome, I'm glad we ran into you and Gloria. Let's get together again soon." He walked around the table so he could shake hands with Tommy. "I like the sound of the plans you have in mind. I look forward to hearing more about them. Will, I'll see you Monday."

I gave a goodbye hug to my mom and dad, and leaned in to press my cheek against Gloria's. "I enjoyed meeting you. Let's keep in touch." She nodded, then smiled in reply.

When we stepped outside the front doors of the club, Harry handed his claim ticket to the valet, who hurried off at a trot. The night had grown considerably more comfortable since we first arrived, and I was enjoying the fresh air. I hadn't realized until that moment how stuffy the atmosphere felt in the clubhouse. Stuffy in more ways than one, I thought. All in all, I had to admit, it had been an interesting evening full of surprises, shocks, and more than a little drama. I was still struggling to process everything.

The valet pulled up in Harry's brother's car and leapt out to open the door for me. When we were both seated, Harry turned to me with a knowing look. "Ready to go home?"

"More than ready," I replied.

I couldn't wait to change into my pajamas and sink into the softness of my bed. More than anything else, I wanted to push the evening out of my mind until I'd had a chance to talk with my dad.

Harry and I barely spoke as he drove me home. It wasn't an uncomfortable silence. In fact, I was pleasantly surprised at how relaxed I felt just sitting quietly next to him. When we arrived at my apartment, he jumped out to open my car door before, once again, offering his arm to me as we made our way up the staircase. At the top, he waited while I dug my door key out of the small clutch I carried, and stepped aside so I could unlock the door.

"I had a great time, Harry. Thank you for inviting me to join you."

"I'm the one who should thank you. I had no idea what a circus I was asking you to be a part of. You were a good sport when Tommy Owen started in on you."

"I guess I wasn't really sure what to make of him. My dad seems quite impressed by what he has in mind for the Nashville music scene, so I guess that's what I should focus on. But on a personal level, he kind of seems like a jerk, if you don't mind my saying so."

Harry's face broke into a huge grin. "I like a woman with a little spunk." He deepened his voice in an obvious attempt to imitate Tommy Owen, causing me to smile in appreciation.

You sound just like him. But, luckily, you're nothing like him."

He glanced down at his shiny black dress shoes, turning them sideways as if he was checking to see if they were dirty. "You're something else, Julie."

"I hope that's a good thing."

"Absolutely. So, tell me. Will you go out with me again? Somewhere more casual, of course."

I was pleasantly surprised at his suggestion and my reply. "I think we talked about a soup and salad night."

He smiled broadly. "Yes, we did! Since my apartment seems to have a little more space to cook than yours, why don't I pick you up next Saturday; say, around five? We can stop by Kroger to get what we need before heading over to my place."

"I like that idea."

He hesitated for a moment before leaning in to give me a quick, but gentle kiss on the lips.

"Good night, Julie."

"'Night, Harry."

I felt like I was floating as I walked into my apartment. The evening had certainly given me a lot to think about. But at the moment, all I could focus on was the feel of Harry's lips on mine. They were soft and warm, and I could still smell the lingering scent of his aftershave, mixed with a hint of something spicy, which was probably a remnant of our Mexican dinner.

I quickly undressed and crawled into my bed, pulling the coolness of the top sheet over me with a sigh. For one of the first nights in a long time, I slept a deep dreamless sleep until morning.

CHAPTER SEVENTEEN

It had been a while since I'd been home for Sunday dinner, and I was looking forward to catching up with everybody. Everybody, that is, who happened to be around on that particular Sunday. I knew I wouldn't see Bill. He'd been back to Nashville only a few times since starting working in Atlanta, choosing instead to spend most holidays and vacations with his girlfriend and her family. Mike's presence at Sunday dinner was also less frequent since he'd moved into his own apartment. Whenever my mom called to ask him if he was going to come over the following Sunday, he usually begged off by saying he needed the time to prepare his teaching lessons for the coming week, or he had already planned some outing with his roommate, Josh.

I met Josh on a few occasions. He seemed to be a really nice guy. He was cute, with reddish-blond hair and a smattering of freckles across his nose that reminded me a little of the TV character, Dennis the Menace. Josh was not menacing in the least. He was kind and always acted as if he was glad to see me. My parents had encouraged Mike to bring him by the house some

Sunday, but Mike always had an excuse for why Josh couldn't come.

Sherry and Carey had calmed somewhat from the energetic, excitable girls I had grown up with. It was hard to believe they were both twenty-years old now. After graduating from St. Bernadette's, they both decided to attend the newly created Music Business program at Belmont College and become quite adept as singers and songwriters. However, since there was no small supply of musical performers with an abundance of talent in Nashville, they felt their best bet for making a living in the profession would be to learn the business side of the music industry. Like Mike, they opted to continue living at home in order to cut costs and focus their attention on their studies.

When I arrived at home on this particular Sunday, the twins were ensconced on the screened-in deck, guitars in hand, bent over a stack of sheet music spread out in front of them. I stuck my head inside the door of the deck to say hello before wandering across the dining room toward the kitchen. Even if I hadn't known where the kitchen was located, I would have been able to find it by following the tantalizing scents that wafted out from that direction. My mother was standing at the stove, stirring something in a pot, and I went over to give her a kiss on the cheek.

"Something smells incredible!"

"Hi, Honey. Thanks! I made roast chicken with new potatoes, some green beans, and I'll slice up some of your dad's tomatoes to go with them."

"That sounds great. Speaking of Dad, is he in the backyard?"

"Where else? Why don't you go on out there and say hello? Take a couple of glasses of iced tea with you. It'll be a while before lunch is ready."

I grabbed two plastic cups from the pantry and filled them with ice before adding tea from the pitcher in the refrigerator. Since my hands were full, I had to back out of the screen door, causing it to slam shut behind me. The sound must have startled my dad, because his head suddenly popped up from behind a row of tomato plants. "Hey, girl!"

"Hay's for horses, Dad."

He laughed heartily. "Fair enough. I hope that's iced tea you got there."

"Mom said to bring you some because it'll be a while before we eat."

He stood slowly from his crouched position, placing his hands on his hips as he stretched backwards. "These old bones are talking to me a lot more than they used to."

"Oh, Dad. You're not old." As I handed him one of the glasses, I did a mental calculation. I knew that my oldest brother, Bill, was born when my dad was twenty-four. Since Bill was now twenty-four, that made my dad...forty-eight! Wow! In another couple of years, he'd be fifty.

He looked at me over the top of his glass as he took a long swallow. "Doing the math in your head?"

I looked at him in surprise.

"What? You don't think I haven't seen you do the same thing a zillion times? I can always tell when you're running numbers through your brain, because your eyes squint and you get this intense look on your face."

"Remind me never to play poker with you," I laughed.

I heard something to my left that sounded like an animal moving through bushes. When I turned in that direction, I was surprised to see Harry pop up from behind another row of plants. He looked up, and gave me a little wave.

"I didn't know Harry would be here."

"It was your mother's idea. She suggested I invite him after last night. I wasn't sure how you'd feel about it, but I gave him a call today and he seemed to appreciate the invitation."

"It's fine. I just wish someone had warned me." I glanced down at my clothes to see what I was wearing. Most of the time, I didn't give much thought to what I put on when I came to see my parents. Not that I was a slob or anything. I just tended to choose comfort over style. Luckily, today I had on a pair of khaki shorts and a short-sleeved white shirt that were, if not neatly pressed, at least clean.

Harry made his way to where we were standing, and looked down at the glass I was holding. "Is that for me?"

I looked at it, too, before holding it out to him. "I guess so. My mom told me to bring out two cups, but she didn't tell me we had a visitor."

He took a long swallow of the tea. "I hope you don't mind me being here. I assumed your parents told you they asked me."

"Well, they didn't mention it, but I'm glad to see you. Although, I doubt you expected to be roped into garden duty." Both of the knees of his jeans were smudged with dirt, and there was a streak of mud across one cheek. I started to raise my hand to wipe it off but stopped myself when I realized the intimacy of that gesture. "Um, you've got some dirt on your face."

He swiped his hand across his cheek. Unfortunately, it was the wrong cheek, which also ended up with dirt smudged from his hand. I tried unsuccessfully to stop myself from laughing, releasing a sound that was somewhere between a gag and a snort.

He gave me a smug look and handed his half-empty cup back to me. "Hold on to this for me. I'll be right back." My eyes followed him as he walked towards the house and entered the back door. I guess I was staring after him a little too long, because I suddenly became aware of how intently my dad was watching me.

"You two seemed to enjoy yourselves last night."

"It was nice. Although, I have to admit, your little announcement tended to overshadow anything else going on. How long have you been talking to Tommy Owen?"

"Not long. Wes Plant, the chair of the CMA, brought his name up during one of our meetings. It seems he's drawn a lot of attention from the Nashville music community because of some digitalized recordings he's been working on for some of the West Coast artists. In an interview on WSM-TV, he mentioned he'd like to try out his technology on some of the Country artists. Wes thought it would be a good idea to get in touch with him and see what he had in mind.

"I don't understand how he fits into all the other plans you shared with me."

"I don't suppose he does, in any direct way. Truthfully, I'm still not sold on the idea of our getting so cozy with the Taylor brothers. I guess I'm hoping that Tommy can help bring everyone's focus back around to where it belongs."

"And where's that?"

"With the music. Everything we've been working on really boils down to the fact that Nashville has the potential of becoming a music empire. Fan Fair, the theme park, the new site of the Opry, there's certainly a lot to be gained financially from those endeavors. However, the true purpose behind each one of them is to bring the world around to realizing that Nashville is THE Music City. Building the most impressive venues to feature that music won't be worth much unless we can also produce a sound that is unparalleled. It's my hope that Tommy Owen can help make that happen."

What he said made sense, but it seemed he was putting a lot of eggs in that particular basket. "I hope you're right. I have to admit, I like him about as much as I like the Taylor brothers."

My dad nodded in agreement. "I know what you mean. But I believe with Tommy, you get what you see. I'm not convinced anything about the Taylor brothers is that transparent."

The screen door slammed, alerting us to Harry's return. I noticed his face was clean and slightly red from where I assumed he had scrubbed off the garden dirt. His hair was also sticking up on the sides, which I now recognized was an indication he had tried to comb it with his fingers. I found it oddly appealing that he could be comfortable enough to wear a tuxedo one night, and the next day be digging around in the dirt with my dad without concern for messing up his clothes or smudging his face with mud. He was tucking his pink polo shirt into his jeans as he approached, which I chalked up to one more indication of his uniqueness and self-confidence. He stopped next to my dad.

"Your wife said to tell you that dinner will be ready in twenty minutes and to bring in some fresh tomatoes."

"Right-O." My dad walked up the yard to where there was a stack of plastic bowls and picked one. He walked back to where we were waiting and held it out to me. "Fill this up with some ripe ones. I'm going inside to clean up a bit."

"Sure, Dad." I started down one of the rows of plants, stopping every now and then to select a tomato from the bushes. Harry walked down the row next to mine, looking to see which tomatoes I selected, then choosing a similar one to add. When the bowl was full, we began to walk in the direction of the house. When we were almost to the back door, he stopped me by placing a hand on my arm.

"I had a really good time last night. With you, that is. I don't think it would have been nearly as enjoyable if you hadn't been with me."

"I felt the same way."

His mouth twisted into a smile as he studied the ground. "So, you don't mind seeing me again so soon? When your mom invited me, I wasn't sure I should accept. But I let my desire to see you again, outside of work that is, override my concern you might not be thrilled to see me so soon."

"I'll admit it was a surprise. But not in a bad way. I'm glad you're here." As I said it, I realized it was true. There was something that just seemed right about finding Harry in the garden with my dad, picking tomatoes with me, getting ready to sit down with all of us for dinner. I smiled at him happily. "I really am glad you're here."

He returned my smile and reached out to take the bowl of tomatoes from me, before taking my hand in his.

CHAPTER EIGHTEEN

By the time summer ended and the faded tones of dried grasses were replaced by the brilliant red, yellow, and orange colors of fall, several other significant events made the change in seasons feel like a prophetic sign. I had been going out with Harry on a regular basis, ever since our unexpected meeting at my parents' house for dinner, and our relationship had grown in both comfort and intensity. It was an odd thing, at least for me in my limited experience with relationships, to feel so at ease with a man, while at the same time burn with such desire that I felt it might consume me.

I don't remember precisely how we progressed from just seeing each other casually to being almost inseparable, but it happened as easily as everything else between us. One day he was kissing me politely at my door, and the next we were falling into each other's arms as if we couldn't get close enough. I suppose the years of observing the ease with which my mom and dad related to each other physically, without embarrassment or any effort to hide their passion for each other, must have affected me on some subliminal level and given me a degree of comfort with my own sexuality.

Harry and I established a regular routine of spending every weekend together from the end of work on Friday to the conclusion of Sunday dinner. On most Friday nights, we would camp out on the landing outside my apartment with a couple of icy drinks and some take-out pizza, and allow our minds to wind their way through the events of the previous week. On Saturdays, we often went for a walk in Centennial Park, except for those times when there was a mandatory class at the bank for me to attend and him to teach. We rode in together on those mornings, although Harry dropped me off a discrete distance away in order to avoid drawing attention to our relationship. Not that our dating was a secret. We just chose not to broadcast it unnecessarily.

Saturday afternoons, we each took time to ourselves before meeting up again in the evening. For me, time to myself usually meant doing the laundry and tidying up my apartment, or stopping by to catch up with Georgia or Mike. It's funny, even though they were both aware of how close Harry and I had grown to each other, neither one of them asked me very much about him. I tried not to take offense at their indifference, instead choosing to chalk it up to the fact that they were both preoccupied with their own personal lives.

Georgia and Jon Barnett had finally acted on the depth of their feelings for each other, which had been helped along by a series of tragic events involving Georgia's dear friend Ida Hood. Ida had suffered a stroke that turned out to be the last of several she had kept secret from her family and friends. She was rushed to the ER at St. Thomas Hospital after a neighbor found her unconscious in her home, and died a few weeks later.

Up to that point, Georgia had been ambivalent about her feelings toward Jon because of his tendency toward secrecy and aloofness. It was an ironic twist of fate that the very thing that devastated Georgia the most, which was the loss of someone who had become a cherished friend and the loving parent she'd never had, was what finally gave her the courage to open her heart to

Jon. When Georgia saw how Jon stepped up to support her through the weeks of painful waiting and anguished loss, she allowed herself to trust him in a way she hadn't before. And on Jon's end, the tragedy of Ida's illness and death seemed to force him to step outside of his brash exterior and become the loving, supportive man Georgia needed.

There had still been times when they each drifted back into their old habits, causing them to get mired down in an emotional tug of war. But those times had grown less frequent. If I allowed that old gut instinct to talk to me about it, I'd have to say I believed they were going to be just fine.

As for Mike, the mystery of why he had become more and more absent at family occasions, and why he always refused to bring his roommate around to meet the family, was solved. He showed up one Sunday with Josh in tow. Well, to be precise, with Josh in hand. He told my parents ahead of time that he would be coming to Sunday dinner and would bring his roommate along. When the two of them walked in holding hands, my mother threw her hands over her mouth in surprise, while my father stood frozen in place, just staring at the two of them. Harry and I arrived shortly before them, and watched the scene unfold as if it was a movie we were viewing from a safe distance away. It had become our habit to come to dinner most Sundays, and my mom made sure we were present at this one in anticipation of Mike's visit. For a long minute, no one spoke or made a move, until Sherry and Carey came hurrying in. When they saw what was happening, they spoke up with their usual aplomb.

"Oh cool! We have a friend at Belmont whose brother is gay, and I always thought it would be so neat if you or Bill were." Sherry ran over and gave Mike a big hug before turning and embracing Josh. "Welcome to the family!" Carey followed suit, which seemed to break the ice for the rest of us. I was proud that no one in my family seemed to be upset at this unexpected turn of events. We were just surprised. Especially since Mike had rarely been around for the last year or so. I was the only one who had seen him with some regularity, and I was silently berating myself for not picking up on the signs. I had only been around a few gay people in my entire life; at least those I knew about. Even they hid their true selves from me until we graduated from high school and went our separate ways.

When everyone else headed to the dining room except Mike, Josh, Harry and me, I walked over to my brother and gave him a firm hug, followed by a punch in the arm. "You could have told me, you know."

He nodded sheepishly. "I didn't know how. I wasn't sure how any of you would react." Tears began to fill his eyes. "You can't imagine how hard it's been to keep this a secret. Not just from the family, but at work, too." He turned to pull Josh close to him. "But I fell in love. As you can certainly understand, that's not something you plan on happening. When it does, all you can do is be open to it."

"My eyes also began to fill as he spoke. "I'm so proud of you. I can't imagine how difficult it's been for you to live this secret alone. From everyone except Josh, I mean. That took a lot of courage."

When he looked at Josh, I could see their eyes link with the same connection I experienced every time I looked at Harry. For the first time, I understood; it's not the person you love that matters. It's that you allow yourself to love.

The four of us stood quietly for a few moments, each lost in thought. Finally, Mike broke the spell. "I don't know about the rest of you, but I'm starving. What do you say we join the others in the dining room?"

Josh rolled his eyes. "Oh, that's a shocker. When have you ever not been hungry?"

Harry grinned at me and whispered in my ear, "Must be something that runs in the family." I punched him good-naturedly and returned his grin with a smug look.

Mike wrapped his arm around Josh's neck in a playful, choking hold as they headed down the hallway to wash up before dinner. I grabbed Harry's arm and steered him in the direction of the dining room, leaning close to him so I could whisper in his ear. "I'm so glad you're here and we found each other."

He looked directly into my eyes without breaking step. "Me, too. It's times like this that make me realize just how lucky we are." I squeezed his arm tightly and glanced back at Mike and Josh, who seemed to be having their own private exchange. I was thrilled that my brother had found love, but I said a silent prayer the rest of the world would be able to accept their relationship without judgment.

CHAPTER NINETEEN
EARLY SPRING, 1973

Construction on the First National Center was finally completed in early 1973. Once we successfully moved all of the contents of our old building, it was demolished to make way for the construction of a new hotel promised to be one of the finest in Nashville. I suppose the idea of adding a brand-new hotel to the downtown was exciting, since it meant that Nashville was growing to the point it needed an additional place for tourists and visitors to stay. Watching the implosion of the First National Bank, which was the first and only place I had ever worked, as well as the place I met Harry, was a heart-wrenching moment in a way I hadn't anticipated.

On the day the demolition was to take place, a small group of us gathered across the street behind a row of barricades positioned to keep people a safe distance away.

The building wasn't enormous by some standards, but its thick stone walls and massive columns made it as impenetrable as a prison. As a result, the wrecking crew arrived armed with enough explosives to level a small city. I was impressed with how they were able to contain the destruction by causing the building to implode into itself. Harry, who I was quickly learning was a veritable encyclopedia of facts about pretty much anything and everything, explained that the explosive devices were really just used to remove the support structure of the building along a previously determined point, causing the section above to fall down into what was called its "footprint". What that meant, he explained, was that gravity was what brought the building down. That was all extremely fascinating, but it didn't change my emotional reaction to seeing it fall, which felt exactly like any other loss of something special.

It also didn't help that our new bank building, the First National Center, was nothing like the old one. The outside soared 28 stories in height and was constructed of glass and steel. That gave it a very modern appearance, compared to our old building, but robbed it of character and warmth.

Harry explained the architectural style of the Center was known as International, which was very popular in Europe but hadn't caught on yet in the United States. It was a point of pride with the architects and owners of the First National Center that they were on the forefront of something still making its way into cities like New York and Chicago.

The interior of the building covered 801,000 square feet. It included a ground floor that contained the main banking area; several upper levels that held offices for the executives; a very large room designed to accommodate an elaborate filing system; three conference rooms; a catering kitchen and staff dining room; and one entire floor that would house the latest in technology, including numerous brand new Fax machines and state-of-the art computers. In addition, there was a level underneath the main floor devoted to employee and customer parking. It was everything anyone could possibly need to conduct the business of banking, and more. It just wasn't as homey or welcoming as our old building had been.

The first time the employees were given a tour of the building, the lead architect explained the inside was designed to appear open and airy, and to give the impression of weightlessness through the use of ample glass and pale colors. Even the walls dividing the offices were made of a special type of soundproof and shatter-resistant glass. According to him, the use of glass walls to divide the various spaces was intended to give an impression of openness, as if the entire floor flowed freely from room to room without obstruction or boundaries.

It was hard for me to understand why the architects choose that particular design, especially given the private nature of most of our transactions. Perhaps their intent was to make us feel we were all equal, with no real or imagined walls separating us from one another. Or perhaps they were just intrigued with the idea of open space and never gave a thought to its effect on the people who would occupy those areas. Whatever the reason, it made me feel uncomfortably vulnerable. For someone who counted on the illusion of control to keep her anxiety in check, that was a worrisome thing to feel.

A few months after our move into the new Center, I was invited by Harry to attend what turned out to be an unusual social event. The bank's involvement with representatives of WSM and the CMA, and our newly formed alliance with Tommy Owen, meant the bank executives were starting to receive a lot more invitations to musically-related events. My inclusion was, of course, peripheral, due to my dad's ranking, as well as Harry being given a promotion to assistant financial manager. That was a great boost to Harry's career, and helpful for our relationship because it meant he was no longer my "boss," at least not directly.

Harry's former position as branch manager had been filled by two financial services representatives from Memphis, who would share the title as co-managers. As the bank grew in size, the requirements of any particular job also increased, which is why it would take two people now to do the job of one. Jerome also received a promotion from teller to FSR–a position he would share with Frank Reed.

The sheer physical dimensions of our new bank had necessitated adding at least fifty new employees, many of whom were slated to work on what was referred to as the Tech floor. That meant those employees came armed with at least a basic understanding of computers. Since the whole idea of using computers to do much of anything in banking was still relatively new, a series of classes had been arranged to help train the new employees. Up to that time, I only had a chance to use a computer for some basic tasks related to my work as a teller. I found the idea fascinating, that a machine could think and perform banking duties as well as or better than a human being. When a notice was posted inviting current employees to apply to attend the computer training sessions, I made sure my name was the first on the list.

I attended one other formal social activity with Harry since the one held at the Belle Meade Country Club. It took place after the official opening of the First National Center and was held at The City Club. Like the Belle Meade Country Club, the City Club was usually accessible only to members, so it was a special treat to be invited to attend an event there.

The City Club was located on the 20th floor of a building on Fourth Avenue in downtown Nashville, with floor-to-ceiling windows that gave it the unique status of having the most panoramic view in the entire city. It also had the status of being one of the most sought-after venues for private events like weddings and holiday parties, as well as a host of corporate functions. Since the dinner I attended took place in the fall, it meant I had to make another trip to Gianna where, once again, Rosa helped me pick out the perfect outfit for the evening.

Even though I found it fun to play dress up on those formal occasions, I was much more comfortable in casual attire. So, when Harry mentioned he had been invited to attend a party at the Carousel Club in Printer's Alley, a place with a storied and very shady history, I accepted his invitation with enthusiasm. Printer's Alley was an actual alley, between Third and Fourth Avenues downtown, which ran from Union to Commerce Street. According to my encyclopedic boyfriend, whom I had begun to call W.B. after World Book, in the early 20th Century the Alley was home to two newspapers, ten print shops, and thirteen publishers. Its trade shifted to nightclubs and bars in the 1940s, at which point it gained a reputation for being the place to go to find "anything and everything you were looking for," including liquor by the drink. W.B. was beginning to rival my father for his "let me tell you about that" comments!

Although it had been legal to buy liquor in stores in Nashville since the repeal of Prohibition in 1939, it was still illegal to sell it in public places like bars and restaurants. But in the early 1960s, patrons were allowed to bring their own bottle to establishments designated as "private clubs". The bottles were supposed to be placed in special lockers assigned to each club member, or stored in brown paper bags on a shelf behind the bar with the patron's name prominently displayed. When the owner of the bottle asked for a drink, one would be poured from their private stash, at a price set by the establishment.

This practice was quite common in private clubs, or "mixing bars", as they were known all over Nashville. But clubs in Printer's Alley were also doling out drinks from their own supply of bottles, giving them the right to tack a more generous price tag to their patrons' bills. This practice went on in the Alley for quite a while before it was stopped, most likely because the clubs were frequented by a bevy of politicians, lawyers, and judges who chose to turn a blind eye to what was going on. As I listened to Harry's account of what was happening in Nashville during that time, I found it curious how, a raid on the Alley threatening to shut down five of them, was overturned. It was also very interesting that the pending charges filed against the five businesses were inexplicably dropped, and business resumed as usual in the Alley.

The Carousel Club was one of several establishments still vibrant in the Alley in the 1970s. It was especially popular with local jazz musicians, who headed to the club after their day jobs ended, which usually involved playing backup to a slew of country music singers. The jazz musicians would wander in and toss down a few drinks before sauntering onstage to jam with other musicians who arrived earlier in the evening. The Carousel Club was also a favorite night spot for Ralph Stein, the editor of the

Nashville News, who had a special table permanently reserved for his private use.

The party we were invited to attend was called the Alley Cat Party, which was slated to be a fundraiser for the Alley and the businesses that still functioned along its length. The party was sponsored by the Nashville News, which was also the chief sponsor of the Music City USA Pro-Celebrity Golf Tournament, which would wrap up earlier that same day so the celebrities and professional golfers could attend the party.

Several articles about the party appeared in the News and, by all accounts, it would be one of the premier social events of the season. I was excited to learn that Georgia and Jon would be attending the party, even though their involvement in the proceedings leading up to the relocation of the Daily Courier had ruffled more than a few feathers at the News and led to her being fired from her job there as a reporter. The Courier had been the only competitor to the News for several years before its planned closure. Due to some fast thinking on the part of Georgia and Ida Hood, who had worked at the Metropolitan Historical Commission before her unexpected death, and string pulling by Jon and Thomas Bookman, head of the journalism program at Belmont College, the Courier had been saved from complete extinction. That was the fate the Mayor and Ralph Stein had in mind for it. Instead, the four proved to be a formidable team, able to commandeer a plan to make the Courier a part of a newly expanded journalism program at the College, which would also serve as a training ground for fledgling reporters, and provide employment for many of the former staff of the paper.

I hadn't been around Jon Barnett very often. I mostly thought of him as the man who captured Georgia's heart after putting her through a ton of grief as she tried to figure out his intentions. I looked forward to delving deeper into the mystery of Mr. Gorgeous; the name I had given him after I first saw his picture in the Nashville News. The Alley Cat party would also be only the third time Georgia had been around Harry, and I was anxious for the two of them to get to know each other better. I was eager for them to get along. Of course, how they felt about each other wasn't something I could control, but I intended to do my best to sway their opinion in the right direction.

CHAPTER TWENTY

The Carousel Club was decked out in its finest for the Alley Cat party. The floors and tables had been scrubbed clean of any remnant of booze or tobacco stains. The outside windows, usually so streaked with soot and dirt they barely let in any light, now fairly sparkled. Even the smell of stale beer and cigarettes was less noticeable after the doors and windows had been left open throughout the day.

I had been in the club one other time, when Jerome and Gloria invited us to hear a musician friend of theirs known for the soulful tunes he was able to coax from his saxophone. My impression that evening was the club was loud, smoky, and fascinating. We had managed to snag two additional invitations to the Alley Cat party for Jerome and Gloria, after my dad did more than a little persuasive arm twisting. So, the six of us: Georgia, Jon, Jerome, Gloria, Harry, and I wove our way through the crowd already beginning to fill the vacant chairs, settling at a table in the far back corner of the room.

We passed no fewer than three open bar stations on our way down the Alley toward the club. Apparently, there were many more people hoping to gain admission than there was room for, so the unlucky ones stood along the Alley's length in order to catch a glimpse of their favorite country music star or celebrity golfer. The regular bar inside the club was also open, but it was lined three deep with people waiting to place their drink orders. Harry started to head in that direction when Jerome stopped him with a hand on his arm.

"I've got this. One of my cousins is a waiter here. He told me to let him know when we arrived, and he'd make sure we were taken care of."

Harry sat back in his chair. "That's great. I wasn't looking forward to fighting that crowd."

Jerome looked around the room and raised his hand to flag down a white-coated waiter, who promptly headed in our direction. When he arrived at our table, Jerome stood so the two men could share a quick embrace.

"Hey, man. I'd like you to meet some friends of mine." He proceeded to introduce each of us at the table, ending with Gloria. "Of course, you know this lovely lady."

The waiter grinned broadly and bent to kiss Gloria's hand. "I sure do. I'm just wondering how long it's going to take her to realize she's getting second best."

Gloria pretended to be offended, but I could see she was flattered by his comment. "Oh, go on Lyndsey Ames. You know you're talking trash."

Lyndsey laughed appreciatively. "What can I get y'all tonight?"

We gave him our drink orders and looked around the room. "There's your mom and dad." Harry pointed at a table toward the front. Tommy Owen was with them, seated next to an attractive redhead who looked barely out of her teens. I recognized some of the executives from First National at other tables, and the men from WSM and the CMA with whom my dad had been meeting. Several music celebrities were also among the guests. Boots Randolph was at one table and Johnny Paycheck, Roger Miller, and Sammie Smith at another.

Lyndsey returned with a tray of drinks and passed them around. "Let me know if I can get you anything else. It's pretty crazy in here tonight." We thanked him and clinked glasses with one another. The room was filled with the sound of high-pitched voices mingled with the music produced by a quartet playing at one end of the room. A few couples had squeezed their way onto a small dance floor in front of the band.

Waiters were weaving their way through the crowd holding trays overhead and miraculously managing not to spill anything. A long table was set up along one wall with an assortment of finger food, and a variety of people kept piling into the already packed room. I noticed that despite the slew of famous people on hand, there was one table in the front row drawing a lot of attention. I pointed it out to Georgia, who leaned in so she could shout in my ear.

"That's Ralph Stein up there. The woman with him is his wife, Dorothy, and the other couple they're with are Timmy and Tina Slyde, the owners of the Carousel Club. I didn't know Mr. Stein was so cozy with the Slydes, but I guess there's a lot I don't know about my former boss."

Jerome nodded his recognition. "Oh, yeah. Ralph Stein and Timmy Slyde are tight. Lyndsey said Stein's down here at least a couple of times a week, and the Mayor is one of the regulars at his table."

Jon leaned across the table. "Timmy Slyde is involved in a lot more things in this city than just running a nightclub. He's one of the chief investors in the Nashville News, and a long-time friend of Ralph Stein. He also made a hefty donation to the mayor's re-election campaign. The three of them are as thick as thieves, and I don't mean that in a trivial way. It's no coincidence that Stein moved from Editor to Publisher of the News so soon after the closing of the Courier was announced."

Georgia's face twisted into a frown. "Do you think Stein was given a kickback for turning a blind eye to the Mayor's plans to shut down the Courier? I remember how he did a 180 after he told me not to continue trying to find out why you were in

Nashville. Then Ida got word the Mansion had been given the status of a historical site, which meant it couldn't be used to relocate the Courier, as you had hoped. Luckily for us, the money Ida's aunt left her enabled us to add a wing to the College. Otherwise, the Courier and writing staff would be right where Ralph Stein and the Mayor wanted them. Gone."

Jon's eyes darkened. "I don't know exactly what Stein gained from the whole ordeal, but there was definitely something more going on than was obvious at the time. Now, Stein seems to be getting cozy with a couple of brothers who've been buying up stock in Tennessee banks like it was gold."

His revelation caused my gut to clench and an alarm went off in my head. "You mean the Taylor brothers? Ralph Stein is friends with them?"

Jon glanced around the room before nodding. "Yeah. That's the name I heard, and the Mayor, too. All four of them have been spotted out together more than once, and not just in the Carousel Club."

I looked at Georgia, whose eyes had grown as round as marbles as Jon spoke. She and I had spent many evenings discussing what had happened at the News in the aftermath of the Courier's relocation. There was still too much about it all that didn't make sense. Now it gave me cold chills to hear that the same people who had likely been involved in some dirty dealings with the newspapers were possibly gearing up to pull a similar coup in the banking industry.

I looked around the room for Harry, who left to say hello to a few of the other bank executives. He was walking across the room in our direction, and I gestured for him to hurry. He approached the table with a worried look and bent down next to me. "Is everything all right? You look like you've seen a ghost!"

"Maybe I have. At least I may have seen something that could haunt my dreams. Can we get out of here?"

He nodded as he turned to the rest of our crowd. "Are you all ready to leave? Something's got Julie all worked up, so I think we should go."

Everyone collected their things as we headed for the door. Along the way, I noticed Hank Taylor standing alone at the back of the room. His eyes followed me as I passed, and that same creepy feeling came over me as I glanced in his direction.

Once we were outside in the Alley, Harry stopped me with a hand on my arm. "What happened? What's got you spooked?"

"Can we just go now? I'll tell you about it later."

"Sure." He turned to the rest of the group. "Anybody up for a nightcap?"

Georgia leaned into Jon, who wrapped his arm around her possessively. "Why don't we go to my place? We can sit out on the patio and let some of the smoke air out of our clothes."

The six of us headed to where our cars were parked. Jon and Georgia were in a two-seater sports car Jon was leasing, and we agreed to meet them at Georgia's house. On the way, Harry and I swung down Charlotte Avenue and dropped Jerome and Gloria off at their apartment. The two of them had begged off joining us at Georgia's, claiming sleepiness and the need to get up early the next morning.

Georgia's house was located in a neighborhood next to Belmont College, and a stone's throw away from the Mansion. It had originally been owned by Ida Hood, but became Georgia's after it was discovered Ida had left it to her in her will. Harry and I, along with Jon, Thomas Bookman and his girlfriend, Mary Alice, had helped Georgia move into the house about a month after Ida's passing. It was a cute, two-story brick, with a patio out back.

It was close to 11 p.m. by the time the four of us settled onto Georgia's patio. There was a slight breeze blowing, and the freshness of the night was a wonderful contrast to the smoky confines of the club. We sat quietly for a while, gazing up at the star-filled sky. Georgia's cat, Ebie, sauntered out to join us and began weaving her way in and out of Jon's legs, mewing insistently until he reached down and scooped her onto his lap. She turned in one complete circle before lying down with a slight grunt and began purring contentedly.

Georgia looked at the two of them and shook her head. "She's become Jon's biggest fan. I never expected my female competition to be of the feline variety. I guess I should be relieved."

Jon stroked Ebie's head and gazed down at her warmly. "I'm afraid I have to admit she's stolen my heart. But since she's part of a package deal, you have nothing to worry about." The look he shared with Georgia smoldered with a passion so intense I could feel the heat wafting off them from where I sat.

"So, what's with you two? Are you planning to make this official any time soon?" I looked from Georgia to Jon, who turned to Georgia as if waiting to see what she would say.

"We're just giving ourselves time to figure things out, but I could ask you the same question." She gave me a look that said how's that for turning the tables?

Harry and I had been holding hands since we sat down, and he squeezed my hand gently. We had talked several times about our future together, but agreed not to say anything about it to anyone until we'd moved past the what if stage. He turned to Georgia. "We haven't made any plans yet, but I promise you'll be one of the first to know."

Even though the light outside was dim, I could detect Georgia's frown. "What do you mean one of the first?"

Harry cleared his throat. "Well, there's her family and mine. We figured when there's something to tell, they should hear about it before anyone else."

"You did, huh?" The expression, if looks could kill came to mind, causing me to speak up quickly.

"Harry just meant, if we were going to announce something monumental, like an engagement, we should probably tell our parents before anyone else. Besides. There's nothing to announce right now."

I could see Georgia's shoulders drop from their position next to her ears. "I'm sorry, Harry. I didn't have what you'd call a very loving childhood, so it's difficult for me to imagine why anyone would place their parents' feelings above those of their closest friends. But that's just me. I guess you could say Julie is really the only family I've ever had, at least in the ways that truly count."

Harry, wonderful Harry, my sweetheart, my hero, and my friend, stood and walked to Georgia and pulled her up into a snug embrace. "I hope you'll allow me to become part of your family someday. I don't know what it's like to feel like you feel, but having grown up with loving, supportive parents, it makes me want to protect you from any more hurt." He pulled back so that he could look her in the eyes. "Are you in the market for a big brother?"

Georgia looked at him as if she wasn't sure how to react. "Well, I've never had one. But if that means I can borrow your truck and call you when I need you to beat somebody up for me, I'm in." The four of us let loose such an explosion of giddiness I was certain the neighbors on either side would be turning on their lights to complain. I guess it was what you'd call nervous laughter. After Harry's question and Georgia's flippant reply, the tension melted away like butter on a hot biscuit. I chuckled to myself as I realized I was beginning to think like a Southerner.

Even Jon, who was usually the most stoic of the group, laughed so hard he had tears rolling down his cheeks. The only hold-out to our hilarity was Ebie, who jumped down from Jon's lap following our outburst and stood glaring at us from the edge of the patio. If cats could talk, I imagined this one would be saying: What's wrong with you crazy humans? Why can't you just curl up in each other's laps and go to sleep instead of making all this racket? Well, I wasn't very good at "cat talk", but I had to admit she made a very good point.

CHAPTER TWENTY-ONE

Sleeping in on Sunday had been a rare luxury after I started attending Catholic school. Once our family moved to Nashville and became regulars at the folk mass service at Holy Angels Church, lazy Sunday mornings became even less common.

I was still gripped with guilt–Catholic guilt–my classmates and I used to call it, if I didn't haul myself out of bed when Sunday morning rolled around, even if it was just to lounge around my apartment.

Harry didn't grow up Catholic. When I asked him what church he went to, he replied "the church of the great outdoors." In other words, his idea of a proper Sunday morning was to load up his truck with a cooler of beverages, lace up his hiking boots, and head to some local park where he could roam the trails to his heart's content. When we started spending most Sundays together, we reached a compromise. One week he would go to church then dinner at my parents with me, the next I would go on a hike and picnic with him. The third we would allow ourselves to lounge around in bed until the urge to get up struck us.

Since the Sunday after the Alley Cat Party fell into the last category, we were still snuggling under the covers at 10 a.m. We decided to stay at Harry's after the party. He had gotten out of bed just long enough to pick the Sunday paper off his front porch and grab two bottles of Coca-Cola from the refrigerator. Neither of us were coffee drinkers. Too much caffeine made me jumpy, and Harry just didn't like the taste. But our "Coke habit" was something we shared. Well, at least it wasn't the worst habit we could have.

I finished reading the sections of the paper I found most interesting, which included the comics and the financial pages. I was deciding whether to go back to sleep or get up and make some breakfast, when Harry rolled over to face me.

"You know, you never told me what was bothering you so much at the party last night."

I grimaced and squeezed my eyes shut at the memory. "I was hoping you'd forget about that."

"Why? Is this another one of those things you can't tell me?"

He was referring to my slip of the tongue at the Country Club.

"Not at all. I just don't look forward to revisiting what happened." I turned so I could lie on my side and face him. "While you were away from the table, the rest of us saw Ralph Stein at a table with the owners of the Carousel Club. Georgia mentioned she hadn't been aware they were friends. Jerome said his cousin had spotted them together several times, and the Mayor was frequently with them. Jon said the Slydes were major investors in the News and made a significant contribution to the mayor's re-election campaign. He also said Ralph Stein and the Mayor seemed to be pretty buddy-buddy with the Taylor brothers. When we were leaving the club, I saw Hank Taylor watching me. I swear there was something evil in his eyes. The whole experience spooked me so badly I just had to get out of there."

Harry's face was only a few inches from mine, and I could see his eyes narrow as he listened to what I said. "I have to admit there's something odd about the Taylors keeping company with the Mayor of Nashville, the publisher of Nashville's only newspaper, and the owners of a Club that's known for attracting some of the most influential people in the city."

"Remember my telling you how Georgia and Jon helped relocate the Courier after the Mayor announced it was going to be permanently closed? Jon suggested the Slydes may have been involved in the plan to shut down the Courier, at least behind the scenes. I still can't figure out what the Taylors are up to."

Harry didn't say anything for a few moments. The troubled look on his face told me he was deep in thought. "Is that what you were referring to at the County Club? Has your dad mentioned anything about the meetings he's been involved in with the Taylors?"

I hesitated before answering. I didn't want to keep secrets from him, but I also didn't want to betray my dad's trust. "All I can tell you is he has concerns about the Taylors, as I do. He's trying to make sure he has hard facts to back up his suspicions. I need to talk to him about what I witnessed last night, and get his take on it. I promise I'll tell you what I think is going on as soon as I have more clarity about it."

He wrapped one arm around my waist and pulled me closer. I could feel the physical evidence of his interest pressing against my leg, and I wondered how he could have possibly gone from one thought to the other so rapidly. As if he had read my mind, he smiled and gave me a lingering kiss. "Being next to you always affects me this way, and I don't intend to let our discussion about the Taylor brothers, or anyone else, interfere with that."

I threw my leg across both of his so I could hoist myself above him, settling down to straddle his lap in a way that was certain to affect him even more. "I think we should do something about that." I shifted so he could enter me, moving slowly in order to prolong the pleasure. As we began to rock in rhythm, a fleeting thought of Hank Taylor flashed through my mind. But it was quickly smashed into pieces by the force of the orgasm that had me quivering and swaying against Harry as he bucked his hips against mine.

When our passion subsided, I slid off Harry to settle against his side. I could feel his heart beating rapidly where my hand lay against his chest, and I stroked the fine hairs that grew there until I could feel him begin to relax.

"Anytime you want to change the subject like that, you have my permission." I smiled into his shoulder.

"Thank you, ma'am. Glad to oblige." He pulled me closer against his chest and was soon snoring quietly. My previous experiences with sex amounted to one episode in the back seat of a car that was over as quickly as it had begun, and a couple of times at the apartment of a guy I briefly considered boyfriend material, until I discovered three other girls regarded him in the same way. The only thing each of these shared in common was a bewilderment about how men could fall asleep so easily afterward, while I was wide awake and full of thoughts. On this occasion, the thoughts were about what I saw the night before, what Jon said about the possible connection among the five men, and what, if anything, it all had to do with the plans my dad helped launch.

I carefully lifted Harry's arm so I could slip out of bed without waking him, and walked over to where my phone sat on the kitchen table. I carried it into the bathroom, closing the door behind me. Luckily, the cord was long enough to reach, and I sat down on the toilet to dial Georgia's number.

"Goo' Mornin,' Jules." Her voice sounded muffled over the line.

"How did you know it was me?"

"Don't know anyone else who'd call this early."

I glanced at my watch and saw that it was almost 11 a.m. "Early? It's almost noon. Why are you still asleep? You're usually up by now."

She cleared her throat and then chuckled. "I was. Then I went back to bed. Jon stayed over last night."

I could hear her smug smile over the line. "I'm at Harry's. What a couple of wanton women we've become!"

"Yeah. What would the nuns think?"

Since we were both products of a Catholic education, the expression "what would the nuns think" tended to come up whenever we were talking about doing something we imagined they wouldn't approve of, which was pretty much anything that didn't involve going to church and wearing clothes that revealed nothing but more clothes.

"Listen. Can you meet me later? I'd like to pick your brain about some things."

"I'm not sure there's much in there to pick from, but you're welcome to try. What time did you have in mind?"

"Why don't we meet in Centennial Park around two? We can walk around the lake while we talk."

"Sounds good. I haven't had much time to get out and walk lately. The new job is really gathering steam."

Georgia had been hired by Thomas Bookman to be his assistant after she was fired from the News. The plan was for her to eventually play a larger role in instructing the new journalism students. There had been a lot of hoops to jump through before they could actually get the program up and running. Just recently, the path seemed to have smoothed out, and the plans were coming together quickly.

When Harry stirred a little while later, we dug around in his refrigerator to see what we could find for lunch, settling on some leftover chicken we made into sandwiches. We worked well together in the kitchen, just as we did pretty much every place else. Harry laid out four slices of bread, which I slathered with mayonnaise. He then added some chicken, which I topped with slices of fresh tomato. We sat across from each other at his kitchen table and dove into the food. It was a simple meal, but it was so good I licked my fingers where the tomatoes had dripped and settled back in my chair with a sigh.

Harry grinned at me. "You want another one? I think there's some ice cream in the freezer, too."

He was used to my big appetite and the way I swooned over good food. Luckily, it didn't bother him that I matched him bite for bite whenever we ate together. He often looked at me in awe when he saw me down the equivalent of a linebacker's portion and still have room for dessert.

"No. I think I'm good for now. I told Georgia I'd meet her for a walk in a couple of hours. Then I thought I could meet you at my place and we could swing by my parents for dinner."

He frowned. "I'm sorry. I forgot to mention I told my parents I'd stop by to see them this afternoon. I could probably meet you there later, depending on how long you plan to stay."

I considered his offer. "You know, on second thought, I think I'll just ask Georgia to drop me off at my parents' after we walk, and I'll head back to my apartment after dinner. I can ask Mike to give me a ride. Now that he's spilled the beans about what's really going on with him and Josh, he's been showing up over there more often."

"Okay, if you're sure, but I know that look. You're going to try to solve the mystery of the unholy trinity, aren't you?"

"If you're referring to the mystery of what the Taylors have to do with Stein, Slyde, and Brill, then yes I am. I'm hoping my dad is willing to give me some insight into what's going on."

"Fair enough. Oh, and my mom keeps asking when you're going to come for dinner? She knows Sundays are pretty full for us already, so she suggested maybe one night next week."

I considered his question. "Wednesday? Tell her I'll ask my dad to give me some of his fresh basil. She told me she'd found a recipe where you grind it up with some oil, nuts, and parmesan cheese, then add it to hot spaghetti. It sounds fantastic!"

He laughed at my enthusiasm. "Oh, Julie Travers. What am I going to do with you?" His eyes turned serious. "Actually, I'd like to talk to you about that. You know, Georgia asked us a very serious question last night, and I think we ought to come up with an answer."

"I agree. But let's wait a little while until I can get this other stuff off my mind. Right now, what's going on at the bank is all I can think about."

"Waiting a little while is okay. But I know how you get when there's something weighing on your mind. Please don't let 'a little while' last too long."

I stood to gather the dishes and leaned in so I could give him a kiss on the cheek. "I promise." I stacked the dishes in the sink and squeezed a little soap on them. "I'll clean these up if you want to head on over to your parents' house."

He came up behind me and enclosed me in an embrace. "I love you, Julie."

I turned so that I was facing him and wrapped my arms around his neck. "I love you, too. Now get out of here before I decide to convince you to stay."

He kissed me firmly and backed away with a lopsided grin. "I wouldn't take much convincing. I'll see you tomorrow morning."

He grabbed his car keys and a jacket and headed out the door. We gave each other copies of our door keys after it became a regular thing for us to stay over at each other's apartments. Harry had even given me a spare key to his truck, although I was yet to get up the nerve to drive it. I learned to drive in a 1959 Oldsmobile. It was long and wide, and had tail fins that made it look like some sort of giant winged bird. It was way too much car for me to handle, given that I could barely see the end of the hood when I looked out the windshield. It had the unfortunate tendency to stall out whenever I tried to drive uphill in cold weather.

One time I even managed to hit the metal strip that lined the bottom of the right side of the car in my attempt to roll back down a hill onto level ground. The strip crumpled up so badly from where it hit the edge of the sidewalk that all I could do was pick it up and toss it in the back seat. After that, my dad decided it would be a good idea to let my brothers share the Oldsmobile. He bought a smaller and more manageable Dodge Rambler for the rest of us to use.

I finished washing our lunch dishes and stacked them in the draining rack. The kitchen clock showed I had about twenty minutes before I was supposed to meet Georgia. That was plenty of time for me to walk from Harry's apartment to Centennial Park. His apartment was on the opposite side of West End from mine, in a red brick building located on 32nd Avenue.

I grabbed my windbreaker, stuffing my keys and wallet in one pocket, and hurried down the steps to the sidewalk. Georgia and I were different in many ways, but one thing we shared in common was a penchant for always being on time. I had no intention of breaking that pattern today.

CHAPTER TWENTY-TWO

My family was already sitting down to dinner by the time I reached my parents' house. I hoped to have a chance to talk to my dad alone before we ate, but my late arrival meant I was going to have to wait until afterwards.

Bill, along with his girlfriend Mitzi, had driven up from Georgia for a rare weekend visit. I met Mitzi Randolph a couple of times before. She was very pretty, but I found her aloof and hard to warm up to, which I considered a poor match for my "never met a person who wasn't a friend" big brother. Mitzi was one of those women who looked as if she woke up each morning in freshly pressed clothes with nary a hair out of place. Whereas Bill usually gave the impression he had slept in his clothes, which had often been the case. I noticed however, his appearance had changed since he'd been keeping company with Miss Randolph "of the Atlanta Randolph's, direct descendants of Sir John Randolph of Williamsburg", as she had informed us when we first met.

Over the years they had been dating, Mitzi managed to turn Bill into a facsimile of one of those men regularly featured in

GQ Magazine. In Bill's case, he looked as if he was wearing someone else's clothes and counting the minutes until he could replace them with his well-worn jeans and raggedy T-shirt. The clothes just didn't fit the man, and neither did the girl.

Mike was also present for this particular Sunday dinner, along with Josh, who seemed to be the target of close scrutiny by Mitzi who glared at him through squinted eyes. The twins were crowded together at the far end of the table, carrying on what seemed to be a monologue, only conducted simultaneously by two people, about their songwriting debut at a college function. My dad sat at the opposite end. My seat was next to Josh, which gave me a direct view of Bill and Mitzi, seated next to my mother on the opposite side. It occurred to me it was the first time our entire family was together for a Sunday dinner in as long as I could remember. I was beginning to regret my decision to tell Harry not to stop by.

My mom had really gone all out in preparing the meal. A huge platter of pot roast with carrots and new potatoes sat in the center of the table, flanked by a bowl of mashed potatoes, in deference to Bill who wouldn't eat potatoes any other way, and a small pitcher of gravy. Another bowl held a large salad made from a mixture of lettuces and herbs from the garden, and the last of the season's tomatoes. There were also two loaves of freshly baked bread still warm from the oven, and a whipped cream topped strawberry pie made from berries canned during the summer.

For several minutes, no one spoke as the various dishes were passed around the table. Finally, Bill lifted his glass of iced tea and took a long swallow before clearing his throat with a glance at Mitzi.

"Mom. Dad. Everybody. Mitzi and I have an announcement to make." My dad leaned back in his chair, his eyebrows raised in expectation, while my mom looked disconcerted. "I've asked Mitzi to marry me, and she said yes. We've set a date for early June."

"Woo hoo!" the twins shouted. We could always count on them for some sort of exclamatory reaction, regardless of the circumstances. "Do we get to be bridesmaids?"

Mitzi frowned and looked at Bill.

"Mitzi wants to ask her sister to be the maid of honor, and her four best girlfriends to be bridesmaids. We thought you two and Julie could help serve at the reception."

I couldn't believe what I was hearing! My oldest brother was getting married, and he expected his sisters to be part of the serving crew while her friends got the honor of standing up for them at the wedding? How crazy was that! I placed my fork on my plate and looked across the table at Bill, who was looking decidedly uncomfortable. "You're kidding, I hope. I can understand why she would want her sister to be the maid of honor, but do you two really feel that Mitzi's friends are more important than your sisters?

Bill shifted around in his chair so he could look at Mitzi, who was staring at the ceiling with her arms folded across her chest. It was easy to see who was calling the shots on these wedding arrangements. My anger began to escalate as I watched my normally fearless big brother cower in the wake of his fiancée's obvious disapproval. Finally, my mother came to his rescue. "I'm sure Bill is just trying to do what his bride-to-be wants. Isn't that right, dear?" She looked directly at Mitzi, who responded with an unblinking stare.

"My mother and I thought it would be best. But if you'd rather your daughters not be servers at the reception, I'm sure we can make other arrangements."

Mike leaned across the table so he could speak directly to Bill. "Who did you have in mind to be your best man, Bill? One of her brothers?"

Bill looked increasingly uncomfortable. "I—I'm not sure. I wanted to ask you, but her father said their family tradition dictates I should ask her oldest brother."

My father, who had been noticeably silent up to that point, tossed his napkin on the table. "It seems Mitzi's family is dead set on dictating everything about your wedding. Doesn't it concern you that the pattern they're setting now could be what you should expect the rest of your married life? It's odd to me that Mitzi seems to have talked all of this out with her family, but it's the first time any of us have heard about it."

Bill's expression was becoming more and more dismal, while Mitzi's had taken on a combative look. "I wanted to tell you sooner. It's just that we see her family more often, and I wanted to wait to tell you in person. I wasn't expecting this sort of reaction to our news. Aren't any of you happy for me?" He looked around the table expectantly.

My mother sighed, and reached around Mitzi to cover Bill's hand with hers. "If you're happy, then we are, too. I just wonder if you've really thought the whole thing through very carefully. I'd hate to see you make decisions you could end up regretting."

Mitzi stood up in a huff. "Come on, Bill. We don't have to listen to this." She strode out of the dining room with her head held high and her back as stiff as a board.

Bill's eyes grew increasingly worried as he watched her leave. "I owe her a lot. Her dad made a place for me in his company, way better than I could have gotten at any other place for several years. He's gone out of his way to introduce me to a lot of influential people who can help my career. Her family has been talking about our getting married for a long time, and since one of Mitzi's best friends just got engaged, she felt it was time we did, too. I honestly couldn't come up with a good reason to put things off any longer."

My dad frowned. "That doesn't sound like a good enough reason to marry her. I think you're confusing gratitude with love, which, by the way, is a word I haven't heard you use once in relation to this young woman."

Bill looked surprised. "Of course I love her! That should be obvious."

Mike piped up. "The only thing that seems obvious in this whole situation is she's got you roped, tied, and tethered. Don't think I didn't notice the way she was glaring at Josh. I imagine she'll have some choice words for you about why you shouldn't invite him, or us, for that matter, to your wedding. What a scandal that would be!"

"That's not fair. She's not a monster. She just has very strong opinions about some things." He stood and ran his fingers through his hair. "I'd better go. She's probably waiting for me in the car. We have a long drive ahead of us." He leaned over to kiss my mom on the cheek as he passed.

The seven of us wordlessly watched him leave. The food sat mostly untouched on our plates. Only the twins continued to eat. In fact, they hadn't stopped eating at any point during the entire exchange. Mike and Josh shared a meaningful look and shook their heads at each other. My mom and dad looked ill, and I imagined my face mirrored theirs. Bill had always been the strong one. At least, that's the way the rest of us viewed him. Maybe the truth was; while he was certainly physically strong, his tough exterior may have been covering a marshmallow center. We just witnessed what happens when marshmallows come into contact with heat. Needless to say, it was a very sticky situation.

CHAPTER TWENTY-THREE

After Bill left, an ominous silence filled the house. Mike and Josh left soon afterward, mumbling something about needing to prepare to teach the next day. The twins helped collect the dishes and stack them in the kitchen, where I set about washing them. My mom and dad stayed at the table for a while, talking quietly. I decided not to disturb them with my concerns and asked Sherry, the better driver of the twins, though that wasn't saying much, to give me a ride home in the Rambler. I couldn't concentrate on anything of substance that night. My thoughts kept running back and forth between Bill's announcement, the likely repercussions of his decision, and the questions I had about the relationship among the three men I had seen together at the Alley Cat party and the Taylor brothers.

By the time Monday morning rolled around, I was feeling exhausted from the combination of too little sleep and the worry that consumed my thoughts. I talked to Harry at length on the phone the night before about what happened at my parents' house and my continuing concerns about what we had heard at the Alley

Cat party. There wasn't much he could say in response. It was a tricky situation, made more so by what was going on at the bank.

I went through the first part of the work day just trying to concentrate on my job, which wasn't too hard considering how busy Mondays tended to be around the bank. I saw my dad pass by a few times. He was always flanked by a couple of men in suits who looked as if they had serious business to attend to; so, there was no opportunity for me to talk to him.

By lunch time, I decided I was going to have to take the bull by the horns, so to speak, if I was going to have a chance to voice my concerns to him. I marched into his office and asked his secretary if I could make an official appointment to see him. She looked at me with surprise but penciled me in for a slot just after my work day ended. That meant I wouldn't be able to get a ride home with Harry unless he waited around for me, which he quickly offered to do when I told him the reason for my delay.

By the time five o'clock rolled around, I was a bundle of nerves from spending so many hours mulling over what I wanted to say to my dad. I had nothing concrete to base my concerns on, so I would have to depend upon my gut to speak for me. Luckily, that was something he valued listening to. He was sitting at his desk with an open folder in front of him when I knocked on his door, and he quickly stood and walked around the desk to give me a hug.

"What a surprise to find my last appointment of the day is with my oldest daughter. To what do I owe this pleasure?"

He sat in one of the two chairs in front of his desk and I took the other. "I've been wanting to talk to you about something I heard the night of the Alley Cat party. Well, actually it's something I heard and saw while I was there."

He frowned and leaned closer to me. "Go on."

"I was sitting with Georgia and Jon, and I noticed a table up front seemed to be drawing a lot of attention. When I pointed it out to Georgia, she said the people sitting there included her former boss at the Nashville News, Ralph Stein, Mayor Brill, and the owner of the Carousel Club, Jimmy Slyde. When she expressed surprise that the three of them were friends, Jerome told us his cousin said Mr. Stein and the Mayor were regulars at the Club, and Mr. Slyde always seemed very buddy-buddy with them. Then Jon said Mr. Stein and Timmy Slyde were not just friendly but were close friends. He insinuated that Mr. Slyde may have had something to do with the plans to shut down the Daily Courier, with the Mayor's blessing. He also said the three of them had been seen cozying up to a couple of brothers who were known to have been buying up controlling interest in several banks. He didn't mention their names, but as I was leaving the party, I saw Hank Taylor standing near the back of the room, and the look that he gave me made the hair stand up on the back of my neck."

My dad let out a long sigh as he straightened in his chair. "That's interesting. I heard Jimmy Slyde had the Mayor in his back pocket. In fact, some people have insinuated he was largely behind the Mayor's successful re-election. I didn't know Ralph Stein was also involved in whatever's been going on with the two of them. Although, I can't say I'm surprised, since Ralph's support of Mayor Brill is common knowledge."

"That's what Jon said. He seems to think the whole thing is connected." I held up one hand and began to tick things off finger by finger. "Jimmy Slyde was a chief backer of both the News and the Mayor's re-election campaign; the decision to close down the Courier, which was supported by the Mayor and Mr. Stein, both of whom stood to greatly benefit from getting rid of the only competition to the News; the Mayor's successful re-election, and Mr. Stein's move to publisher of the News. What I can't figure out is how the Taylor brothers fit into this whole ball of wax. From what you've told me, they don't seem to have anything to do with the newspaper business. Since they live in Knoxville now, it doesn't make sense they would care about the political scene in Nashville."

My father looked grim. "Unfortunately, there are a few things I haven't shared with you about the Taylors that raise some real concerns about what you've just shared with me. I recently learned Hank Taylor plans to run against William Lunt for the

Governor's seat in Tennessee. If he were to pull that off, it would mean he would control not only the majority of banking reserves in the state, but also the purse strings of the state. That's a pretty scary thought. Since no one has managed to make a successful run for the Governorship of Tennessee without having a significant amount of support from the movers and shakers in Nashville, it makes sense that Hank Taylor would be doing his best to cozy up to people like Ralph Stein and Jimmy Slyde, not to mention the Mayor.

"There's one more interesting piece of this puzzle. I've been told the Taylor brothers are trying to drum up enthusiasm for holding the next World's Fair in Knoxville. I would imagine the recent success we've had with Fan Fair and Opryland USA would be of great interest to them, in that regard."

His revelation struck a chord of alarm within me. "Do you think Hank Taylor is aware of how much you know about his plans? Because I don't think I imagined the evil look he gave me when I saw him at the Alley Cat party. Maybe he's hoping that if he can scare me, it will make you back off from trying to find out what he's up to."

My dad stood abruptly. "Let's just say I have a few things up my sleeve, too. I don't intend to let Hank Taylor, or anyone else for that matter, intimidate me into backing away from doing what I know is right."

I stood slowly and studied my father. I knew him so well, yet I felt, at that moment, I was seeing him for the first time. He wasn't just a respected businessman, an enthusiastic gardener, and a loving dad. He was a shrewd diplomat who knew how to keep his own counsel, and who possessed a strength I was only beginning to comprehend. I walked closer so I could wrap my arms around him and rest my head on his chest.

"I trust you know what you're doing, but please be careful. I have a feeling these people will do whatever they have to in order to get what they want."

He pulled away from me gently and gave me a slight smile. "That's how I'm different from them. I'll do whatever it takes, but I won't compromise my integrity, or the integrity of this bank, in order to make it happen." He placed a hand on the small of my back and steered me toward his office door. "Is Harry going to give you a ride home? Otherwise, I can call a cab for you."

"Thanks, he's waiting for me in his office."

"Okay then. I have some things I need to take care of before I leave, so I'll say goodbye now." I started to turn away until his voice made me turn toward him again. "By the way, I'm glad you came to talk to me. As I've said before, don't ever hesitate to tell me what you're feeling. You've always had good instincts. You just need to allow yourself to trust them."

His compliment brought tears of joy to my eyes. "That's something I'm still working on. I love you. 'Bye, Dad."

As I closed the door behind me, an image of Harry, as he looked deeply into my eyes and implored me to allow myself to consider our future together, came to mind. Did trusting my instincts also apply to matters of love and marriage? If so, should I just give myself over to what I felt toward Harry and stop trying to make sure everything was in perfect order before we took that next step? After all, as Dr. Blackburn pointed out several times, having the illusion that one could control the future was probably one of the least reliable illusions of all. My years of therapy helped me succeed in letting go of many of the illusions I sought to control. Perhaps this was the next one I needed to add to the list.

CHAPTER TWENTY-FOUR

After that conversation, I found myself watching everything that happened around the bank with an uneasiness that came from knowing there was more going on than was apparent. I couldn't make my observations directly, since the conference rooms and offices of the executives were located on the floor above where I worked. However, my spot behind the teller's window gave me a direct view of the elevators, allowing me to keep an eye on anyone who came in and out of the building. Occasionally, I could also hear snippets of conversation that drifted down from the mezzanine. It was a little tricky to do my job while simultaneously keeping my eyes and ears attuned to what else was going on, but I had become fairly adept at multitasking. As a result, I was able to pinpoint the exact moment things began to spiral into a vortex so powerful only an extreme act would be capable of halting it.

One of the first things I noticed was that Tommy Owen began to appear at the bank on a daily basis. He was usually flanked by one or two guests whose manner of dress shouted "music business" to anyone who had spent any time living in

Nashville. That meant, at the minimum, cowboy boots with finely tooled designs, shirts or blouses with elaborate embroidery and rhinestone decorations, and well-worn, faded blue jeans or knee-length prairie skirts. Sometimes, the entire ensemble was topped off with a denim jacket that fell to the waist or a fringed coat made of suede. Tommy had a way of striding in as if he owned the place, with his accompanying visitors trailing a few steps behind. He looked from right to left as he walked, offering a toothy grin and shouted greetings to anyone he encountered. His meetings usually lasted at least an hour, after which he would leave the building in the same fashion as he arrived.

On one of his visits, he surprised me by stopping by my teller's window on his way out, bringing two visitors with him as he bypassed the waiting line and strode up to lean across my counter.

"Hello there, darlin'. You're looking as pretty as a picture today."

I glanced behind him at the customers he had cut in front of, expecting to see at least confusion, if not outright anger on their faces. Instead, I was surprised to find them looking spellbound with curiosity at the trio standing in front of me. "Hello, Mr. Owen. It's nice to see you again."

The smirk on his face suggested he was doubtful of my sincerity. He turned to look at the man and woman who were with him. "I'd like you to meet a couple of friends of mine. Dottie. Kenny. Say hello to Julie Travers."

My mouth fell open as I realized who his "friends" were. The woman was a striking redhead with wavy hair that fell to her shoulders, and smoldering deep, brown eyes. In fact, she was the same redhead I saw him with at the Alley Cat party. The man standing next to her had salt-and-pepper hair that covered his ears and collar, and a neatly trimmed beard. There was no mistaking who either of them was. I recognized them from the covers of albums I had seen at my parents' house and from concerts I'd watched on TV. I had never seen the two of them together. My face flushed as I nodded at them in greeting.

"Miss West. Mr. Rogers. It's a pleasure to meet you."

They returned my greeting and accepted the scraps of paper and pens thrust in their direction by the customers anxious to take advantage of a rare autograph opportunity. Tommy glanced with amusement at the autograph seekers before shifting his attention back to me. "I've just come from a meeting with your daddy, and I was hoping you can point me in the direction of that young man I met with y'all at the Country Club the other night."

"Do you mean Harry Simpson?" I asked.

"No. That's not the name I recall. It was something like Gerald, or Jeremy."

"Jerome? The dark-skinned man who was at our table?"

He laughed deep in his throat. "Well, that's one way to describe him. Yep, that's who I meant. Jerome. Can you tell us where to find him? I meant to ask your dad, but I forgot until I was in the elevator. I figured you'd be able to help me out."

"He's one of our FSRs. Sorry, Financial Service Representatives. You can find him in that office at the back of the room."

He looked in the direction I was pointing. "All right then. We'll leave you to it." He casually moved between Dottie and Kenny, placing a hand on the back of each so he could maneuver them away from their fans. I had to admit, the man was smooth. But he still had a way of making me feel I needed to wash my hands after being around him.

"What was that all about? Was that who I think it was with Tommy Owen?" I turned to find Harry standing behind me.

"If you think it was Dottie West and Kenny Rogers, you'd be right. As for the rest, all I know is he was looking for Jerome."

"Jerome, huh. Well, that's interesting."

Just then, the front doors opened, disgorging a troop of men, all wearing black suits, white shirts, black ties, and sunglasses. They stopped just inside the building in a semi-circle, as they scanned the room in all directions. The door opened again, and another man walked through, stopping just behind the others. He was older and noticeably paunchy, with a prominent double chin and thinning hair combed straight back. He was dressed differently from the rest, in a light gray suit with a white shirt and a red-and-white striped tie.

"Jesus! Do you know who that is?" Harry whispered in my ear. "That's J. Edgar Hoover. He's the director of the FBI. This can't be good."

J. Edgar Hoover was one of the most powerful and feared men in the United States, best known for his attacks on organized crime. He had a long and storied history directing the FBI, but was now in his seventies and considered near the end of his career. His presence in our bank, with his bevy of agents forming a protective barrier around his entrance, was puzzling, to say the least.

Activities in the bank had come to a standstill, as everyone watched the scene unfolding before us. One of the agents moved ahead of the others and approached the information desk. After a brief conversation with the employee on duty that day, who responded by placing a call from the phone on her desk, he turned on his heels and marched to Mr. Hoover, speaking briefly with him before returning to his position in the line. Mr. Hoover stepped in front of the agents and stood ramrod straight, with his hands clasped in front of him, as he stared expectantly at the elevator. In a few minutes, the door to the elevator opened, spilling out the president of First National, Mr. Browning, the bank manager, Mr. Carson, and my dad. Mr. Hoover nodded at the three men before turning to leave the building as the agents stepped aside to allow his retreat. After glancing uncertainly at each other, my dad and the other two men followed him out the front door.

There was a stunned silence that trailed their exit, followed by a clamor as everyone began speaking at once. Harry rushed up the stairs as soon as the men departed, and I could see his head emerge on the second floor as he moved quickly toward the executive offices. In what seemed like no time at all, he was hurrying back down the stairs, followed by the two branch managers, joined by Jerome. Harry turned to speak briefly to Jerome before rushing out the front door.

I watched him leave in shocked silence with a feeling of dread in the pit of my stomach. What could the FBI possibly want with my dad, not to mention the other executives of the bank? I tried to focus on the customers in front of me who were attempting to finish their transactions, but my eyes kept darting back to Jerome who was talking rapidly on the telephone. Finally, I couldn't wait any longer to find out what was happening, so I closed down my teller's window and walked to where he stood.

"Jerome. What's going on? Where have they taken my dad and the others?"

He glanced around him before answering. "I don't know very much, but it has something to do with the Taylor brothers and their business with the bank. One of the branch managers is trying to reach our attorney now so he can get down to the courthouse. Harry went ahead to see what he could find out."

The Taylor brothers. I knew they were trouble from the moment I first met them. Now, it looked as though they had involved the bank in something pretty ominous if it caused the head of the FBI to show up at our door. My head was spinning with the possibilities when I realized Jerome was still talking to me.

"I'm sorry, Jerome. What were you saying?"

He smiled sympathetically. "Not that it will do much good to say this, but try not to worry. I can't imagine your dad allowing himself to get wrapped up in anything unlawful. They probably just want to question the three of them to find out what they know."

"But if that's all it is, why didn't they just arrange a meeting? Why go to all the trouble to parade in here and march them out as if they were criminals?"

"I don't know. But we just have to believe everything will be okay. When Harry was leaving, he told me to tell you he'll call you as soon as he knows anything. He said to tell you it's your turn to trust him. I assume you know what that means?"

I nodded reluctantly. "I guess I don't have much choice. But it's going to be hard to concentrate on anything until I hear from him."

He took me by the arm and led me back to my teller's window. "Staying busy is usually the best distraction when you're waiting for news. By the looks of that line, you're going to have plenty to keep you busy."

I looked up and was surprised to find at least ten people standing in front of my station, with just as many lined up at the other five windows. Word must have spread fast about our visitors. Or maybe it was a delayed reaction to the music celebrities who had been with Tommy Owen earlier. I almost forgot about that odd occurrence in the midst of the more recent excitement.

"What happened with Tommy Owen and the others? The last time I saw them, they were heading for your office."

He shook his head. "He wanted to talk about those music clubs over on Jefferson, but as soon as the FBI showed up, he suddenly remembered another meeting he had to go to and took out of here like he'd been fired from a cannon. He was practically pushing Dottie and Kenny out of his way. That man is strange!"

That was putting it lightly! I thought to myself. But, at that particular moment, what Tommy Owen was up to felt like the least of my worries.

CHAPTER TWENTY-FIVE

By the time I arrived home that evening, Harry had called to tell me my dad was fine after his trip downtown, and he was on his way back to the bank. Apparently, he and the others had been aware of the planned visit by the FBI. A contact from the Bureau got in touch with Mr. Browning a week earlier to let him know the agents would be coming to the bank to escort him, Mr. Carson, and my dad to the courthouse in order to interview them regarding their knowledge of the financial activities of the Taylors. They had been sworn to secrecy about the plans, which is why it came as such a shock to the rest of us.

Harry said the three were unaware the Director of the FBI would also be part of the escort party, and the reasons behind his inclusion remained a mystery. The only explanation anyone could come up with was he had a politically driven ulterior motive. That idea was also suggested in an article that appeared in the Nashville News the next day. The piece recounted what took place at the bank and suggested J. Edgar Hoover's surprise appearance was a clever ploy to shift focus away from recent accusations that he had used illegal investigative techniques to accumulate derogatory personal information on several prominent political figures, including Martin Luther King Jr., John F. Kennedy, and Robert Kennedy. Placing him on the scene where serious criminal actions had been uncovered would help cast him in the role of a hero instead of a villain. The reporter portrayed the visit in a manner that suggested the executives at First National had been party to some shady dealings. The article even included a photo giving the impression they had been strong-armed by the agents as they entered the Courthouse. The only thing that appeared evident to the rest of us, was someone had a pretty hefty ax to grind. They were determined to hone it against the reputation of the First National Bank.

I wasn't really surprised by the suggestion that Mr. Hoover's intentions were self-serving. Ralph Stein was a long-time friend of the Kennedy's. The Bureau Director's attacks on them wasn't something I imagined he would take lightly. But his printed insinuations about the bank's involvement in criminal activities was deliberately slanderous, and it brought to mind my recent discussion with Georgia and Jon about the peculiar friendship among Ralph Stein, Mayor Brill, Jimmy Slyde, and the Taylors. Was the article intended to shift suspicion to innocent parties in order to mask the involvement of the others? If so, it did a pretty good job.

I looked at the clock in my kitchen and realized I still had a little time before I needed to leave for work, so I dialed Georgia's number.

She picked up on the second ring. "I've been waiting for your call."

I sat on the edge of my bed. "I guess you've read the article in the News?"

"Twice. I can't believe the gall of Ralph Stein to suggest your dad was involved in something illegal."

"Of course, Mr. Stein didn't write the article, but he had to approve the copy. What do you think he's up to?"

"Jon thinks he's trying to cover his own tracks. He's convinced Stein and the others are up to something suspicious.

When they sensed the FBI might be closing in, they decided to make it look like the First National executives are the guilty ones."

"What can we do about it?"

She sighed. "You're not going to like hearing this, but Jon said he thinks you and everyone else at First National should just sit tight and let the truth surface in its own time."

"Uggh. No, that's not what I want to hear. There has to be something I can do." The phone went silent for a few seconds. "Georgia? Are you still there?"

"Yeah. I was thinking about something. Look. I don't know if there's anything we can do, but you don't have to try to figure this out by yourself. Why don't you and Harry come over after work? We can at least put our heads together and see what we can come up with."

I smiled in relief. Leave it to my old friend to find a way to lighten my load just when it became too heavy to bear. "When do you want us there?"

"Six o'clock. Ask Jerome and Gloria to come, too, and I'll invite Thomas and Mary Ellen. There's strength in numbers, as they say."

I hung up the phone and prepared to leave the house. The sense of dread that filled my heart and tugged at my gut began to ease slightly, and I actually smiled at myself in the mirror as I gave my hair a final brush. I wasn't sure what I was smiling about. I felt as if a little of the weight I had been carrying around since I watched the FBI agents escort my dad from work, was lighter.

By the time seven o'clock rolled around, the eight of us were comfortably settled on Georgia's patio with a drink in hand and our feet resting on the new fire pit Jon had built in the center. Since the air was chilly for April, I placed mine on the wall as soon as I sat, and I could feel the warmth beginning to penetrate the soles of my shoes.

Harry and I were the first to arrive, followed by Jerome and Gloria. Thomas and Mary Ellen pulled up a short time later, armed with four boxes of Shakey's sausage and pepperoni pizza, which they passed around to the rest of us. Georgia's cat, Ebie, appeared on the patio, sniffing the air before weaving her way between everyone's legs in an obvious attempt to coax a sympathetic morsel from someone. Jon pulled off a small chunk of sausage to give her before handing out cold beers and soft drinks to the rest of us. For several minutes, the only sounds came from the groans of enjoyment as everyone devoured the pizza. Finally, Georgia broke the silence.

"Okay, gang. Anybody have any ideas?"

Thomas and Mary Ellen exchanged a look before Thomas spoke. "I think we need to lay out all the facts as we understand them."

Jon nodded emphatically. "I agree. A lot has been happening, and it's all starting to run together in my head."

Thomas reached into his back pocket and pulled out a small notepad and pen. He spent years as an investigative reporter, first in upstate New York and then at the Daily Courier, before taking a position at Belmont College as Chair of the Communications department. More recently, he had been one of the key players in helping to relocate the now defunct Daily Courier to Belmont College.

The Courier was now the Belmont Post, a campus run paper, staffed by the former employees of the Courier, which provided a training ground for students enrolled in the newly expanded Journalism program at the College. While it didn't pose the same level of threat to the Nashville News as before, it was still a vehicle for providing another point of view to readers that, at times, was dramatically different from that voiced in the News.

Thomas flipped open the cover of the notepad and sat with his pen poised to write. "Who wants to start?" He glanced around the group.

"Why don't we use the Journalism formula?" Georgia suggested.

I groaned audibly. She was referring to a practice that used to be popular among newspaper reporters gathering facts for a story. It involved posing questions that began with 5 W's and 1 H: What happened? Who did it? When did it take place? Where did it take place? Why did it happen? And how did it happen? The reporter's task was to come up with a factual answer to each question. Most recently, I had been party to Georgia using this particular approach to figure out how she felt about Jon. As I remembered too clearly, the process had only managed to get both of us bogged down in our search for the answers. Of course, this time we would be using the technique in a more objective manner, rather than with something as subjective as matters of the heart.

Thomas frowned at the suggestion. "I've never been very keen on using that approach in journalism, though it was widely taught when I went through school. The practice actually originated with the ancient Greeks, who definitely knew a thing or two about problem solving. Maybe we should give it a shot."

Jon shrugged in agreement. "It can't hurt." He frowned and tapped his finger on his chin. "The first four are pretty clear. The FBI showed up at First National on Thursday; escorted Julie's dad, Mr. Browning, and Mr. Carson to the courthouse; and interviewed them about their business dealings with the Taylor brothers. The other two questions aren't so easy to come up with. Why are they targeting the Taylors, and How did they find out about their dealings with First National?"

"There are actually more facts that go along with the first four W's," I added. "Some other 'Who' could be Ralph Stein, Mayor Brill, and Jimmy Slyde."

"Tommy Owen, too," Jerome offered. "He came to see me at the bank on the same day the FBI was there. He wanted to know if I could recommend some jazz musicians who might be interested in playing on a recording he was planning with Kenny Rogers and Dottie West. It may have been a coincidence he was there at the same time as the others, but when all of the commotion with the agents began, he hightailed it out of there."

"Maybe he has something to hide." I suggested. "He always seemed a little fishy to me."

Thomas nodded. "Let's put him down as a question mark for now. Jon? You seemed to have some pretty strong feelings about what the other three were up to. Do you think they're involved in whatever has the FBI sniffing around the Taylors?"

He paused before speaking. "I don't have any facts. But I have a strong suspicion there's a connection there."

Harry "WB" Simpson spoke up. "Historically, the FBI has been mainly involved in investigating issues of national security. They turned their attention to organized crime in the late '50s and '60s, targeting those considered professional criminals, mostly in relation to racketeering and drug traffic. Regulation of the banking system is under the jurisdiction of another Federal organization; the FDIC, Federal Deposit Insurance Corporation. Their governing body is appointed by the President of the United States, with the consent of the U.S. Senate.

"Their main function is to protect investors by insuring deposits in banks and thrift institutions and restoring confidence in the banking industry as a whole. One of their responsibilities is to periodically make unplanned visits to banks that may be involved in suspicious activities involving their balance sheets, in order to assess their viability. I've been told several of the banks run by the Taylors have been under close scrutiny by the FDIC for some time, but so far, they haven't been able to uncover any illegal dealings. My guess is that the FDIC requested support from the FBI to try to beef up their investigation."

Gloria raised her hand timidly. Neither she nor Mary Ellen had spoken a word since we had started in on the 5 W's and H. I was curious what they were thinking. "You don't have to ask permission to speak, Gloria. In this crowd, you just have to raise your voice loud enough to be heard," I said.

Jerome gave Gloria a warm smile and nodded his encouragement. "I'm not sure I have anything of value to contribute, but it might be worth mentioning something I heard at work a few days ago." Gloria had been working part-time at the hair salon at Cain Sloan department store in Green Hills while studying for an Associate Degree in Nursing at Tennessee State University. "A woman came in for a cut and color. I'd seen her at the shop before, but I didn't know her name. She sat at my station to have her hair washed.

"You know how everybody gets real chatty when they come into a hair salon? Well, she no sooner sat down than she started in about her husband, and how upset she was because he was letting his brother push him out of the family business. As she told it, the brothers had been buying up stock in a bunch of banks, but now his brother decided he would be better off managing them on his own. It seems this was creating some bad blood between him and his brother. She said her husband was talking to some powerful men who just might give the brother a taste of his own medicine. After she left the salon, I asked the hairdresser for her name. It was Shirley Taylor."

Mumbled exclamations could be heard in the group. "That must be J.R.'s wife." Harry said. "I noticed he hasn't been showing up in meetings with his brother anymore."

"Okay. So, the brothers are less of a dynamic duo than they used to be. How does that fit into the rest of the picture?" Thomas asked.

Jon spoke up. "If Hank is working independently from his brother, then he has more reasons to recruit support from people like the Mayor and Ralph Stein. No one can make a go of it alone in this town, and it makes sense he would want to align himself with people in power. I don't think there are very many people in Nashville who wield more power than Ralph and the Mayor, except perhaps for some folks in the music industry. Julie? Didn't you tell me a while back your dad has been having meetings with the presidents of the CMA and WSM?"

I looked at Harry before answering. I hadn't managed to tell him the things my dad shared with me about those meetings, but it seemed like the time had come to put it all out in the open. "He was meeting with them about some projects they needed to secure funding for. You all know about most of it by now: Fan Fair, Opryland USA, the new Opryland Hotel and Convention Center, and a few other projects.

"As Gloria mentioned, the Taylor brothers have been accumulating stock in several Tennessee banks since the late '60s, and they were looking for a way to get their foot in the door at First National. Somehow, they found out about Fan Fair and the other projects being discussed, so they approached Wes Plant from the CMA. Wes came to my dad and asked him to hear the Taylors out about what they could offer. My dad told me when he met with them, they informed him that in addition to holding stock in several banks, they also held controlling interest in the National Life Company. They said they could arrange for money to be transferred from NL&AIC and several other banks to First National in order to fund the projects. By moving the money from more than one place and depositing it over an extended period of time, they would meet the requirements set by the FDIC for that type of transaction. Apparently, Wes was totally sold on the idea, although my dad had his doubts about the whole thing."

Harry looked at me with raised eyebrows. "Brokered deposits! The FDIC set a $100K cap on those a while back in order to protect investors. It sounds like the Taylors have been doing their homework. But I still don't see how all of this benefits them?"

"If, like Julie said, they've been trying to get their foot in the door at First National, this certainly would have accomplished that," Jon said. "Julie, did your dad say whether they were able to buy enough stocks in the bank to give them control?"

"He didn't say. The last thing he mentioned was he had a few things up his sleeve, but he didn't intend to lose his integrity in the process of acting on them, or something like that."

Georgia sat up straighter in her chair. "It just occurred to me, if it's true Hank has been separating himself from his brother, who, from what Gloria said, is none too happy about it, it's possible J.R. is the informant to the FBI."

"But that would be pretty stupid, wouldn't it?" I asked. "He'd be calling attention to himself as well as to his brother."

Jon nodded. "Unless he's made a deal with the Feds in exchange for his own protection."

The story was growing more ominous and complicated as we spoke, and my gut level fear for my dad returned.

Thomas flipped to another page of his notepad. "Here's what we have so far. The Taylors first appeared on the scene when they came to the bank to meet with Julie's dad and representatives of the CMA and WSM. They'd already been buying up controlling interest in several banks by that time, so it makes sense they were collecting facts on the projects being discussed to see how they might benefit from being involved. They offered to facilitate securing funds to complete the projects, which was likely a "good faith" gesture to win the support of Julie's dad and the others. Their ulterior motive seemed to be to position themselves to be able to buy a significant amount of stock in First National, but we're not sure if that has happened.

"In the meantime, the Taylors must have been meeting with the Mayor and Ralph Stein with the likely intent of gathering support for Hank's run at the governorship. Then Tommy Owen shows up in town, following an invitation from your dad and encouragement by the presidents of WSM and the CMA, Elliott Waldell and Wes Plant. I'm not sure if Owen fits into the rest of this picture. It may just be that Waldell and Plant were looking for a way to boost the music business in Nashville and capitalize on the attention that Fan Fair and Opryland brought to town."

I remembered something else my dad said. "I think you're probably right. My dad said he was hoping that by bringing Tommy Owen into the picture, he could help shift the interest back around to where it belongs, which he said was the music Nashville can produce. I think we're getting confused by the fact that some of the same key figures are on both sides of this story, but the only ones who really seem to be in the middle of it are the Taylors."

I noticed Harry had been frowning through much of the discussion. As things grew silent again, he stretched his arms over his head, and laced his hands behind his head. "If I were J. Edgar, or any other member of the Federal government, I'd have eyes on the Taylors, too."

His comment triggered unanimous nods from the group. Mary Ellen, who had remained silent through the entire evening, stood and began collecting paper plates and empty cans. "This is all very fascinating, but I'm beat. I've been working swing shifts the past few weeks, and my body clock is all messed up." Mary Ellen was a nurse in the E.R. at St. Thomas Hospital. In fact, she was the one to alert Thomas when Ida Hood had been admitted, an action that almost cost her job. It was against hospital policy to tell someone who was not a direct member of the family about a patient's medical condition. Since that time, the two of them had been going out regularly, and seemed well suited to each other.

Thomas jumped to his feet. "I'm sorry, Mary Ellen. I lost track of time." He handed his notepad to Georgia. "Why don't you take this and devote that investigative brain of yours to what we've uncovered tonight. Maybe something will occur to you that we've missed so far."

Georgia took the pad from him, and carried it into the kitchen so she could place it on the table. Everyone else began slowly to get to their feet, mumbling their thanks, and exchanging good night hugs before heading to the front where the cars were parked. I hung back a few steps behind so I could walk side by side with Georgia. "I really hope you can come up with something. I have a bad feeling about this whole thing, especially since my dad appears to be caught up in it."

She gave me a sideways hug and smiled. "The investigative team of Ayres and Barnett is on it. I'll call you tomorrow."

Harry was standing next to his truck, holding the door of the passenger's side open for me. I climbed into the cab and locked my seat belt securely around my waist, letting my head fall back against the comfort of the headrest. It seemed we had come up with more questions than answers as the evening progressed. I suppose that was a necessary step in the whole process. It was difficult for me to wait for things to be resolved, and I had a nagging urge to call my dad o find out what he knew. Something told me to hold off on making that call. Whatever he was willing to share with me could wait until morning. I doubted if I would get a wink of sleep until I was able to talk to him.

Harry leaned across the seat and covered my hand with his. "What's going on in that brain of yours?"

I smiled. Sometimes his ability to read me was irritating when I didn't want to admit to myself what I was thinking. "I want to fix this. I can't stand not knowing what's going on. It's driving me crazy because it feels so completely out of my control."

He squeezed my hand gently. "I know. But we have a pretty formidable team behind us now. I have a feeling things are going to start coming into focus very soon."

I looked at him doubtfully. "I hope you're right."

Although his reassurance was comforting, I was still filled with an uneasiness I knew was unlikely to disappear until the entire situation had been resolved. God! What a time to have to deal with this whole need for control thing. This was one time I'd just as soon give up that need to anyone else who wanted it. As soon as that thought came into my mind, I realized with a start that I had seven other people willing to take it on. It was a wonderful feeling to know they were there.

CHAPTER TWENTY-SIX

I was standing at my teller's window the next morning, attempting to focus on serving the customers lined up in front of me, when a trio of policemen entered the front door. They stopped in their tracks for a moment and seemed to scan the surroundings before walking purposefully in the direction of the elevator. My heart felt as if it had stopped with their arrival, and I held my breath as I waited for them to return.

When the elevator door opened again, it revealed my dad, accompanied by the three policemen. One of them had a grip on his left arm, while the other two followed behind. The foursome passed, and I noticed with alarm that my dad's hands were cuffed behind him. He walked with his head held high and gave me a reassuring smile as he passed.

Mr. Carson and Mr. Browning came down the staircase a short while later, pausing near the bottom as they watched the men leave the building. Mr. Carson stepped aside to allow Mr. Browning to move to the center of the floor, raising his arms to get everyone's attention.

"I don't want any of you to be alarmed. What you've just witnessed is the result of an unfortunate misunderstanding that will, hopefully, be remedied very soon. In the meantime, I want to assure our customers this bank is as sound and trustworthy as you've always known us to be. I encourage all of you to go about your business as usual and not give this matter another thought."

His announcement did very little to ease the nervous tension that filled the air as we all, customers and employees alike, struggled to comprehend what was going on. A few of the customers left the building swiftly as though they were afraid they would become the victims of a crime. Others glanced around with concern before resuming their transactions. I noticed several of the customers at the tellers' windows were requesting withdrawals of large sums of money; larger than was typical for a normal daily transaction. The employees were not handling the situation much better than the customers. Having the police in our building the day after the Federal agents was a tremendous shock, and we looked at one another with hesitation as we struggled to perform our jobs.

By the time my lunch break arrived, I was feeling exhausted from pretending nothing unusual had gone on that morning. I was trying my best to set aside my fear, and follow my dad's advice to place my trust in him. But the battle to allow faith to take precedence over fact was not one I was sure I could win. I flipped the "closed" sign around in my window, and picked up my purse from the floor. I hadn't had time to put together anything for my lunch that morning, in the aftermath of the previous night's discussion, so I decided to walk across the street to a café on the corner to grab a bite to eat.

A television behind the counter was on when I walked in the front door of the café, and everyone seemed to be focused on what was on the screen. The place was fairly full, so I headed toward a vacant stool and studied the menu posted on a blackboard directly in front of me. A waitress noticed my arrival and wandered over to take my order. "What can I get for you, Hon? The meatloaf's selling pretty well today."

"That sounds fine. And a Coca-Cola, please." I wasn't very hungry, but I was feeling a little light-headed and knew I'd better eat something. While I was waiting on my order, I glanced up at the TV to see what had everyone's attention. My heart stopped as I caught sight of the image of my dad being escorted into the police station above a caption that read financial manager of First National under investigation for accounting fraud.

I looked up as the waitress sat my plate in front of me. "I'm sorry. Can you wrap this up to go?" My voice was barely a whisper, and she looked at me oddly.

"Sure, Hon. You all right? You look kinda pale."

"I'm okay. I just remembered I have to be somewhere."

She removed the plate and returned shortly with a Styrofoam container and a paper cup. "I got you the Coke to go, too. You look like you could use it."

I laid some bills on the counter and muttered my thanks. Once I was outside, I tossed both containers in a nearby trash can and hurried back across the street, nearly running into Harry as I rushed up the front steps.

"There you are! I've been looking for you." He grabbed hold of both my arms and studied me closely. "What's wrong?"

"I was across the street at the coffee shop. There was something on the TV about my dad committing fraud."

He let out his breath in a whoosh and let go of my arms.

"That's why I was looking for you. Mr. Carson just held a meeting of the bank officers and told us what was happening. He still thinks it's all a mistake, but I could tell he's worried."

"What does Mr. Browning say? Have you spoken to him?"

He shook his head. "He's been in meetings most of the day. I tried to get in to see him, but his secretary said he gave her strict instructions that he didn't want to be disturbed. There is one bit of good news, or at least it could be. Jon called to say he and Georgia have something they need to talk to us about. Apparently, she's been trying to reach you. When she couldn't, Jon phoned me."

My mind was still spinning out of control, but his mention of Jon and Georgia made me suddenly remember our conversation from the night before. "What did he want? Did he say if they've come up with anything that might help?"

"He didn't say, but he asked if we could meet them right away. It sounded urgent."

I looked around as if I was waiting for someone to tell me what to do.

Harry took my hand. "Come on. I told him we'd meet them in the lobby of Union Station. I got Jerome to cover for you while we're away."

I was still struggling to comprehend what I was hearing. "The train station? Why would we meet them there?"

"I don't know, but Jon said it's important we get there before one p.m." He glanced at his watch. "It's 12:30 now. Luckily, it's close enough for us to walk, so we should be able to get there in twenty minutes or less."

There wasn't much else I could do but follow him as he led the way at a brisk pace. It felt good to allow the infusion of oxygen and sunshine to shake lose some of the panic that had consumed me ever since the FBI showed up at our door the previous morning. As we came within sight of the station, I looked up at the clock tower. It was ten minutes to one.

We entered the main doors and walked into an area with a boarding platform on one side, and ticket offices and waiting rooms on the other. I had been in the train station only once before, when my parents drove me there to pick-up a former high school friend who traveled back to visit me from her new home in St. Louis. I remembered the feeling of excitement that filled me then, as I stood in the middle of the floor, allowing myself to be caught up in the swirl of activity as people hustled by in all directions. Now, all I could feel was a sense of foreboding.

As we were walking there, Harry explained how Union Station previously served as a shipping-out point for tens-of-thousands of soldiers during World War II. In the past few years, it had fallen victim to the same fate that transpired in many other train stations across the United States following the arrival of Amtrak; the national railroad company that had taken over most of the remaining passenger rail services in the United States. Since Amtrak's arrival in Nashville, passenger service there had been reduced to a single line served by only a few trains a day. The outcome of that decline was painfully evident as I looked up at the holes in the skylights, and down at the bird-droppings covering the dusty floors of the main building.

Harry pointed to our right, where I spotted Jon and Georgia standing off to the side. My sadness at seeing the condition of the building was lessened when I noticed the gleam of anticipation in their eyes. I waved at Georgia as we walked quickly toward them.

Jon shook Harry's hand and leaned forward to give me an uncharacteristically friendly kiss on the cheek. Jon and I were not what you'd call close friends, though we shared a love for Georgia. I had begun to notice him warming up to me the more time we spent in each other's company. "I'm really sorry about your dad, Julie. Even if it's a huge mistake—and I'm sure it must be—this can't be easy for you or your family."

Georgia moved beside me and linked her arm through mine. "I've known Will Travers for several years, and I would bet my first-born child that whatever he's being accused of is a complete and total mistake."

I smiled at her gratefully. "I'm trying to hold on to that belief, too."

Harry squeezed my hand and looked at Jon. "Why did you ask us to come down here?"

"I don't know if you're aware of it, but the passenger train line that runs through Nashville these days is called the Floridian. It goes back and forth between Miami and Chicago, with several stops along the way, Nashville being one of them. I have a friend, David Savage, who used to work for the Birmingham Post until he got an offer at the Chicago Tribune. David's been assigned to write a story about the demise in passenger rail travel in the United States, so he's spending a week riding the rails on the Floridian, interviewing passengers and railroad personnel about their experiences.

"After our discussion the other night, I remembered an article he once wrote about a scandal at the Birmingham Southern Bank. I dug back through my files and pulled out the article. The story described a situation very similar to the one that's unfolding at First National right now. Unfortunately, the outcome wasn't very good. The bank's financial manager was accused of participating in an illegal cover-up allowing several banks to avoid being discovered insolvent by helping them shift funds. The source of the money also came into question, since the depositor who brokered the funds turned out to be representing a company that existed only on paper.

"The financial manager claimed he was misled, and therefore, was not guilty of any wrongdoing. The scandal caused a run on the bank's available cash, eventually forcing it to sell off valuable assets to stay afloat. The FBI launched an investigation, eventually leading to the acquittal of the bank officer. It was drawn out for such a long time that his reputation, as well as that of the bank in general, never recovered.

"Since there were a lot of details never disclosed in the article, I placed a call to David to see if he could fill in some facts. It turns out he's arriving on the Floridian at one o'clock today and will be staying in Nashville overnight. He's pretty booked up with scheduled interviews for the time he'll be here, but I convinced him to join us for a late lunch before his first appointment." He looked at Harry and me. "You haven't eaten yet, have you? If so, you can at least order a drink."

As if on cue, my stomach emitted a low, growling noise that reminded me of the fate of my take-out lunch order from the café. Jon smiled as he registered the sound as coming from me. "I'll take that as a no. David booked a room at the Savage House Bed and Breakfast on Eighth Avenue. There's a Tea Room on the main floor that serves lunch. We can head there as soon as the train arrives."

The Floridian was not known for its punctuality, but on this particular day, it arrived only a few minutes past its scheduled time. The train alerted us to its approach by releasing one long blast from its horn, after which it groaned to a stop as the wheels squealed along the metal tracks. Attendants hurried to the exit doors, placing a set of steps at each to assist passengers stepping onto the platform. Although I knew that train travel had greatly declined over the past year, I was still surprised to see only a dozen or so people disembark.

Jon yelled a greeting and waved in the direction of a sandy haired man with dark rimmed glasses, who returned his wave and headed in our direction. As he came nearer, I noticed he was carrying a worn, leather suitcase and wore wrinkled khakis and a white dress shirt with the sleeves rolled up past his elbows. His eyes looked red-rimmed, as if he had gone without sleep for some time. His face broadened into a smile as he dropped his suitcase and grasped Jon's hand as he clapped him on the back.

"Barnett. It's great to see you again. Where have you been keeping yourself?"

Jon returned his handshake vigorously. "That's a long story, Dave. Let me introduce you to some folks. This is my girlfriend, Georgia Ayres, and our friends Julie Travers and Harry Simpson."

David nodded in greeting, and then peered at Georgia with a crooked grin. "Girlfriend, huh? Now it's all beginning to make sense."

Jon dipped his head and glanced at Georgia with a smile. "Georgia's in the newspaper business, too. She used to work for the Nashville News before she got involved in helping run a new publication at Belmont College. The paper is a joint venture between students from the college's journalism program and former staff members of the Daily Courier."

David's eyes narrowed as he registered what Jon said. "I think I heard something about that. It caused quite a scandal in Nashville, as I recall." His eyebrows lifted as he turned to Jon. "And you were in the middle of it? Wasn't your family's company trying to buy the Courier until something went wrong with the plans?" A light bulb seemed to go off in his mind as he turned to look at Georgia again. "Or maybe I should say, until something went very right! I guess we do have a lot of catching up to do."

"I'm afraid that will have to wait, since you said you won't have much free time while you're here. We have a situation unfolding that we're hoping you can help us get to the bottom of."

David lifted his suitcase again. "Then let's get going. I need to get checked in at the B&B, and I'd like to wash up a little before my three o'clock meeting."

Jon pointed the way to the exit. "We can walk to where you're staying. They have a pretty nice lunch place in the lobby where we can meet when you're ready."

"Sounds good to me. The food they serve on trains these days resembles something you'd get out of a vending machine. Anything fresh would be a huge improvement."

Jon filled David in on the recent events at the bank while we were walking, with occasional input from the rest of us. David listened quietly until we were finished, then shook his head. "I feel like I've just had a déjà vu. This sounds very similar to what happened at Birmingham Southern a few years back."

Jon nodded. "I know. That's why I thought of you. There are too many pieces to this puzzle that don't fit, and I'm hoping you'll be able to give us a hand at figuring out what's missing."

We arrived at the Savage House and David agreed to meet us in the Tea Room in half an hour. While we were waiting, we chatted with the manager on duty, who gave us a detailed account of the history of the building. My mind was too full of worry for my dad to pay close attention to what he was saying, but I heard enough to understand the Savage House had a pretty impressive history. According to the manager, it first served as a boarding house in the mid-1800s, before becoming the private residence of an affluent banker. A few years later, the banker leased his home to an exclusive private club called "The Standard," frequented by some of the most influential and prominent residents of Nashville. Eventually, the club became so popular it was forced to relocate to a larger venue in nearby Franklin, Tennessee. The downtown Nashville site resumed function as a private home until its present reincarnation as a Bed and Breakfast.

The manager gave us a quick tour of the rest of the building before escorting us into the Tea Room. The room was fairly small, with a few tables for two lined up along the walls and six round tops with seating for four placed down the middle. Ivory colored cloths with crocheted designs covered the tables and small pewter pitchers containing cream and sugar sat in the middle next to a glass vase of flowers. The walls were painted a pale blue and decorated with an assortment of blue and white plates suspended from wire holders. The lighting was subtle, which gave the entire room a cozy, but cheery feeling.

The hostess quickly pushed two of the round tables together in the center of the room, and indicated we should be seated. A waitress handed us menus before heading back toward the kitchen, returning quickly with two small plates containing miniature muffins. The muffins gave off the enticing scent of cinnamon, sugar, and lemon, and I felt my stomach respond in anticipation.

"Can I get y'all anything to start? Our specialty is iced fruit tea, but we also have coffee and hot tea."

Jon and Georgia opted for coffee, while Harry and I asked for the fruit tea. David arrived shortly after we placed our order and told the waiter to also bring him the fruit tea.

We all sat quietly for a few minutes studying our menus, before unanimously deciding to select the special of the day. The special was a Monte Cristo sandwich, which was described as ham, turkey, and Swiss cheese layered inside white bread that was dipped in an egg and milk batter and fried in butter. The finished product was dusted with powdered sugar and served with a side of strawberry preserves.

While we waited for our food, Jon asked David to give us a more thorough account of what happened at the Birmingham bank. He described how the bank's financial manager handled a large deposit of funds from a man claiming to represent a real estate development firm out of Florida. The money was deposited in the form of a series of checks that came into the bank on the first of each month, for six months. The depositor explained that breaking the total amount into several deposits was necessary because the money was coming from the sale of different condominium developments with staggered closing dates.

"The financial manager didn't see any reason to question the source of the funds. The deposits came in regularly as promised, and the checks cleared the originating account quickly. Unfortunately, it turned out that the real estate firm existed only on paper. The actual source of the money was a series of illegal loans and stock manipulations at the banks from which the funds were withdrawn. These fraudulent activities were hidden through the use of creative bookkeeping overstating the banks' assets and understating their liabilities. If anyone decided to look into the bank's financial situation, they would appear to be solvent due to the falsified accounting ledgers. In fact, money that was supposed to contribute to the bank's working capital was being secretly funneled out into a private account established at Birmingham Southern."

"I don't understand. Why would anyone think that moving the money from the banks where these illegal dealings were taking place to one totally outside of their control would help hide what was going on? Wouldn't it have been smarter just to shift the money around to the banks that were part of the fraud?" I asked.

Harry spoke up. "I think I can explain. In 1970, a piece of legislation was signed that required banks to file a report with the Treasury Department whenever they processed a transaction exceeding $100,000. I suspect the total deposit we're talking about exceeded that by a considerable amount. By moving money out of different banks, and re-depositing it over several different transactions into Birmingham Southern, it would have been possible to keep each withdrawal and deposit below $100K."

Georgia shifted in her chair. "That's a lot of money moving. Even if they performed some creative bookkeeping, it seems someone would have noticed something was off. Wouldn't the FDIC have been able to detect the books had been falsified?"

Harry leaned his elbows on the table. "If the FDIC spots some irregularity during one of their unannounced visits, they have the authority to force the bank to correct its situation or risk being shut down. That's assuming they're able to find something. You have to remember; we're dealing with criminals who know all the ins and outs of covering their tracks."

David nodded his agreement. "Except in this case, someone made a grave error. The depositor must have been aware of the law restricting the transactions to under $100K, because most of the deposits came in just under that amount. However, the final payment was a little bit over. Whether that was a mistake or he just got too self-assured, no one knows. When the financial manager at Birmingham Southern noticed the higher amount of the final deposit, he followed the rules and filed the required paperwork. That alerted the FDIC, who passed on the information to the Treasury Department.

"At that point, things got more interesting. Since there had been an upsurge in money laundering activities involving banking officials during the past several years, some of which were linked to drug trafficking and risks to national security, the Treasury department contacted the FBI. Unfortunately, the depositor must have realized his mistake because he disappeared without a trace. That left the financial manager in hot water. Whether or not he was guilty of any wrongdoing, he was a party to the transactions, making him a very viable suspect. The FBI was never able to prove his involvement, and by the time the trail grew cold, the list of other possible suspects dried up, too."

"Were they ever able to track down the man who first approached the bank? The guy you referred to as the depositor?" Jon asked.

"Unfortunately, no. Although the investigation hinted he was a front man for someone inside the banking industry. The depositor only brokered the money."

The pieces of the puzzle had begun to fall into place, but I didn't like the picture they were forming. "So that's why the FBI was at First National. They must think my dad was involved in something similar to what happened in Birmingham."

David sighed and nodded his head. "I'm afraid you may be right. The FBI doesn't take it lightly when they have the wool pulled over their eyes. If the situation at First National gave them any reason to think it might be related to what went down at Birmingham Southern, they would be all over it like a dog on a bone."

David tossed his napkin on the table and pushed back his chair. "I'm afraid I have to head out if I'm going to make my meeting on time. Let me leave you with this last fact to add to everything else we've been tossing around. The financial manager of Birmingham Southern said the individual who brokered the funds told him he represented a private company called SS&B Enterprises. He said he'd never met the actual representatives of the company, but had spoken on the phone once to a man who called himself J.R."

My eyes flew open wide at the sound of the familiar name, and I noticed it had a similar effect on the other members of our party. David looked around at us before standing. "I can see that something I said has struck a chord. Jon, I hate to leave things like this. Why don't I call you when my meetings are over for the day, and maybe we can hash things out a little more over a couple of beers?"

Jon readily agreed to his suggestion. We thanked David for his time and sat quietly, watching him leave the café. Harry was the first to break the silence.

"It's pretty obvious who he was talking about. But the question still remains how all of this is connected to First National."

Jon pushed back his chair and stood. "I've got some things I need to do before I see David tonight. Georgia, do you mind if I drop you off at work? I want to take a drive down to the newspaper archives and do a little digging."

We stopped at the hostess stand to take care of the bill before heading out the door. Harry and I waved goodbye to Jon and Georgia who agreed to call us if they came up with any more facts on this increasingly disturbing case. We walked slowly back in the direction of the First National Center. As we came within sight of the building, I could feel the now-familiar twinges of discomfort filling my stomach. It was true, I never really "warmed up" to the place, but now it made me feel as if I was gripped by an icy panic. In this case, the feeling was triggered by the realization that whatever was going on at the bank, my dad seemed to be knee-deep in the middle of it. I wasn't sure what to do to help him back onto solid ground.

CHAPTER TWENTY-SEVEN

The next morning, I received a call from Georgia telling me to hurry and turn on the television. I laid down the receiver so I could keep her on the line and rushed to the set, flipping the knob until the news appeared. The screen was filled with the image of two police officers knocking on the door of a room in the Hermitage Hotel in downtown Nashville. After a few insistent poundings, the door was opened by a sleepy looking man I didn't recognize, but who quickly slammed the door after he spotted the camera man behind the police. Another man stepped forward, who appeared to be an employee of the hotel, and used his key to open the door.

The next scene was of the officers escorting the man from the hotel room through the hotel lobby and into a patrol car. A newscaster described what was happening: "Late last night, local police received an anonymous tip that led them to the hotel room of Jesse Carr who, pending further investigation, is being held on charges of money laundering and the illegal transfer of insider loans. Mr. Carr was arrested in 1967 for illegal banking practices, for which he served a year in prison. Since that time, it appears he has been secretly functioning as a consultant to Hank and J.R. Taylor who, over the past four years, succeeded in obtaining controlling interest in eleven banks in Tennessee, plus six others scattered across Alabama. The tip came in after an investigation was launched by the FBI on the activities of William Travers, the financial manager of First National Bank of Nashville. Mr. Travers has not been charged with any wrongdoing at this time. We hope to have more details about this ongoing investigation later this morning."

I felt stunned by what I heard, and was struggling to make sense of it, when I became aware of Georgia's voice coming faintly from my telephone receiver. I picked it up and placed it against my ear.

"Georgia?"

"Thank God! I was afraid you'd passed out at the news."

I shook my head. "I don't understand. Has my dad been arrested? The newscaster didn't say he had, but it sounded like it was just a matter of time. Who's this Jesse Carr? I've never heard his name mentioned before."

"I know it's a lot to take in, but I have more facts about the whole thing that should put your mind at ease. Jon and I will be over in about half an hour. Is Harry there, or can you call and ask him to join us?"

"He stayed at his place last night. We were both exhausted after all of the excitement of the past couple of days. I'll phone him and see if he can come over."

I hung up the phone and sat staring at the TV. The news had switched over to a story about a local high school student being scouted by the Atlanta Braves. I turned off the set and placed a call to Harry, who said he'd be right over. He had been watching the same news report, so he wasn't surprised by my call.

While I waited for everyone to arrive, I busied myself with making the bed and getting dressed. I opened the refrigerator with the intent of having some breakfast, but ended up just taking out a Coke, which I poured into a glass of ice. I had just taken a sip when I heard a knock on the door.

Harry, Georgia and Jon arrived at the same time, and the three of them stood outside on the landing. Georgia hurried to embrace me, followed by Harry, who kept his arm around me as the four of us stood in a circle in the kitchen. Jon looked around my apartment, letting his gaze rest on the table.

"Georgia, why don't you and Julie have a seat? Harry and I can stand."

"I'd rather stand, too." I said.

He nodded and walked around us to lean against the kitchen counter with a sigh. "It's been a long night." He looked at each of us before continuing. "After I left you yesterday afternoon, I went down to the newspaper archives building across from the State Capitol. I wanted to pull up anything on record about what happened at Birmingham Southern around the time of the FBI's investigation. Most of what I could find was a repeat of the details Dave filled us in on yesterday. I was about to give up hope about discovering anything else, when I decided to dig back through the files that preceded the investigation. I came across an article from 1968 mentioning a man from Birmingham who had just been released from prison for illegal banking practices. Since the place and the crime were a good fit for what we were talking about, I went back through the archives during the years that followed his release. There wasn't much, but I hit the jackpot when I found a photograph of that same man standing beside another person on the steps of the Birmingham courthouse shaking hands with none other than Hank and J.R. Taylor. According to the caption, the two bankers from Tennessee were sealing the deal on a business arrangement they had just made to acquire controlling stock in two local banks. The man they were shaking hands with was identified as John Crayton who, at the time, was the director of the Southern Banking Corporation. The man standing next to him was Jesse Carr."

My head jerked up at the last name. "So, you're the anonymous tip!"

Jon shook his head. "That's where things get strange. I was planning on taking my information to the police this morning.

I wanted to talk to Dave first, to see if he remembered anything about a connection between Crayton and Carr. When we talked last night, he wasn't able to put the two of them together, but I decided it was worth taking my information to the police anyway. Before I could do anything however, I saw the news report about the arrest at the Hermitage Hotel. I recognized the man as Jesse Carr."

Harry shook his head in disbelief. "If you didn't say anything to the police, who did?"

"I talked to a buddy at the Associated Press to see if they had any more information about the arrest. All he knew was the call came from a woman."

Georgia and I exchanged a look. "Do you remember what Gloria said about the woman in the beauty salon?"

I nodded slowly. "Do you think it's possible she's the one?"

"Shirley Taylor?" Harry spoke the name out loud that had been on our minds. "Why would she want to do something that could get her husband in trouble?"

Jon shrugged. "Maybe she thought they'd leave him alone if she gave them information on the other parties involved. Of maybe she was just tired of her husband letting his brother push him around."

"That's a lot of maybes." Harry said. "I think it's time we find someone who can help us make sense of all this."

Everyone turned to look at me. "My dad, if we can talk to him. Otherwise, my mother. I'll bet you anything she knows more about what's been happening with my dad than she's let on."

"Then let's find out." Harry said. "Grab your things and let's head over to your house. I checked with the bank's legal rep before I came here, and he said they were planning to release your dad this morning. My guess is he'll head home afterward."

When we arrived at my parents' house, there were two unfamiliar cars parked out front. I hurried up the front steps with Harry, Jon and Georgia close on my heels. The door was unlocked, so we headed inside and followed the sound of voices coming from the kitchen. My dad was sitting at the table with a cup of coffee in front of him. He looked haggard, which was not surprising given what he had probably gone through the past few days. My mother was standing at the kitchen counter placing muffins on a plate, which she sat on the table beside a bowl of freshly cut fruit. A man I didn't know was also sitting at the table.

My dad looked up at me tiredly and smiled in greeting.

"Julie! I'm so glad you're here." He looked past me as the others came into view. "And I see you've brought reinforcements. Hello, Georgia. Harry. Jon."

"Hi, Mr. Travers." Georgia said. "I hope you don't mind us barging in on you like this."

"Not at all. It's good to see friendly faces."

"I've just spoken to Mr. Browning. He said to tell you to take the rest of the day off, and not to worry about a thing."

I turned in the direction of the hallway, as I recognized Tim Carson's voice.

"Why, hello, Julie. Harry."

Harry held out his hand in greeting. "Mr. Carson. We just came by to see how Julie's dad is doing."

"And to find out what's going on." I added. "These are our friends, Georgia Ayres and Jon Barnett."

Mr. Carson nodded at them in recognition. "We met a while back at the Alley Cat party. Nice to see you both again."

"I've just made a fresh pot of coffee if anyone would like some. There are banana nut muffins, too." My mom could always be counted on to have something hot and tasty ready at even the most difficult times. It was just part of what she did: she nourished people. Sometimes that meant preparing food, other times it meant she fed us with her loving comfort and support.

I walked to her and wrapped my arms around her shoulders. "Thanks, mom. How are you doing?"

She looked at me with tired eyes. "Your father's the one who's been through the wringer. I'm just glad things are finally getting sorted out."

I turned my attention back to my dad. "We saw the report on the morning news, but there's so much that wasn't explained. I was hoping you or Mom would be able to fill in some facts. I wasn't sure if you'd be here, but I'm so glad you are."

"Me, too. Things got a little sticky a time or two, but I had a good team in my corner." He gestured at the other man sitting at the table. "This is the bank's attorney, John Baker. He and Tim, and your mom of course, have been by my side through this whole ordeal."

"I can't imagine what you've been through, and that's the problem. There's so much about what has happened that I don't understand, and not just over the past few days. You've seemed on edge about something for quite a while." I said.

"That's true. I have been. Some of it I've spoken to you about. There's a lot I wasn't able to say for legal reasons." He looked over at Harry. "I wasn't even at liberty to tell my second-in-command about it. I'm sorry it had to be that way. Now I'm finally able to answer your questions. So, fire away." He looked at me expectantly.

"I'm not sure where to start. Why did the FBI arrest you? Who are Jesse Carr and John Crayton, and what do they have to do with the bank? Did you know all along the Taylors were mixed up in something illegal, or did you just find out? I guess what I'm saying is I'd like to hear the entire story, from start to finish."

He looked at me with a glimmer of something familiar, that I hadn't seen in quite some time. Finally, he gave me a tired grin. "Well, let me tell you about that." I knew everything was going to be okay.

CHAPTER TWENTY-EIGHT

In the weeks that followed, the story my dad shared with us became the hottest news item in both printed and televised media. The reports traced the illegal actions of the Taylor brothers back several years to the time they were still working for their father's newspaper. Without his knowledge, they had quietly set in motion a plan that would allow them to acquire a string of private banks across Tennessee, eventually extending their reach into Northern Alabama. Unfortunately for them, by the time they created a sizable financial empire and were living lavishly off the proceeds of their acquisitions, the very mountain upon which they built their kingdom started to crumble.

Beginning in the early seventies, banking conditions all across the United States were significantly worsening as the steadily growing population was faced with the likelihood of a recession that would stretch their already dwindling financial resources to the max. Legislation restricting banks from offering an interest rate competitive with money markets forced those within the banking industry to come up with more creative ways to avoid closure. For men like the Taylors, "creativity" turned out to equal "illegality".

The only way the banks run by the Taylors could survive, was by offering loans promising a good return on the investment, but which lacked sufficient capital to back them up. Since the FDIC had already put in place a system of accountability designed to safeguard against this illegal practice, it was necessary for the Taylors to find a way to shuffle money around to their various banks so they could create an appearance of financial solvency. In order to pull that off, they recruited the aide of two men known for their savvy at such bookkeeping gymnastics: Jesse Carr, a former banker who had spent a year in prison for illegal banking practices, and John Crayton, a financial advisor who served as president of the Southern Banking Corporation and had inside information that allowed him to be tipped off ahead of time when the FDIC was planning an "unannounced" visit on the local banks.

For a time, the Taylors managed to fly under the radar of the FDIC, but at some point, Hank Taylor let greed get the best of him. He came up with a plan in which he could siphon off part of the interest held by his brother, J.R., which would give Hank majority control of the banks. By the time J.R. caught on to what Hank was up to, it was too late to prevent it, but not too late for J.R. to plot his revenge.

J.R. tried to enlist the aid of Timmy Slyde, the owner of the Carousel Club. Slyde was known for his success in skirting legal issues in Nashville, largely due to his close ties to the Mayor. However, what J.R. hadn't counted on was that Hank had already approached the Mayor and struck a deal that would prove very profitable for the Mayor, Slyde, and Stein, who turned out to be the silent members of the fictitious SS&B Enterprises David told us about. When J.R. told his wife, Shirley, what Hank had pulled on him, and that he felt he had no alternative but to allow him to buy out the rest of his interest in the banks, she flew into an angry rampage and stormed out of the house.

While all of this was taking place, my dad had a plan to help trap Hank and J.R. in their own nets. He was aware of what happened at the Birmingham Southern bank. He'd attended several regional meetings with their former financial manager and knew the manager had lost his job and his reputation, because of the questions raised about his possible involvement in the scandal. My dad said he'd spent a few hours sitting in a bar listening to his colleague bemoan the fact he had been duped by the depositor and the fictitious company he represented. Since no one in the investigation managed to trace the roots of SS&B Enterprises, the key players in that puzzle piece remained unknown. However, a serendipitous discovery by Jerome finally uncovered the true identity of this "paper" company.

Jerome's cousin, Lyndsey, had picked up a cocktail napkin one night from the table recently vacated by Timmy Slyde, Ralph Stein, and Mayor Brill. Lyndsey thought it odd how one of the parties had sketched out a logo using the initials of each of their last names. He kept the napkin and showed it to Jerome, who asked if he could keep it on a hunch. When news of Jesse Carr's arrest caused the media to rehash the details of the scandal at Birmingham Southern, he overheard mention of SS&B Enterprises and hurried to the office of Mr. Carson with the napkin. Mr. Carson approached the bank's attorney with the evidence, who rushed it to the courthouse.

After that, things began to move quickly. The three men behind SS&B Enterprises were called into a private meeting with the chief of police, who agreed to sweep the matter under the table if they would give up any information they had on the illegal activities of the Taylors. Of course, they were more than eager to comply. The anonymous call was traced to a telephone that belonged to Shirley Taylor's sister. When Shirley was brought in for questioning, she willingly gave up enough facts to enable the police to put two and two together. They determined that the Taylor brothers were the chief players behind what happened at Birmingham Southern. The FBI informant turned out to be John Crayton, who functioned as the depositor in Birmingham, and was smart enough to realize his involvement would not stay secret for long after Jesse Carr had been apprehended.

As for my dad's arrest, it was all a pretense to give a false sense of security to the Taylors. He believed they would relax their defenses if they felt the authorities had shifted their focus in another direction. His plan worked, but not before his name and image had been splashed across the front page and television screen of every TV station in Nashville, and had begun to make its way into the national news. Since his quick thinking and desire to turn wrongful deeds into right was the catalyst that finally brought an end to one of the worst banking crimes of the past decade, his good name and reputation remained unscathed in the aftermath of the arrests of the true criminals.

Four arrests followed in the aftermath of my father's release. Jesse Carr was found guilty of conspiring to commit bank fraud and was sentenced to three years in prison. Hank Taylor pleaded guilty to Federal charges of bank fraud and was given a 20-year term. His brother, J.R., was also sent to state prison for state securities fraud, and given a sentence of eight years. Shirley Taylor was charged with withholding state and federal evidence, but was allowed to work off her one-year sentence through community service.

John Crayton received immunity from prosecution due to his role as an FBI informant on both the Birmingham and Nashville cases. He entered into a witness protection program, but after two days in an undisclosed location managed to slip away from the police officers assigned to keep him under observation. He disappeared from sight. As for the men behind the SS&B Enterprises, they walked away free of any legal action on their involvement in the criminal activities. Timmy Slyde decided to focus his attention on boosting the business of his Carousel Club. Mayor Brill continued to serve out his term in Nashville and became a key supporter of the Governor's run for re-election. Ralph Stein received national recognition for his achievements as the publisher of the Nashville News and was regularly seen at major society events around Nashville—but without the company of his former partners in crime.

The weeks following my dad's exoneration from any criminal activity, and the arrest and conviction of the true criminals, was a happy time for my entire family. When my brother, Bill, found out what was happening to my dad, he seemed to snap out of the apathy that enveloped him in the aftermath of his engagement to Mitzi Randolph. As he later explained to us, he woke up one day with a clear conviction of what he should do. Later that same morning, he marched into her father's office and announced that if marrying his daughter was a requirement for him to keep his job, he was officially turning in his resignation. To his great surprise, Mr. Randolph came around the desk and clapped him on the back, and congratulated him for having the good sense to stand up for what he wanted.

Mitzi, however, didn't take things so well when he informed her he was breaking off the engagement. According to Bill, she "turned into an evil monster before my eyes, spitting venomous phrases as she approached me with her claws bared." Bill managed to get out of her sight before she could do major damage, but not before she launched her engagement ring at him, catching him just below the right eye. In typical Bill form, he remarked that sporting a battle scar was a fair exchange for freeing himself from a bad situation, and he got his ring back. That's the brother I love!

The only part of the whole banking drama I couldn't make sense of was where Tommy Owen and the CMA, WSM executives fit. When I posed this query to my dad, he shrugged his shoulders and gave me a crooked smile.

"They fit exactly where they were supposed to; out of harm's way of the whole mess! There was never any connection between what I was working on with Wes, Ronnie, and Elliott, and what was going on with the Taylors. It just looked like there might have been because we allowed the Taylors to think the others were involved. At first, Wes was snowed by their promises. But he wised up quickly, once some facts were put in front of him. We did allow the Taylors to deposit a sizable amount of money into an account set up to fund our various projects. But we never used a penny of their money for any of those things."

"But if you didn't get any financial support from the Taylors, where did the money come from?"

"Let's just say that Tim Carson's frequent golf outings managed to impact more than just his handicap. During one of the times he was playing with Former President Eisenhower, he happened to mention that some plans he had to bring Country Music to the world were likely to fall through because of insufficient funds. It turned out Eisenhower was a devoted fan of Country Music. By the next afternoon, he managed to round up a couple of private investors more than willing to front the money in exchange for a private handshake and photograph with a couple of their favorite music stars. So, the bank was able to keep its hands clean of the whole Taylor mess and still move forward without the Taylors being any the wiser about where the money really came from."

I shook my head in disbelief. "What about Tommy Owen? I thought for certain he was up to something." I said.

"That was just Tommy being himself. He's like that old Amos McCoy TV character that 'roars like a lion, but is gentle as a lamb'. Except Tommy is more like a lion in sheep's clothing. He's actually quite an astute business man. He just likes to act like he's a good ol' Texas cowboy to throw people off the scent of what he's really up to.

"He was up to something, all right. But it was something to our advantage. While the rest of this was going on, he managed to convince Wes and Elliott to support the development of a state-of-the-art recording studio to be built in the new Opryland Hotel. He's already convinced Glen Campbell to switch his recording to that location, and Dottie West and Kenny Rogers have signed on to use the studio to record a joint album. I'm not sure what else he has in the works, because all this mess has distracted me from keeping track of it. But I imagine there'll be a line of music stars waiting to follow in the footsteps of the others."

So, I was wrong about Tommy Owen. That meant I still needed to work on listening to what my gut feelings were really telling me. In this case, maybe they were just saying that brash, swaggering men, an accurate description of my impression of Tommy Owen, made me feel uncomfortable. Which is a whole lot different from saying he was a crook.

My dad and I were sitting on the bench in his backyard talking about these things. It was an unseasonably mild day for early July. We were enjoying that the temperatures had dipped down from their customary ninety degrees to give us a brief respite from the steady heat likely to linger until sometime in early September. Harry drove my mom to Kroger to pick up the ingredients for his "now famous" gazpacho, which she had insisted he show her how to make. They gave my dad and me the task of collecting whatever vegetables we could from the garden to contribute to the dish.

We collected a bowl of peppers and tomatoes that had managed to survive the heat. Barkster and Sunny were sniffing around the edges of the yard, staying as far away from us as they could to avoid being forced back into their enclosed space. At least, they had been getting more exercise than usual since I started seeing Harry. On those Sundays when we spent the day tramping around in the woods somewhere, we would swing by my parents' house first and load the dogs into the back of his truck. The dogs were thrilled with the opportunity the outings gave them to romp and hunt, and Harry clearly cherished a chance to share time with "man's best friend", times two.

I could also hear the faint strains of guitar music wafting out of the open windows of the screened-in deck where the twins were practicing for an upcoming stint at the House of Pizza. They had become regular performers there after the usual entertainer moved to New York City in search of the brighter lights of a bigger city.

Mike and Josh were due to come by a little later for dinner. They had wrapped up another year of teaching at the end of May and were excitedly planning a trip to visit some friends in

Savannah, Georgia. Bill surprised us by announcing he had accepted a job as an engineer with a construction company in Nashville and would be moving back to the city in a few weeks.

All in all, life was settling down, and it felt good to know the band of worry that held us in its firm grip for far too long had begun to loosen.

I turned to look at my dad, and found him studying me discretely.

"What?" I asked.

"Yes, exactly." He answered.

"I was just thinking how things have worked out for the best in a lot of ways. Bill seems to finally be headed in the right direction. The twins are making progress with their music, and more importantly, they're really enjoying what they're doing. And Mike and Josh seem really happy together." I turned sideways on the bench so I could look at him more directly. "You and mom seem good, too. Of course, you always seem good, even when there are things going on that you aren't telling us about."

"That's a parent's job; to make sure our children are safe and secure, and protect them from worries whenever possible."

"But, in case you haven't noticed, none of us are actually children any longer. Well, except for maybe the twins. I have a feeling they're going to play the child-card as long as they can get away with it."

He harrumphed his agreement. "You haven't answered my question. What about you?"

I frowned as I considered how to respond. "I'm good. I've signed up for a computer training course at the bank. I'm hoping I can eventually switch over to working on the Tech floor."

"I heard about that, and I think it's a great idea. Computers are the future of every business, whether some of us want to admit it or not. But what I'm really asking is how you are on a personal level?"

I could feel my face break into a silly grin. "That's good, too. Harry is an incredible person. I didn't know it was possible to find someone who could be my best friend, and for whom I could also feel such an intense physical attraction. Oh, sorry! Maybe that's not something I should be saying to my father."

He shifted on his seat. "I have to admit that thinking of you, or any of you kids, having a physical relationship with someone is not something I find totally comfortable. On the other hand, your mother and I have not exactly made our physical response to each other a secret over the years."

I rolled my eyes. "You can say that again!"

His eyes crinkled at the bluntness of my comment. "We've always felt it was good to show all of you that a good relationship between a husband and wife, or I guess I should say between two committed partners, should include an emotional, intellectual, social, and physical connection."

I appreciated that he was so quick to remember that what was between Mike and Josh didn't fit the definition of a traditional relationship, and he had altered his comment to make sure they were included.

"I agree. I think Harry and I share all of those connections. He allows me to express my feelings without judgment, yet he challenges me to understand myself better. He's sharp as a tack. In fact, I call him my walking encyclopedia because he's always giving me facts about something I'm interested in, which makes me want to learn more about it, too. He fits in easily with my friends, and makes friends quickly with people we meet. He's close to his family, which is really important to me, since our family has always been close. As for the physical…well, let's just say I have no complaints in that department!"

He leaned back against the bench and stretched his arms across the top. "Should I assume you're in love with him?"

His question took me by surprise. Harry and I had expressed those feelings to each other. We had even used the word love on several occasions. But I never admitted out loud to anyone else, even Georgia, that I was in love with him.

"I guess I am. I mean, yes, I am. I love him a lot, and I'm in love with him."

He patted my shoulder with the hand stretched across the back of the bench. "Well, that's just great. I'm happy for you, Jubie. All your mother and I wish for each of you kids is for you to find satisfying careers, and someone to love who loves you back. I'm glad you seem to have found both in your life."

I suddenly felt giddy. His helping me admit I was in love with Harry made me want to shout it out loud. I jumped up from the bench. "Where are they? Shouldn't Mom and Harry be back by now?"

Just then the back screen door slammed, and Harry emerged from the house. I froze in place at the sight of him. My Harry. The love of my life.

He stopped his approach and looked at me curiously, then glanced at my dad, who nodded.

We started walking toward each other at the same time, meeting halfway at the point where a large oak tree cast shade across the yard. Harry grinned at me, and I could feel the smile on my face match his own. He reached forward and took both of my hands in his.

"Julie, I think I have loved you since the first time you walked in the bank when your dad asked me to show you around. I couldn't believe my luck that day. Here was this gorgeous girl, with the most amazing blue eyes, looking at me as if I had the answers to all of life's question. I think you scared me a little that day, because I felt I never wanted to let you down.

"Since that time, I've gotten to know all the different things about you that make you who you are. The uncertainty that freezes you with doubt when you're faced with having to make a tough decision. The anxiety that comes over you when you feel things are out of your control. The way you squint your eyes when you're working out a problem in your head. You sing in the bathroom because you think no one can hear you…"

My mouth flew open in surprise.

"Yep, I've heard you. You have a much better voice than you think. I'm amazed by the love and devotion you have for your family, and the incredible kindness and compassion you show to anyone who is in pain because they are feeling different, or rejected. Mostly, I've come to realize you're the person I've been waiting for. I don't want to let another day go by without showing you just how much you mean to me." As he dropped to the ground on one knee, he reached in his pocket and produced a small, black box, opening it to reveal a diamond ring. "I choose you to be with for the rest of my life. I've already run this by your mom and dad, so what I need to know is, Julie Travers, will you choose me? Will you be my wife?"

My hands flew to my mouth in shock, and for a moment I wasn't sure I was going to be able to make a sound. Finally, I managed to choke out an answer. "Yes! Absolutely. Are you kidding me?"

Harry stood so he could slip the ring on my finger. It was a simple, classic design, with four delicate prongs holding a single diamond above a gold band. It was perfect, and it assured me all over again; the man standing before me had taken the time to understand who I am. "I love it! I love you!" We wrapped our arms around each other in a mutual embrace then pulled apart slightly to share a deep kiss. My mother must have slipped out the back door at some point during his proposal, because I became aware of applause coming from two directions at once. I looked over Harry's shoulder at my mother and extended my hand in her direction, beckoning her to come closer, while at the same time my father walked up behind us and encircled us in a hug.

I turned into my dad's embrace, letting my head rest on his chest as tears of joy streamed down my face and made wet splotches on his blue shirt. "So, this is why you were asking me all of those questions. I guess you knew what Harry had in mind."

He nodded against the top of my head. "He called last night and told us he wanted to ask you to marry him, but he wanted to know how we felt about it. Of course, we told him nothing could make us happier, as long as that was what you wanted, too. I had a pretty strong feeling what you would say, but I wanted to make sure your feelings for him are as strong as his for you." He turned sideways so my mother could be included in our embrace.

My mother looked at me with an expression of sheer joy. "We are so very happy for you both. If the two of you manage to find even half of the joy and pleasure together your father and I have, you will have a wonderful life."

"Hey! What's going on out here? Is somebody getting married?"

I glanced up to see Mike and Josh jogging towards us, followed closely by the twins. Pretty soon, everyone was hugging, crying, and laughing with delight. Even the dogs got into the action as their excited barking punctuated the air while they ran circles around us.

It was a day I would never forget. I was surrounded by some of the most important people in my life, although there were a few significant absences. I leaned close to Harry so he could hear me above the din of dog barks, and laughter.

"I wish Bill was here. And we need to tell your family right away. Oh, and..."

"We need to let Georgia know," he quickly added. "I remember what she said at her house that night, and I thought of her right away. But let's not tell her by phone."

"I agree. The Fourth of July party is tomorrow. We can talk to your family tonight and make the announcement to our friends at the party."

Harry nodded his agreement and pulled me close again. As our eyes locked on each other, it seemed as though all the other sounds and commotion around us fell away. This is how I hoped it would always be between us, like everything else came in second to our devotion to each other. As that thought filled my head, I remembered something my dad had once said to me when I questioned whether he and my mom could love the rest of us as much as they loved each other. He had answered, "Love doesn't get used up when you give it to another person. It's circular, so there's always enough to go around."

At the time, I wasn't sure what he meant. As I looked around at the faces of the loved ones who surrounded me, and I listened to the joy circling us like a swirl of sunlight nudged by a warm breeze, I suddenly realized what he meant: Love has no bounds, unless we choose to impose some upon it. It brings hearts together that sometimes drift apart. It fills us with hope and makes us believe in possibilities. It gives us the courage to listen to our inner voice, our gut instinct. In essence, love is the language of the heart. For the first time, I found myself able to hear it clearly. I happily made the choice to let it flow out of control.

EPILOGUE
THE FOURTH OF JULY, 1973

Choosing a holiday that celebrates independence as the occasion to announce the pending union of two individuals might seem strange at first, but Fourth of July celebrations usually include fireworks, parades, picnics, and concerts; all things one might want to include when announcing an engagement. Harry and I waited until our party of six, which included the two of us, Georgia and Jon, and Thomas and Mary Alice, were all settled in a perfect spot to enjoy the fireworks, against the backdrop of the Parthenon in Centennial Park, before we let everyone know our news. Jerome and Gloria were invited, too, but they'd already made plans with Jerome's family.

When we casually mentioned we became engaged the day before, Georgia was a bit ticked off I hadn't called her immediately after Harry put the ring on my finger, but she quickly shifted into planning mode when I asked if she would be willing to let us have our wedding reception on her patio. Harry and I decided to have a small wedding with only family and our closest friends. Neither of us was very comfortable in large crowds, which we learned after attending a few of the bank's social events with a hundred or more people. Since our guest list came to a grand total of thirty-five, Georgia's patio seemed to us to be the perfect spot for the reception. Sure, it would be a tight fit. But cozy was what we were going for.

Georgia agreed to be my maid-of-honor, and Harry asked his older brother Brian, to be the best man. The rest of our siblings would serve as groomsmen and bridesmaids. We scheduled the ceremony for the first Saturday in October, giving us plenty of time to plan everything, and a pretty fair chance for good weather. My mother suggested we use the church at Holy Angels, since it was the most regular place for our family to attend Mass. But when Mary Alice mentioned that St. Thomas had a "cozy little chapel," we quickly opted for that instead.

Cozy was always better in our minds, although, if we'd left the choice of locations strictly up to Harry, we probably would have gotten married in a park somewhere. That would have been perfectly fine with me, too, except for the reaction I knew we'd get from some of our family. The chapel at St. Thomas was a good compromise. It had plenty of room for the number of people we'd invited, and space near the altar for Sherry and Carey to perform the music for the ceremony.

I decided to spend the night before the wedding at my parents' house, partly because they asked me to, and partly because I thought it would make my transition into married life seem more real. Harry and I agreed it made more sense for us to live in his apartment than mine, so we moved my things there during the previous two weeks. It felt odd to see my clothes hanging in his closet and my books stacked on his shelves, even though I had been spending as much time at Harry's as my own apartment for several months. The sight of my things merged in with his made everything seem final; like putting an exclamation mark at the end of a sentence. We were getting married! And as much as I tried to pretend it was going to be just another ordinary day in my life, I was filled with excited anticipation of the actual event.

I awoke on the morning of the wedding to the sound of rain pounding on the bedroom window. At first, I couldn't figure out where I was, until I sat up and spotted the sewing machine in the corner where my desk used to be. After I moved into my own place, my mother turned my bedroom into her sewing room, keeping the bed in case I ever wanted to spend the night. My dad cut a large piece of plywood to fit over the top of the mattress so she could lay out her patterns. The plywood was slightly smaller than the bedframe, allowing it to be easily slid underneath the bed when it wasn't needed.

I got out of bed and pushed aside the curtains to look outside. I groaned as I spotted the rain splattered window and a gush of water running down the sides of the road. At least the wedding is indoors, I thought. But that idea was quickly followed by alarm when I remembered where the reception would be held. I looked at the clock, and saw that the 10 a.m. wedding was in less than three hours. I planned on arriving at the chapel by 9:00. My dad was going to drive to St. Thomas to drop off Sherry and Carey, my mother, and me, before heading to Harry's to hang out with the groomsmen while they got ready. This rain changed everything, including where the reception would take place.

I hurried out the bedroom door to where a telephone sat on a small table and dialed Georgia's number.

"It's raining!" I exclaimed.

"I know. I've been up since six-thirty watching it. But don't worry. Jon ordered a huge canopy tent that will cover the entire patio. It even has sidewalls that can be dropped in case the rain gets too intense."

"He did? What made him decide to do that?"

"Jon is a weather buff. He listens to weather reports like some people watch sports or politics. When he heard a few days ago there was a good chance of thunderstorms for your wedding day, he decided to order a tent for the patio. It arrived yesterday, and he and Thomas are out there right now putting it up."

"They are?" I realized my questions made me sound as baffled as I was feeling. "But it's pouring out there. They'll get drenched."

I could hear Georgia chuckle over the phone in that low rumble that told me she was shaking her head at me. "Oh, you know what they say. Boys, will be boys! He and Thomas look as happy as a couple of ducks in a pond, which was actually what the patio was beginning to look like before they got to work. They've managed to sweep most of the water out of the way, so everything should be fairly dry by the time of the reception."

That's wonderful! Be sure to tell them how much I appreciate what they're doing."

"Will do. So, how are you? Got any pre-wedding jitters?"

I paused to consider her question. "Surprisingly, not a one."

"Hum. Must mean you're doing the right thing. Not that I'm surprised. I could tell you and Harry were meant to be together from the first time I met him."

"Really? You never told me that."

"I didn't? Well, I thought it. You still want me to come over to help you get dressed?"

I considered the repercussions of wearing my dress out in this downpour. It was made out of ivory silk, strapless on top, and cut in an A-line with a dropped waist. It was the most glamorous creation my mother had ever made. She surprised me with it one day when I was flipping through a bridal magazine and moaning that all the dresses were too frilly. When she produced the box containing the dress and held it up for my inspection, I could see instantly it was exactly what I wanted. It was so beautiful it even rivaled anything I had seen at Rosa Decavanta's boutique. It was the epitome of sophistication, and truthfully, a little too formal for the simple ceremony we had planned. But once I saw it, I couldn't imagine wearing anything else.

"No. I don't think silk and rain are a good combination. I'd better wait and get dressed at St. Thomas. Mary Alice mentioned there's a room behind the altar I can use. You can wait and get dressed there, too, if you want."

"Deal. I'll meet you there around 8:30. That should give us plenty of time. Don't worry. We're not going to let a little rain ruin this day."

Her statement turned out to be prophetic. The rain stopped just as the guests began arriving at the chapel, and by the time the ceremony ended, the storm clouds that had darkened the sky most of the morning, began to shift aside to allow a hint of blue to appear.

I walked down the aisle on the arm of my dad. I could tell he was a little nervous, because he kept clearing his throat and fiddling with his collar. When we reached the altar, he placed one warm kiss on my cheek and whispered in my ear: "You'll always be my Jubie. Your mother and I love you very much," before turning to nod at Harry. I could hear a symphony of sniffles from the guests, and that, combined with my dad's sweet message, threatened to make me break down. When I looked at Harry, suddenly everything else disappeared.

We had written our own vows, and I vaguely remember reciting them. It wasn't until Father Johnson pronounced us husband and wife that I felt the room come back into focus. We stood beaming at each other for a moment before Harry leaned forward and kissed me gently on the lips then grabbed me and swung me in a circle, as the guests clapped and shouted their approval.

The reception at Georgia's was perfect. Even though the rain had stopped, Jon and Thomas decided to leave the canopy in place, in case of a pop-up shower. It provided a welcome relief from the glare of the midday sun. Sherry and Carey convinced a couple of boys from one of their music classes to join them for the reception, and the quartet filled the air with the quiet strains of classical music. A bar was stationed to one side of the tent, and trays of food were passed among the guests by some students recruited by Thomas.

As the afternoon continued, the music shifted into a more energetic beat, prompting several of the men to push aside the tables and chairs covering the patio to create room for dancing. Eventually, a pile of discarded jackets and purses began to accumulate on one of the tables, as the crowd sought to free themselves of any restriction to their movement.

As the day grew longer, I finally collapsed onto one of the vacant chairs and gratefully accepted a glass of cold water from a passing waiter. Georgia came over and fell into a chair beside me. We looked at each other, our faces glowing from the combination of exertion and exhilaration.

"You sure throw a good party." I said.

"I'm glad you're enjoying it."

We looked around at the crowd, which had dwindled down to our closest friends and some members of my family and Harry's. Pretty soon, a group of tired dancers dragged chairs to form a loose circle around us. Harry carried a chair over and positioned it between Georgia and me.

"I'm beat! I don't think I've ever danced that much in my entire life!"

Georgia looked at him with a wicked grin. "Well, I hope you saved some energy!" She wiggled her eyes at him, eliciting a blush that began at his collar, and spread up his neck.

"Uh, yeah. Sure. No problem there." He glanced at me and pretended to study his fingernails.

I stared at him in surprise. I had never seen Harry blush before, and I couldn't imagine what made him react that way now. It certainly wasn't as if we had never been intimate. The man continued to surprise me. "Why, Mr. Simpson! I do believe that Georgia has finally found a way to get your goat."

He dipped his head as the blush made its way further up his face. "It's strange, I know. But it feels like we're about to begin a phase of our lives that's completely new. I guess that makes me a little nervous."

His honesty touched me. Sometimes I tended to forget how special this man was and how willing he was to show his vulnerability. It drew me to him even more, and made me melt in places only he had really ever awakened. I looked around at our assorted friends and family members and felt my heart fill so completely I felt as if it was pressing against my ribs. Josh and Mike sat with their heads bent towards each other as they shared a whispered conversation. Sherry and Carey were chattering happily with the two young men who made up the other half of their musical quartet. Bill was talking to a young woman I recognized as one of Harry's cousins and, by the looks of things, already had his full attention. Mary Alice and Thomas were giggling at some shared joke, while Jerome and Gloria looked on with barely suppressed laughter at their antics.

My parents left a short while earlier, explaining they were going to drop my grandparents off at the Holiday Inn where they were staying and go back to their house to play cards with Harry's parents. Harry's brother, Brian, and his sister, Angie and her family, left at the same time, headed to Shakey's Pizza Parlor for a belated birthday party for Angie's daughter, who turned three the day before. Jon had been making the rounds of the crowd most of the day, checking the availability of food and drinks and making sure the wait-staff was clearing up. Georgia gave him a silent wave and he headed in our direction.

"Are you two going to be next?" I asked.

She looked at me as if she had no clue what I meant, which, having known her as long as I had, I could see right through.

"Don't act as if you have no idea what I'm talking about. I've seen the way the two of you look at each other. It's always been pretty steamy, but lately there's something else."

She looked at me like the Cheshire cat in Alice in Wonderland. "Let's just say things have been heating up."

This was not a time to be speaking in riddles. I decided not to let her off the hook. "Does that mean what I think it does?"

She paused to look up at Jon sitting beside her, then turned back to me. "This is your day. Everything else can wait."

I was about to push the subject further when I remembered something Dr. Blackburn had given me earlier in the day. She had been at our wedding, but left as soon as the ceremony was over. Before leaving, she slipped me a piece of paper I had forgotten about. I fished it out of the sash at my waist, where I had tucked it for safekeeping.

> *Julie. I am so happy for you! It has been a pleasure for me to see you grow into the strong, successful woman you are today. I'm thrilled you have found such a good man to share your life with. In the days and years ahead, there will be times when you will find yourself besieged with uncertainty, because life is a mystery we are constantly seeking to solve. I know it still makes you anxious when you feel like things are out of your control, but I want to remind you that the only things we ever really have control over are the choices we make and the chances we take in making those choices. Those are the things that define our destiny.*
>
> *I believe you've made a good choice to commit yourself to the man you're marrying today. Trust your heart (and your gut!) If you allow them to speak to you, they will guide you through whatever challenges life may bring your way. Be happy, but remember that even when you're sad, you're still destined for a wonderful journey. – Dr. Blackburn.*

My eyes filled with tears, and I nodded firmly to myself. I could always count on Dr. Blackburn to help me see things more clearly, even when what I saw wasn't exactly what I was hoping for. In this instance, it was as if she was reminding me I didn't need to know right this minute what the future held in store. Not for Harry and me, or Georgia and Jon.

Georgia looked over my shoulder at the note. "What's that?"

"Some good advice." I stood and held my hand out to Harry. "Ready to go, Mr. Simpson?"

He took my hand and stood next to me. "Absolutely, Mrs. Simpson." We made the rounds of everyone, giving hugs and accepting kisses, until we were once again by ourselves in Harry's truck. I sighed quietly, but not quietly enough to prevent Harry from noticing. He turned toward me and took my hands in his.

"What is it, Julie?"

"Something Dr. Blackburn said to me in a note. The choices we make in life define our destiny. Do you think that's true?"

He squeezed my hand firmly. "Yes, I do. When you chose to visit the bank and to forego college in order to start your career, I believe that placed us on a path that would inevitably lead us to each other. What you may not have realized is; I was also making choices at the same time." I raised an eyebrow to indicate I wanted him to explain. "I didn't have to teach the classes at the bank. I offered to teach, once I knew you were going to be in them. I hung around after class that day you got caught in the rain, hoping you'd let me give you a ride home. That's why, when I proposed to you, I started by saying I choose you. I wanted you to know I've been making that choice every day since I met you. I'm just so glad you finally decided to choose me, too."

I suddenly realized what Dr. Blackburn had been trying to tell me, both in the note, and during my many sessions with her. It's our choice, ours absolutely, without a doubt, choice, whether or not we allow ourselves to listen to those gut feelings that resound most clearly in our hearts. The only thing in life we really have control over is whether or not we allow ourselves to act on our choice, without fear of where it may lead us.

I slipped my hands free of Harry's, and looped my arm through his, pulling him close. "I'm ready now."

His answering smile told me everything I needed to know.

ANNELL ST. CHARLES

Following a long career in the medical profession, Annell St. Charles turned her attention to writing fiction and producing photography. Her first two novels, "The Things Left Unsaid" and "The Choices We Make", were published in 2016. She also has two books of photography: "Sunrise On Hilton Head Island: Coligny Beach" and "Island Life"; and a book of poetry: "The Clam Shell", also published in 2016. She has been a member of the self-proclaimed "Greater Nashville Book and Wine Club" for around 20 years (who she describes as her toughest critics and greatest friends), and holds a certificate in digital photography from the Shaw Institute. Now a full-time Hilton Head Island resident, she is an avid walker and can usually be found roaming the streets and beaches with her camera slung over one shoulder while she ponders her next work of fiction. She is married to Constantine Tsinakis and borrows her friend's "Ebie-like" cats every chance she gets.

If you enjoyed this book, she would love to hear from you at annellusa@gmail.com. You can also place a review of the book on Amazon.com.